THE
CURSED AMULET
CROW MAGIC BOOK TWO

ELIZABETH FOREST

ARBORI BOOKS

The Cursed Amulet

Crow Magic Book Two

Arbori Books

https://www.arboribooks.com

Print ISBN: 978-0-999-6894-2-4

Ebook ISBN: 978-0-999-6894-3-1

LCCN 2019912580

Cover illustration by Julie Dillon

PROLOGUE

Eʙ Wɪɴɢ sᴛᴏᴏᴅ in the doorway of the carpentry shop, watching the soldiers march past. He'd never seen soldiers in Beeshome before, or anywhere else for that matter. He hadn't known Teveral *had* an army. But here they were in his village, cursing loudly, threatening the market women, and generally behaving like angry bullies.

It was time to go—he had a delivery to make. He loaded a table and chairs onto his master's cart and set out for a farm outside the village. He forgot about the soldiers until he was on the dusty road on his way back to the village.

Up ahead, small bundles lay on the grass beneath the trees. At first he thought they were rags. He squinted against the late afternoon sunlight, trying to make out what they were. The wind shifted, and the smell of decay reached him.

As the cart drew closer, he pulled the kerchief from around his neck and tied it over his nose.

Scattered beneath the trees were the tiny yellow, black, and brown corpses of dead birds. Eb recognized finches, sparrows, nuthatches, and chickadees.

Had they been killed deliberately, or was it some kind of disease? There was no reason to kill songbirds; you couldn't eat them. It was a disturbing sight. He told the horse to halt, and climbed down from the wagon to look more closely.

He picked up one tiny body and turned it over. There was no mark upon it. *Not deliberate killing, then*, he thought. *A disease?* He laid the body back on the grass and took off the kerchief to wipe his hands with it. He'd have to tell Hedith. The wise woman would want to know if animals were dying of disease near their village. He climbed back into the cart and shook the reins.

That's when he remembered the soldiers, marching into the town square as though they owned the place, pushing the farmers and old women out of their way, and cursing the villagers. Had they done something to the birds?

Eb clucked to the horse, urging it to go faster, passing the trees planted as windbreaks for the village's fields.

He returned his master's cart and horse to the stable and hurried home to see that his grandmother was all right.

"I'm fine, Eb, thank you," Grandmother said, when she heard his tale. "But you run and bring Hedith back here. I've heard about these soldiers; they're taking all the wise women away. Don't tell anyone what you're doing or where she's going."

Eb sprinted down the path behind the row of thatched cottages. As he ran, he wondered if his sister Suli knew about the soldiers. If they were looking for wise women, then she was in danger, too. She'd become a wise woman two years before, in the village of Weatherstone in the mountains. How could he warn her? A letter would take too long.

He'd passed three cottages and finally reached Hedith's, the last one by the river. He helped Hedith pack a few belongings. She threw her satchel of remedies over her shoulder, and they hurried back to Eb's house. By the time Grandmother had welcomed her, and taken her to the guest room, Eb had decided.

He'd leave for Weatherstone as soon as his master would let him. If he found a wagon traveling to the mountains, he'd arrive there sooner than any letter.

1

FLYING WITH THE FREE FOLK

SULI WAS FLYING with the wild geese, her human life left far behind.

Her wings beat of their own accord; she felt she could fly forever, a weightless spirit, free of the earth and all its heavy responsibilities. Free of her work as a wise woman, if only for a few weeks. The cold air, knifing in and out of her lungs, was the only reminder of her body.

How many times had she dreamed of flying with the wild geese, floating above the world and traveling across oceans? Now here she was.

A river, at first a mere gleam in the distance, became a wide ribbon of bright silver, surrounded by darker marshland. A streak of pink appeared on the horizon, the first sign of dawn. The leader gave a piercing cry and the flock replied in a ragged chorus before they wheeled above a field of marsh grass, colorless in the early light.

Suli glided down and landed with the others. They would rest and eat and wait for the sun to warm them before continuing their journey. She'd never been this far from Weatherstone before, and saw nothing familiar. The wild geese, or the Free

Folk, as they called themselves, were traveling north to visit relatives, and they'd invited Suli to come along.

The two wild geese beside her sidled away; they'd spoken against inviting her on the journey, saying she was tainted by humanness. Her own flock of shape-shifting humans, Sigur's people, was scorned by most wild geese. It didn't matter that she looked like them; to those who thought as they did she would always be a human who merely pretended to be one of them, the unwelcome changeling.

But Grisa, their leader, had invited her to come, just as she'd invited Tala, Suli's teacher, years before. It was a great honor and Suli knew it. She was careful to do as she was told, to be polite and deferential, even to those who made it plain they didn't want her there. Her behavior would reflect on her people.

Others could take care of things in Weatherstone while she was gone. Orion would remember to feed the goats and the chickens, and to send for Mistress Agat in the next village if anyone got sick.

It was the other niggly things wise women were responsible for that would be neglected while she was gone, such as health of the animals, or protecting the fields from disease or storms. And she hadn't yet discovered why so many children were having nightmares lately. That bothered her. Still, no one died from nightmares.

Suddenly she laughed, startling a goose cropping grass nearby. She was free! Free of responsibility for the first time in two years, or she would be when she stopped thinking everyone needed her. The village would be fine without her.

Everyone was eating, so she should too. She didn't like eating wild grass and bugs but they would sustain her on the journey. *All in a good cause,* she reminded herself. *Freedom has a price.* She dutifully plucked at the coarse marsh grass. In the two years since she'd begun her apprenticeship as a wise woman and learned to change shape, she'd never become used to the food. If she became a human again too soon, it would upset her stomach, but she'd be flying for weeks yet.

She forced herself to swallow, wondering where her teacher Tala was and what she was doing. Tala had declared Suli a wise woman long before Suli felt ready. Then Tala promptly left with her sister Magda to travel to the coast, saying they had to learn more about the Outsiders and their strange attitudes toward magic. Suli had become the wise woman of the village.

As Weatherstone's wise woman. Suli healed the sick—no matter whether they were human, plants, or animals—and protected her village from witchcraft and accidents. Mostly she used magic for routine things, like protection spells, healing corn blight, or setting the occasional broken limb. The life of a wise woman wasn't what she'd thought it would be. It was boring. So when the wild geese invited her on their annual migration, she'd said yes right away.

The sun broke through the clouds, instantly flooding the marsh with color. The grasses seemed to come alive before her eyes, glowing green, gold, or russet. She spread her wings, enjoying the sudden warmth, and relaxed.

The wind shifted. The smell of wood smoke drifted toward her and she heard the sound of bells tinkling and the insistent bleating of a goat demanding to be milked. Then human voices: someone shouting in anger, followed by a shriek of pain and a child's voice crying. She searched for the source, but tall reeds and marsh grass blocked her view.

The flock was busy eating, with some taking the chance to sleep. There was time. She'd just take a quick look.

She rose into the air and flew toward the sound of the voices until she saw a cottage on a rise of ground in the middle of the marsh.

She hung in the air above it, beating her wings. Below her, a small girl of nine or ten with dark curly hair and a pale face sat on a stool, trying to milk a goat. Half the milk was on the ground and the girl was crying too hard to notice that the pail was overturned.

A man watched her, making no move to help. He was tall and beefy, with enormous arms like smoked hams. A thick black beard covered his face, from his chest to his frowning eyebrows. "Shut yer caterwauling," he yelled, glowering at the girl, "and mind what you're doing this time!"

He moved toward her and she scrambled to her feet, overturning the stool, her eyes wide. The man had a whip in his hand, the kind drovers used to beat oxen. The goat bleated and skipped out of reach. The girl backed away, no longer crying but holding her breath, watching him.

"Don't malinger, girl! Get back to work!" the man ordered, but he was smiling.

The girl seemed transfixed by his gaze, as though he were a snake and she his prey. He came toward her, arm raised.

With a sinking feeling, Suli felt the responsibility of being a wise woman settle around her like a heavy cloak. She didn't need her Seeing to read the man's heart. He felt contempt for the child. Worse, he seemed to enjoy her fear.

It was clear what a wise woman should do. Tala's voice sounded in her head, telling her she had to take care of this, one way or another. She couldn't simply walk—or fly—away. Perhaps if the man knew someone had seen him it would discourage him from beating the girl, but she doubted it. If she used the Voice, she could make him feel ill and ashamed when he hurt the girl, or even thought about it. But even that might not be enough.

The girl hadn't moved. She was crouched like a rabbit, her arms over her head.

Suli landed behind the cottage. The pigs watched with interest as she became a girl of fourteen in a faded blue dress. Her bare legs and arms were brown and her hair was the color of a raven's wing.

Of course, she was no match for the man physically; he'd laugh when she intervened. But she knew she could stop him.

By the time Suli came around the side of the house, the girl had scrambled away, until her back was against a fence post. The whip rose in the air, its shadow on the girl's face.

"Excuse me," Suli called. "I seem to be lost."

The man turned. His look of surprise quickly turned to one of fury. "You're trespassing!" he shouted, the blood rushing to his face. He gestured with the whip for her to leave.

"Sorry, but I've lost my way."

The man strode toward her, curling the whip in his hand. "Get out of here! Spying on me and mine. Shove off, or I'll set the dogs on ye!"

"Don't do that," Suli said. "I don't know where I am. *And I'm so tired*," she said, beginning to chant softly with the singsong rhythm of the Voice. *"Could you set me on my road? Yes, I really must sleep. I need directions. My eyes are so heavy. A nap would be so wonderful. So pleasant, to lie down and rest. Rest and sleep. My eyes won't stay open,"* she murmured, her voice rising and falling, now loud, now soft.

The man blinked in confusion, his eyelids fluttering. "Eh?" he said.

The girl stared, open-mouthed.

"So tired, so very tired, I could curl up right here, and rest. So relaxed, so comfortable, so warm. Sleeping would be marvelous. So tired, so good to sleep."

The girl watched in amazement as the man lowered himself down to the muddy ground, curled on one side, his arm pillowing his head. He began to snore loudly.

The girl rose to her feet. "Who are you?"

"My name's Suli. What's yours?"

The girl blinked, as though she didn't understand the question. Finally she said, "Arta. My name is Arta Phos. What're you doing here?"

Suli climbed the rails of the goat pen, and sat on the top rail. "Pleased to meet you, Arta. Why was this man about to beat you? Is he your father?"

Arta glanced at the man snoring in the mud. "That's Master Munro. I'm s'posed to be his apprentice, but I just do all the farm work. He's never taught me anything, and he beats me all the time, no matter what I do." This last was said in a small voice.

"Where are your parents?"

"Da is dead, and Ma lives in Kaliska. She said she couldn't feed me, so she 'prenticed me here."

"I see." Suli thought for a moment. "Does your ma know that Master Munro beats you?"

"No. But I don't expect it would make much difference. She can't feed me," Arta said again.

Suli frowned. She couldn't leave the child here. Munro had already broken the apprenticeship contract by not teaching her anything, never mind the beatings. But where could she take her? She resented the girl for making her feel responsible. She'd dreamt of the journey with the Free Folk for months. She shook her head. All she had to do was take the girl to her mother. Then, if the flock left before she could return, she'd fly hard to catch up. She *couldn't* stop her journey. If she left now, the Free Folk might never give her another chance.

"How far is it to Kaliska?" she asked.

Arta's eyes narrowed. "Ma won't like it if I come back. She had to borrow to pay the fee to Master Munro."

Suli nodded. Yes, in this hard place there would be money involved. Suli's own apprenticeship was the traditional kind, her work for her mistress all the payment required. But paying a master or mistress to take a child for training was becoming more common. If the child's mother was poor, she could ill afford to pay a fee to a master who not only didn't teach her anything, but would likely kill her in the end, even if he didn't mean to.

Suli shook her head. "I'm not so sure. Your ma doesn't know Munro isn't teaching you anything; the way I see it, he's broken the contract and has to give the money back. You can find a better master or mistress."

Arta's pinched face wore a shrewd expression. "That was magic you did, wasn't it, Mistress? Maybe you could take me as 'prentice. I've always wanted to learn magic."

For a moment Suli thought she hadn't heard correctly. "You don't know any magic? Didn't your ma teach you to See?" Suli knew there were places on the coast where girls weren't taught magic, thanks to the strange ideas of the Outsiders, but she'd assumed every village girl was taught to use their natural ability to See. If girls didn't learn to see into other's hearts, how could they protect themselves and their families from trouble?

"No, she didn't. But if I was your apprentice *you* could teach me." Arta sounded pleased.

"I don't need an apprentice! My journey is important to me, and I have to leave soon. I'll take you to your mother, and *she* can teach you, as she should've done."

"I'll do the chores, and learn at the same time," Arta said, excitement in her voice. "It can't be any worse than being here."

"Listen to me! That's not possible. What was your mother thinking, not even teaching you basic magic?" Suli asked, exasperated.

"But *you* can teach me, so it doesn't matter," Arta said calmly. "I don't need to know advanced magic, only what I'm s'posed to know."

Suli bit back an angry retort. Instead she said, "We're going to see your Ma. Collect your things. Hurry."

Arta hesitated, then ran to the house. While she was gone, Suli bent down and whispered into Munro's ear; she could at least make him pay the money back. She straightened up as Arta came running back with a basket and a sack over her shoulder.

"Ready? Good. Which way to Kaliska?"

Arta pointed toward a path that disappeared within the marsh grass. It would pass near the field where the Free Folk were resting.

"You don't have to bother Ma," Arta said as they walked. "I'm a fast learner. You'll be amazed how much easier your life will be with me to do the chores."

Suli wasn't listening. She was trying to decide what to say to Grisa. She didn't want to give up the journey. She wanted to see the strange white lands and frozen seas the Free Folk had boasted of. She *had* to go with them. She'd explain that she'd be delayed, but would catch up as soon as she could. Surely they would understand. Once she'd delivered Arta to her mother, that would be the end of it.

They followed the path deeper into the marsh, the reeds towering over their heads. They arrived where paths branched off in different directions. "Wait for me here," Suli said. "I'll be back in a moment. I have to talk to my companions."

Concealed within the tall grass, she changed shape and flew to where the Free Folk were forming up to leave. She found Grisa and explained hurriedly, saying she had to delay her journey to deliver a fledgling to her mother. She apologized, and promised to catch up with the flock afterward.

Grisa, a grey goose with black feathers on her head, considered before replying. "Of course you must take care of the child. You would never catch up, Suli, so this is farewell. This may be a lucky accident: I was about to suggest you return home, anyway."

Suli frowned. "Why?" Had there been more complaints about letting her come?

"Our southern cousins have arrived, bringing strange news. Some animals are behaving strangely, forgetting who they are, and many eggs aren't hatching. If this is a disease, I suspect the cause is magical. If so, the wise women must take care of it.

"Once the child is home, you should go home, too. All may not be well there."

Suli was too surprised to argue. She didn't want to go home; the freedom she'd tasted was slipping away. "I thought you were going to say others have complained about me."

"Well, it's true some of my advisors will be delighted you're leaving," Grisa said. "They'll say they were right all along, that you are not worthy to watch herds of narwhals playing in the northern seas, while the lights dance in the sky. They will say Sigur's people are no different from other humans: arrogant and flighty, heedless of the honor we do them."

Suli's breath caught in her throat. She'd heard these slurs before, but not from Grisa herself.

"Don't worry, I don't agree," Grisa reassured her. "You will fly with us again someday. But go home now, Suli. If the wise women don't stop this sickness, whatever it is, it may be that none of us will see the northern lights again."

Suli took a deep breath, shaken by Grisa's words. Now she *had* to go home to check that all was well in her village.

Grisa was already turning away, calling for the flock to gather in formation.

"Farewell!" Suli called after her. "Safe journey."

With the deep-throated cries that made Suli's heart ache, the wild geese leapt into the air. She watched them fly away from her, some calling farewell, the pattern of their flight beautiful in the clear autumn light.

Suli returned to the field beside the crossroads, careful to land where she was hidden in the grass. She changed and became human again, feeling angry and disappointed. But if Grisa was worried, she should be too.

Arta was waiting where she'd left her.

"Ready?" Suli said curtly, hiding her disappointment. "Let's find your mother."

With a thoughtful expression, Arta fell into step beside her.

2

SULI'S APPRENTICE

No path ran straight across the marsh. Arta led Suli to one that backtracked oddly, looping around the boggy places where an unwary step meant sinking to your death. The sun was heading toward the western horizon when they finally reached the village of Kaliska, a mean little settlement of pebble-and-dash huts, their thatched roofs in disrepair. Garbage lay in heaps beside the only street.

Arta pointed toward a small cottage with bald spots in the thatch and holes in the flaking walls. A blanket covered the door, and the wind blew freely through the only window.

Arta hung back. Suli stood outside the door and called, "Mistress Phos?"

A small grubby hand appeared and pushed the blanket aside. A dirty baby boy, dressed only in a shirt, tottered into view. He smiled broadly when he saw Arta, displaying his single tooth. "Artie!" he cried happily.

A thin, weather-beaten woman with a sour expression followed him. She took one look at Arta and demanded, "What're you doing here?" Then her gaze narrowed on Suli. She placed her fists on her hips and said, "I give naught to beggars."

"Good morning, Mistress Phos," Suli said, forcing herself to be polite. "My name is Suli Wing. I'm the wise woman in Weatherstone. I was traveling near Master Munro's farm when I saw him beating your daughter. I stopped to see how she fared and she says he's not taught her anything at all. Since he's broken the contract, and was beating her for no reason, I offered to bring her home. That man should give you back your fee, and I've told him so."

Mistress Phos stared at her in disbelief. "Do you mean to say you took her out from under Munro's nose? How on earth could a slip of a girl like you do that? Master Munro is a hard man, I know, and doesn't take kindly to interference, no matter where it comes from. Wise woman indeed!" Mistress Phos spat in the dirt, perilously close to Suli's foot.

Suli forced herself to smile. "It wasn't that difficult, Mistress. He knows he's a bad master and part of him is ashamed, although not a very big part, I grant you. Still, I made sure he'll give you your money back." Her voice hardened. "If you knew he was a bad man, why did you give him your little girl?"

Mistress Phos looked down at the toddler clinging to her skirts and said in a low voice, "I didn't want to, but it was that or all of us starving together. Our crops died before harvest, and the goats all died. We don't have much left. I suppose I hoped he wouldn't treat her badly, her being so young."

Suli took a deep breath. "Well, he did, and he broke the contract as well. I've brought her back so you can find Arta a new mistress or master. But teach her to See, first, so she can protect herself!"

Mistress Phos narrowed her eyes and stepped toward Suli, her right hand balled into a fist. "No one talks to me like that."

Arta spoke quickly. "It's all right, Ma. We'll leave. I want to be *her* apprentice. She knows magic."

"Is that so?" Mistress Pho asked suspiciously. "Is that your game? Don't think you can take advantage of us because we're poor. I'll not give you any money. You chose to interfere between master and apprentice; that makes the girl *your* responsibility now. If you want her, take her, but you won't get a squal from me."

"She was old enough and I apprenticed her, like I was s'posed to," she continued bitterly. "No one asked *you* to break a contract I paid good money for. If you think Munro will give me anything, you're a fool. The money's gone and there's the end of it. I can't take her back and the girl knows it, too."

Suli shook her head. "I don't want an apprentice. I've already had my journey interrupted and my plans ruined. She's your daughter and your responsibility."

Mistress Phos laughed. "You're all high and mighty about saying what others should do, but you don't care whether the girl starves, is that what you're saying?" She turned to her daughter. "Are you sure 'bout prenticing with her? I'm sorry to hear Munro was wicked to you, but there's not a crust in the house to eat and I can't keep you. If you want to go with this *chit* of a girl, 'tis fine by me, but she doesn't seem all that clever."

Suli bit her lip at the insult. She wasn't used to being insulted, not by humans, anyway. Mother and daughter behaved as if they'd decided the matter without her. "I told you, I don't need an apprentice."

Arta looked from her mother to Suli. "It will be all right, Ma," she said. "She's smarter than she looks, and she can protect me with advanced magic."

"Listen to me! I don't *want* an apprentice. Arta, I'm sorry, but you must stay with your ma."

Mistress Phos nodded. "I don't approve of magic—it only leads to trouble, but if that's what you want, on your head be it. And you," she glared at Suli, "treat her well, wise woman or no." She went to Arta. "You'll be better off than many, daughter."

"Can't you understand..." Suli began, but no one paid her any attention.

Arta slipped her hand into Suli's. "Goodbye, Ma," she said softly. "Thanks for worrying about me."

"Don't forget your ma and Tedy."

"Bye, Tedy," Arta said. She waved at her brother and he began to cry. Mistress Phos bent over and hoisted him onto her hip, making soothing noises. "Don't you worry, pet, your sister will be fine."

"I'm sorry," Suli said, pulling her hand free of Arta's. "I've done what I could. But I've no need for an apprentice. Take care of your child, Mistress Phos." She turned and walked away, not looking behind her.

A few minutes later, Suli heard the sound of bare feet running on the path behind her.

"The first thing to do is buy food for the journey," Arta announced breathlessly as she fell into step beside her. "Sibley's farm's up the road. He'll likely sell us sommat."

Suli whirled around and glared at the girl. "I told you, I can't take you."

"And I told *you*, Ma won't take me back," Arta shouted angrily, her eyes bright with tears. "Besides," she continued calmly, "I need to learn magic. You said so yourself; I need to learn to protect myself. You took me away from Munro, so I'm yours now. And don't you worry about feeding me. I'll find my own food and a place to sleep, too. But I won't go back."

Suli noticed the expression in the girl's eyes. With a sinking feeling she realized she hadn't paid attention. She'd been so upset about leaving the Free Folk and losing her journey, so *sure* of herself, she'd forgotten to use her Seeing on Mistress Phos. Now, remembering what had passed between mother and child, Suli understood that for Arta, living with Master Munro hadn't been much different from living with her Ma. The girl was used to beatings.

She sighed deeply. "All right. *Tonight* we travel together until we reach Weatherstone. But this isn't permanent. Once I'm home, I'll find you a new master or mistress." A few tradesmen in Weatherstone might be willing to train the girl. The cheese maker, for one. He'd lost his apprentice when the lad decided he'd rather be a soldier.

She'd find something for the girl. However annoying she was, Arta was right. Suli created the situation so it was up to her to solve it; she couldn't let the girl starve. She only had to put up with Arta until she found someone who needed help.

They passed a gate to a lane snaking up the hill. "Is that Sibley's farm?"

Arta nodded. "Better let me go first. Master Sibley sets the dogs on you if he thinks you're trespassing. He's not a bad sort if he knows you. He'll recognize me, and once you show him your coin, he'll be agreeable." She grinned. "Don't worry, Mistress. I'll be useful. You'll see."

IT WAS MORE than a day's journey to Weatherstone, and for all her boasting, Arta was too worn out from overwork, scanty food, and constant beatings to travel quickly. She was obviously lagging and weary. Although she was impatient, wanting to fly home quickly to check on her village, Suli decided they'd travel in easy stages. On the way, she could learn more about the girl.

Master Sibley was happy to sell them bread, cheese, half a roasted chicken, a sack of wrinkled apples, and a jug of cider. They found a sunny clearing beside a stream not far from their road and stopped to eat.

Suli lay back against the cracked bark of the oak they sheltered beneath, and tried to forget her disappointment. It was hard to let go. In her mind's eye she saw the Free Folk flying without her. But Grisa's warning about a sickness among the animals worried her. She reminded herself she probably would have returned home anyway. She wished she knew more.

"Tell me about yourself," she said, handing an apple to Arta and biting into one herself. It was sweet and good.

"Not much to tell," Arta replied. "I'm eldest so Ma always said I'd have to make my own way. Two of my sisters died when they were babies, and Tedy is the first boy."

Suli lay back, staring up at the sunlight shining through the leaves. "So what *did* your Ma teach you about magic?"

When Arta didn't reply Suli turned to look at her. The girl wouldn't meet her eyes.

"Nothing at all?" she asked, shocked. She'd never heard of such a thing. She knew folk on the coast had begun to reject magic, calling it witchcraft, but hadn't thought such attitudes existed in the countryside.

Arta shook her head.

"I see." It seemed Arta's mother had neglected her in more ways than one.

"Ma didn't want a girl," Arta said. "She said it was too much work, teaching me things, and she was feeding me for someone else in the end."

Suli didn't trust herself to reply for a long time. Then she said quietly, "There are three kinds of magic. Where I come from, all girls learn the first kind, called Seeing. It's a way of reading other people's hearts, to learn their intentions, to know if they mean you harm. It's an innate skill that most girls have. I can't remember not being able to do it, so I don't know if I can teach you how."

"You will," Arta said, her eyes shining. "What are the other kinds?"

Suli grimaced. "The second kind is Healing. You start by using your Seeing to discover what a plant, animal, or person needs to make them healthy again. Then you use the magical energy all around us to Heal them. Only wise women learn that."

Arta nodded, her face rapt. "And the third kind? That's the kind I want to learn."

Suli glanced at her. "I thought you said you didn't know anything about magic."

"I've heard stories," Arta said defensively. "I want to be able to do what you did to Master Munro."

Of course you do, Suli thought. But the village Elders might not allow it. She was too far behind others her age, and her motives were wrong. *But mine were, too,* she reminded herself.

"Well, that's what people think, that magic makes you powerful, enabling you to force people to do what you want. But it's really not like that. Not if you use it correctly."

Arta's face was scrunched in concentration. "What do you mean?"

"I used the Voice on Mr. Munro. The Voice is one example of the third kind of magic, the dangerous kind."

"I don't see why it's dangerous; you helped me. And why call it the third kind of magic? Why don't you just call it the Voice?"

Suli sighed. "It's dangerous because it controls people. Do you want someone to control *you?* And it has consequences for the wise woman who uses it. The third kind of magic includes other ways to control people or animals, besides the Voice. Magical objects can influence you, too, changing you, controlling you."

Arta shook her head. "Nobody's going to control *me.* So if it's dangerous, why did you use the Voice on Mr. Munro?" She looked at Suli suspiciously. "Is it really witchcraft? Ma says teaching magic is the same as teaching witchcraft."

Suli nodded. "That's a good question but your ma is wrong. If I had used the Voice on Mr. Munro only because I didn't like him and wanted him to do what I say, that would be witchcraft. But because I did it to help you, it won't affect my ability to See. *Why* you use it matters. If I put him to sleep to steal all his money, and if I did this often, sooner or later I wouldn't be able to See or Heal at all. There's a price to be paid for misusing magic. Do you understand?"

"Not really," Arta said. "What's the point of magic if you can't use it?"

Suli sighed. It had taken *her* a long time to learn this. And even longer to understand the difference between magic and witchcraft.

"Wise women focus the energy of magic that comes from everything around us. When that energy is used correctly, you can Heal others by rebalancing their energy. So you use magic to protect yourself and others, to heal an animal that's sick, or to take care of your garden by keeping the pests out. That's the safe, useful kind of magic. Does that make sense?"

Arta looked skeptical. "Maybe. It sounds like you're trying to warn me off the kind that makes you powerful, 'cause you don't want to teach me."

"No, but only wise women learn the dangerous kind of magic. Most villages are careful about who they allow to learn it, to keep girls from becoming bullies. Even if you were to apprentice as a wise woman, it would be years before you'd be allowed to use that. Too many things could go wrong.

"But I will teach you to See, so you can avoid dangerous people. If you can do that, then I'll teach you to Heal." But she thought the girl would be apprenticed to someone else by then, and would probably forget all about it.

To change the subject Suli asked, "Was there ever something you wanted to do? Something that makes your heart happy when you think of it?"

"Yes," Arta said. "Only it was long ago now."

Suli tossed the apple core away and wondered what "long ago" meant to the girl. Last year? A time when she thought her ma would take care of her? "What was that, then?"

Arta spoke so softly Suli had to strain to hear. "I'd like to work with horses. They're so beautiful."

Suli sighed. Girls and horses; a typical answer for a girl her age. She'd outgrow it when she learned no one would hire a girl as a stable boy. "There's no hurry. Think about it. I have friends in the village with different trades. I'm sure there'll be something you'll want to learn."

A girl who didn't know *any* magic or even what she wanted to do (besides using magic against brutal men) certainly wouldn't be allowed to learn the third kind of magic. Or be apprenticed to a wise woman. No sense in telling the girl that. She'd find out soon enough. *Besides, being a cheese maker wasn't a bad life.*

"Come on," Suli said, rising to her feet. "Let's put a few more miles behind us."

3

ON THE RUN

It was in Winton that Benno first heard the rumors about the king and queen.

He was passing the tables set out beneath the plane tree in the yard of the Compass Rose Inn. Someone had risen from a table, leaving a few coins and a half-full mug of ale.

Glancing warily around him, Benno slid onto the trestle bench and began drinking from the mug. He hoped he looked like a customer. His stomach growled loudly, awakened by the ale. He wished he had bread to go with the ale; he'd settle for day-old bread, or week-old come to that. Even a moldy potato. The rivers of food that flowed through the palace kitchens seemed a distant memory.

Once he'd drained the mug he sat quietly, listening to the talk drifting from the other tables. The serving woman set down two bowls in front of the farmers at the table next to his: mutton swimming in broth and onions. The tantalizing aroma drifted toward him and his stomach growled again.

"T'ain't right, and ye can't tell me it is." The farmer's battered straw hat bobbed above his leathery face as he addressed his companion across the table.

The second man rubbed his ruddy face and took a long pull of ale before he set down his mug with a sigh. "What do ye mean?"

"Animals abandoning their young, most of 'em born dead anyway, and some not even afraid of people but walking right up to 'em as though asking for help. Something's going on, I'm telling you."

"You're not wrong—my goats are acting peculiar. They crowd together and stare at something, only blessed if I know what. There's nothing there. Some forget to eat. Who ever heard of a goat who won't eat?"

"Soldiers took away our wise woman," the first farmer muttered. "My missus says bad things are happening because the wise women are gone."

The second farmer glanced behind him and whispered, "Best not talk about it."

"Then there's talk of the king and queen. Word is they're both so ill they're dying; no one's seen 'em in public for weeks," the first farmer continued.

"What *I* heard was, 'tis witchcraft, and the prince is already dead, only no one will admit it."

"Nonsense," the first farmer said. "I heard 'twas grief made them ill, not magic. No one's seen the prince for weeks, though, so mayhap he *is* dead."

Benno saw the maid had noticed him. She scowled and walked over to whisper to the farmers. They turned to stare at him.

Benno couldn't move; his legs felt leaden. The maid started toward him, her mouth opening. He forced himself to his feet. Without looking back, he walked around the side of the inn, toward the kitchen garden and stables behind it. No one came after him.

Long rows of beans and hops on tall poles stretched the width of the garden; the Inn must brew its own ale. He walked until he was hidden by the vines, then sank down onto the sun-warmed dirt and wrapped his arms around his legs. The rumors were probably more of the prime minister's lies. Benno wanted to be strong, but hot, angry tears came and he couldn't stop them.

If the rumors about the king and queen were true, he'd have his revenge, even if it took the rest of his life. He muttered his vow to the Sisters, fiercely. Then he wiped his eyes and nose on his sleeve and began to laugh. A snot-nosed boy, hiding in the dirt, vowing revenge.

It was time to move on.

He rose to his feet, his mind clear. He'd find food and keep moving, to keep the dogs from picking up his trail. Flying had saved him once, but he couldn't count on it again. He wasn't even sure he could change again. Maybe he had to be desperate for it to work.

He'd discovered he was willing to steal. The penalty was harsh if he was caught; some towns still chopped off the thief's hand, but it had been four days since he'd had enough to eat and he was weak from hunger. First, food, then a place to sleep, out of reach of the dogs. A tree maybe. Perhaps he'd better try to change after he'd eaten something. If he couldn't, it was better to learn the worst now, rather than wait until he was in danger.

If he *was* able to change again, could he roost in the trees? He didn't even know if geese did that. His mother had had no chance to teach him more than how to change shape and the basics of flying. He knew so little of winged life he wasn't even sure what he could eat. He would stick to human food; that was what he craved anyway—fresh bread, roasted meat, even a roasted potato or leek would be welcome, dipped in new butter...

He had to stop thinking about food or he'd do something stupid and get caught. If he could fly again, maybe it wouldn't take that long to reach Weatherstone.

He walked into the stable, avoiding the tack room where the

grooms were talking. He found a bin of oats and grabbed a handful, stuffing it in a pocket, while murmuring an apology to the horses watching from their stalls. He took a few more handfuls and left, chewing as he walked. The oats were dusty dry and mostly tasteless, but they would keep him going until he found something better.

4

THE HUNT

"Do you know where to find the Western Road?" Suli asked. They'd been trudging for hours, and Suli thought they should head in that direction soon. She hadn't come by road, so she had no idea how to find the right one.

Arta grimaced and Suli wondered if she'd ever see the girl smile. "There's a crossroads at Winton," Arta said. "That's where Master Munro takes his goods to market. But I've never been, myself."

"Then we'll go to Winton, and hope it's not market day. How far is it, do you think?"

Arta thought for a moment. "I'd guess something like fifteen miles. He took three hours to get there, on his mule cart."

Suli calculated they'd already come five miles from Kaliska, but maybe they were only now abreast of where Munro's house was in the marsh. "Let's assume it will be fifteen miles from here. We may not get there before nightfall and we'll have to sleep somewhere. Did he spend the night?"

Arta scoffed. "Not him! He was afraid of robbers attacking him while he slept at the inn, so he made sure he came back, even if it was late."

Suli sighed. They'd have to sleep wherever they could, then. Someone would have a barn or a stable they could use. Without Arta, she could've roosted as a goose, and no one the wiser. With the girl in tow, she needed to find somewhere both warm and safe and she didn't have much money left. She hadn't thought she'd need it, flying with the Free Folk—in fact, it was lucky she had any at all. When she'd put a comb in her pocket, she hadn't noticed the coins there.

The sun floated through a cloudless sky as they walked. Now and then a cart or a rider on horseback would pass, staring curiously at two girls traveling by themselves, but no one stopped them. Maybe the rest of the journey would be uneventful.

Something darted across the road and into the trees, moving so rapidly it was gone before Suli turned to look, hidden by tall grass. She caught a flash of something brown before it disappeared.

Immediately a pack of hunting dogs, baying loudly, followed swiftly behind it, spreading across the road until they too plunged into the woods.

Arta and Suli exchanged glances. "Did you see what it was?" Suli asked. Arta shook her head.

A flock of crows was settling in the branches of a tall sycamore where the dogs had entered the woods. Telling Arta to wait, Suli walked over to the tree, the prickly seedpods crunching underfoot.

Suli called a greeting in Crow.

An old crow with a white cast in his eye yelled back, "Begone human! How dare you speak our language!" The other crows brayed their agreement.

"Murderer! Thief! Your hands are bloody! Humans should die and then we'll eat you!" the old crow cried. "We shall never forgive what your magic has done, never!"

Completely bewildered, Suli called, "I'm Suli, from Weatherstone. What magic are you talking about?"

The old crow fumed. "As if you didn't know, wise woman. Oh yes, I can see what you are. I am Blackwing, and this is my flock. We have sworn death to humans!"

"Death! Death! Death!" The flock of crows took up the cry until the air was filled with their angry calls.

"But why?" Suli called loudly, to be heard over the chanting.

Blackwing extended his wings. "You have killed our children! We shall never forgive you!"

"Never! Never! Never!" the flock cried.

Covering her ears, Suli ran into the trees, wondering what had happened to their children. Whatever it was, it was clear who they blamed.

Once hidden from the road behind the tall ferns and under-growth, she changed shape and flew up above the forest canopy, landing on a branch that overlooked the meadow beyond.

The dogs were there, yelping a different call, announcing they'd cornered their prey.

The meadow grass was flattened where the dogs had surrounded the boy. He was about eight, in ragged and dirty clothes, and he looked desperate. He turned this way, then another, searching for a way to escape the snapping and growling dogs.

Where are the hunters following the pack? No one else was in sight yet, so she landed and changed, then ran to the circle of dogs. "Lie down!" she commanded, using the pidgin, the language the animals used to talk to each other. Those nearest her obeyed, still staring at the boy with their tongues hanging out. Cautiously she stepped over them and into the center of the circle of dogs with the boy.

"Why are they chasing you?" she asked.

The dogs growled at her. One snapped at her leg, barely missing it.

Suli was about to command the dogs using the Voice, but then

Arta was running toward her, passing the dogs, and turning to face them.

What in the name of the Sisters does she think she's doing? To Suli's amazement, the dogs whimpered and backed away, lowering themselves to the ground, their eyes on Arta.

"Run!" Arta said to the boy. "I'll hold the dogs here while you get away. Go! Do you want the hunters to find you?"

The boy stared at her blankly. She gave him a push. "Go!" she commanded.

He set off running, disappearing into the trees.

"What did you do?" Suli asked. It wasn't the Voice—Arta hadn't said a word. Now she simply scowled at Suli.

They'd better leave, too. Arta was right: the hunters would be there soon. She heard the sound of horses on the road. Did they know the dogs were chasing a child?

Before she could move, three men rode out from beneath the trees, their horses sweating and lathered.

"What have you witches done to my dogs?" a man yelled. He wore a leather jerkin studded with metal rings and carried a whip in his hand.

A second man, in a blue uniform, said, "Never mind that— where is that thrice-cursed child? Did you see where he went?"

Three armed men on horseback hunting a child with a pack of hounds. "Don't say you've seen the boy," Suli whispered. Her Seeing revealed these men would follow any order, no matter how cruel, as long as they were well paid. And now they were angry with Suli and Arta.

"Are these your dogs?" Suli called. "My sister and I thought we'd be killed and eaten! It's a good thing the dogs heard you coming, and lay down to wait."

"They've tamed 'em somehow," the third man said. From what could be seen past the dark beard, he had a brutal face. He too wore a uniform, but with a sergeant's gold braid on the sleeve. Suli guessed he was the leader.

"Tamed!" exclaimed the first man. He gestured at Suli with his whip. "Those are my best trackers. What've you done to 'em, witch? Some evil magic to make them lose the scent, I'll wager." He glanced at the leader. "They look like witches, Sergeant."

Suli didn't like where this was headed. She said quickly, "They were biting and snapping at us! We were terrified! It was only when you arrived that they calmed down. There was no witchcraft, good sirs."

The sergeant examined Suli coldly. He threw a leg over the saddle and slid off his horse. "They simply stopped?" he asked, coming up to the circle of dogs and striding though them to stand over them. "The dogs stopped hunting, for no reason? Then where is the boy?" He watched Suli and Arta intently.

"What boy? There's no one else here—the dogs surrounded us! Please! Take your dogs away and leave us alone! We're both shaking."

"What about you?" He turned to Arta. "Which way did he go?"

Arta stared at him silently, her face pale. Three of the dogs growled softly in the back of their throats.

"Tanner! Keep your dogs in line!" the sergeant called over his shoulder. "Can't you hear they're threatening me?"

Tanner dismounted, throwing his reins to his companion, and approached the pack. He whistled and waited for them to come to him. The dogs raised their heads to glance at him, then turned their gaze back to Arta.

Now we're in real danger, Suli thought. They had to distract them. "Master Tanner, are you the dogs' trainer? Because if you are, I think you should be ashamed. Why haven't you trained them *not* to chase children? If the local mayor hears about this you'll be in trouble."

The man on horseback chuckled. "Best watch out, Tanner, or you'll be in trouble."

"What do you mean, children? So you did see the boy!" the sergeant exclaimed.

"I mean they chased my sister and me through the wood," Suli said. "We thought they'd kill us! Aren't you even ashamed? The least you can do is apologize."

The man on horseback laughed. "Yeah, Sarge," he said in a falsetto voice, mocking Suli, "you should apologize. Imagine setting dogs on children." He grinned, and rode nearer. "C'mon, we're wasting time. The boy's long gone, if he was ever here at all. I think the dogs followed the wrong scent and treed these witches instead."

Tanner shook his head. "Not possible. They've never made that kind of mistake. He *was* here and the witches are lying." He stepped closer, just outside the circle of dogs, to hiss at Arta, "Where is he?"

Now *all* the dogs growled, the fur rising on their backs. Tanner took a step back, bewildered. "It's witchcraft, right enough. They've never done *that* before. We'd better take 'em in, Sarge. They fit the profile."

The sergeant stood within arm's reach of Suli. He was watching her thoughtfully. Suli put her arms around Arta and pitched her voice low, for his ears alone. "Can't you go and leave us alone?" She couldn't control him with the Voice, not with the others watching, but she could try to confuse him. She chanted softly, "You should go. Please, go away and leave us. *Go find this boy, whoever he is.* Why are you hunting a boy?"

Against his will, the sergeant answered. "You'd like to know that wouldn't you? It's as much as my life is worth to say. I'll not reveal my master's secrets. You'd better be on your way before we take you to a witch camp." His expression shifted from anger to confusion and back again.

The man on horseback called, "Shouldn't we take 'em in? If we were on normal patrol that's what we'd do."

The sergeant shook his head, as though to clear it. "Witches they may be, but we can't be sidetracked. Our mission is more important than a couple of underage witches, and now we've lost the scent. We've got to find the boy, or we're for punishment. Let 'em go."

Suli didn't need telling twice. Grasping Arta's hand tightly, she pulled her through the watchful circle of dogs, and began to run.

They kept running, even after they were hidden by the trees, stumbling over roots and deadfalls, their faces scratched by the branches around them. If the sergeant changed his mind, Suli wanted to have disappeared.

She pointed to a luxuriant bed of new ferns. They crawled beneath the arching fronds, where a tunnel of dead and crackly ferns lay concealed inside the new growth. They lay in the warm bracken and waited, listening for sounds of pursuit.

When the sound of the horses had faded away, Arta whispered, "Wasn't it lucky you had me with you? I stopped the dogs from attacking you. Admit it: I'm useful."

Suli laughed and sat up, her head brushing the rustling ferns. "All right. Thank you for saving me. But how did you do that? Do you know magic after all?"

Arta didn't meet her eyes. "Animals like me, that's all. They do what I ask."

"I see," Suli said. "That sounds useful." But it wasn't an explanation. If Arta was using magic, it was nothing she'd ever heard of. "Can you tell me more?"

Arta shrugged and looked away. "I don't know more. I don't think it's magic."

Suli sighed. "Don't mention we saw the boy or those soldiers to anyone."

Arta rolled her eyes "I'm not a fool. I know about such men."

"What do you mean?"

Arta gave her a pitying look. "You haven't heard about the soldiers rounding up witches for the camps? I thought you were supposed to be a wise woman. Mayhap you're not as clever as you think."

Suli wanted to wipe that smug expression off the girl's face. But she had to humor her, to find out what the girl had done to the dogs. Unknown magic was a threat, even if it had saved her from being attacked. If the girl knew advanced magic after all, then Arta had been lying to her. Worse, it meant Suli's Seeing, the most basic kind of magic, hadn't revealed it. That could mean her magic no longer worked. "Why would soldiers catch girls and put them in camps?" *Not just camps—witch camps.* A lump of ice settled in her belly.

"Cos they're learning to be witches, aren't they?" Arta said. "The soldiers are afraid of women in the countryside, and the young ones what learn magic. Only the namby-pamby girls in town are safe."

"What about the wise women? The ones who actually use magic—"

"Rounding them up first, o' course. I thought Ma would say something. Mayhap she doesn't know either. They'll come for you, too, once they get 'round to it."

Suli looked at her curiously. "How on earth did *you* know about it, living in the middle of nowhere?"

"I hear things," Arta said evasively.

"If you know they're rounding up wise women, why would you risk being apprenticed to one?"

Arta drew a circle in the dirt beside her. "I figured knowing magic would be useful. Besides, you took care of Master Munro, right enough." She looked up. "And you might've talked that sergeant 'round, only he wasn't alone so you couldn't." She smiled at Suli's expression. "I want to do that, too."

The girl was perceptive and had some kind of magic Suli didn't know about. *She's not only annoying, she's dangerous.* The sooner they got off the road and found a safe place to spend the night, the better. She was afraid the soldiers would change their minds and come after them. That threat about putting them in a camp was real. But why were they chasing a boy? The sergeant had said it was a secret worth his life, and he'd been telling the truth, she was certain.

"About the inn in Winton—" she began.

"Master Munro said it was full of thieves and con men."

Suli didn't give a fig for Master Munro's opinion. She couldn't afford a room, but they could sleep in the stables or barn. No hayloft tonight; she wanted a place with a door.

Once they were safe, she'd tackle Arta about how she'd controlled the dogs. Strange magic was just as worrying as the threat of being put in a "witch camp."

If she was going to make it home, she'd better find out about both.

5

MASTER SWIFT'S CARAVAN

THEY ARRIVED in Winton sooner than Suli expected, just as the sun was setting. Using her Seeing, she found a trustworthy woman who gave them directions to the Compass Rose Inn.

The inn seemed a comfortable sort of place, clean and well run, with a steady stream of locals leaving the main dining room after their dinners. Suli drew the landlady aside and asked if they could sleep in the stables for a couple of squals.

"Well, you don't look like horse thieves, so I don't see why not," she said briskly, tucking a loose strand of dark hair behind her ear. "You have to use a safety lantern though. I'll not have the place set on fire." She handed a shuttered lantern to Suli. "Go ask Daniel to show you an empty stall."

Suli thanked her and took the lantern.

In the stable, Daniel showed them a clean and empty stall. Suli set the lantern on the top of the half door and they ate the last of the pie before piling hay up in mounds and settling into the piles. It was prickly, but warm.

"Why did the dogs lie down and obey you?" Suli asked, wriggling deeper beneath the hay. "You say you don't know magic, but that's what it must've been. How did you do it?" She spoke in a low voice. It was unlikely they'd be overheard, but there was no point in taking chances.

"I don't know," Arta said. "I told the dogs not to hurt the boy and they stopped and lay down. That's all."

"You told them? I didn't hear you."

"In my mind," Arta said, as though it were obvious.

Suli shook her head. Her Seeing told her Arta wasn't lying—if it still worked—but her teachers had never mentioned anything like this. It sounded like another form of the third kind of magic, commanding others to obey, like the Voice, but in silence. "Have you ever done this before?"

Arta bit her lip. "Maybe."

"Give me an example."

Arta hesitated, then shrugged. "The first time it happened at Mr. Munro's, I was feeding the goats. They crowded against me and knocked me down. I thought they'd trample me, so I yelled at them in my mind to get back, and they did. They cleared a space around me."

"Did Mr. Munro see that?"

"Oh no, I never let him see anything."

"Oh? Did you do other things? I don't mean to pry into your secrets, Arta." *Except that I do, or the Sisters only know what trouble we'll be in.*

Arta met her gaze. "Will you tell me what you can do, too?" she asked. "Would you tell me, for instance, if you were able to change shape and fly?"

Caught off guard, Suli laughed nervously. "What do you mean?"

"Fair's fair," Arta prodded. "I saw you fly, twice. The first time was in the marshes: a goose flew up from where you'd gone into the grass. The second time, a goose flew over the trees after you talked to that crow. How can you talk to crows?" she asked, wonder in her voice. "Tell me the truth: are you a wise woman, or are you really a witch?"

Suli stared at her. Arta was so thin her clothes pooled around her like a bundle someone had left behind. But now her chin was lifted and her eyes blazed as she waited for Suli to tell her the truth. The frightened girl she'd rescued from Munro was gone. She wasn't afraid anymore, at least not of Suli.

Suli smiled to herself. The girl was observant and smart. She'd saved Suli and that boy from the dogs, all by herself. She might be small, but she'd proven she was brave, with powerful magic. Maybe she *should* treat her like an apprentice.

Arta had already guessed she was a shape-shifter, so there wasn't much risk in admitting it. They needed to trust each other. They were both in danger of being accused of witchcraft.

"I'm not a witch. I'm the wise woman in Weatherstone, as you'll see when we get there. Yes, I can change shape, but that's something I inherited from my family. My friend Orion and the crow flock in Weatherstone taught me Crow. Anyone can learn it. I'm more interested in how you can talk to an animal silently and make it obey you. I've never heard of anything like that before. What do you know about it? Can others in your family do it?"

Arta shook her head. "No one's said naught to me. I only found out I could do it this year. Can you teach me to fly?" she asked. "I'd like to fly."

Suli suddenly felt too tired to keep her eyes open. She rose and put out the lantern, then lay down, her head resting on her sack stuffed with hay for a pillow. "I told you, changing shape is something I inherited from my family." She yawned. "I can't teach you; it doesn't work that way."

The straw rustled; Arta had curled up beside her. "I suppose we both have secrets we can't tell anyone. And that little boy, what was his secret?" she asked sleepily.

Suli turned but couldn't see Arta's face in the darkness. She'd like to know the answer to that too, but there was no use worrying. They'd probably never hear anything more about it.

Right before she fell asleep she remembered the anger of that flock of crows. She'd never seen them before, yet they called her a murderer. Something about human magic murdering their children. Had a witch murdered their fledglings?

Grisa had warned her that she needed to go home because of a strange sickness among animals. Was that related to the crow fledglings? She felt a moment of fear. She wanted to fly home right away, to see that everyone was safe, especially Coalfeather's flock.

But she couldn't. Arta was her responsibility now.

And even though she was beginning to like this perceptive and stubborn girl, the sooner she found out whether Arta's magic was a danger to others the better.

THE NEXT MORNING all their food was gone and all Suli's money spent. Suli and Arta threw their nearly empty sacks over their shoulders, brushed off the hay, and went to ask directions to the Western Road.

With Arta waiting outside, Suli entered the common room of the inn. The landlady had seemed trustworthy enough the night before, and Suli wanted to ask if she'd heard anything about the soldiers they'd met.

But when she entered, two men stopped eating to watch her, and the landlord never stopped staring. Better to leave before questions were asked. Girls on their own were suspicious these days.

The landlady directed her to the market square. Her husband, pretending to polish a glass, edged closer, trying to overhear their conversation. She couldn't prevent the landlady from telling everyone where they were going. Besides, anyone could follow them and figure it out.

They crossed the busy market square, passing stalls selling

rolls and pies that made Suli's stomach rumble. The sooner they reached home, the sooner they'd eat. They found the Western Road easily, and joined the steady flow of foot traffic, horses, and wagons.

The morning was cold, but the sun felt warm on their backs as they walked. Women pushing handcarts filled with vegetables or homespun wool were arriving in the square. Farmers drove past, their carts stacked high with cabbages or casks of ale. The merchant traders had a lane to themselves, their heavy wagons filled with sacks of wool, salt, or coal, the oxen plodding more slowly than the horses.

Suli felt safe for the first time since they'd encountered the hunting dogs. That might be an illusion, but anyone who wanted to question them would have to do it in front of a crowd of witnesses.

By the time the sun was high overhead, and their stomachs were growling with hunger, they were dusty and tired. Suli searched for a place to stop and rest, hoping for water to refill their jug.

A long caravan of brightly colored wagons had parked beside the road. Many of the wagons were really cottages, gaily painted with flowerpots hanging from the windows. Suli and Arta stopped to watch the men and women cooking food over a fire. A sandy-haired man in a tunic of midnight blue came over to greet them.

"Hello, my dears, are you hungry? We have plenty to share if you'd like to stop and sup with us." He gestured at three fires with large cooking pots. One of the women stirring a pot, with a kerchief over her hair, waved and smiled.

Suli was about to refuse, afraid of prying questions, but Arta said loudly, "Yes, please. I'm *very* hungry."

The man laughed. "Good. Come with me."

Suli's stomach growled. She decided not argue. "Thank you, Master…?"

The man bowed. "Master Swift, at your service. This is my caravan, and these are my people."

"Thank you, Master Swift," Suli said, curtsying. "I'm Suli Wing, and this is Arta Phos. You're very kind." Her Seeing revealed his kindness was genuine.

Master Swift led them to a group of people sitting on a cloth spread on the grass. They nodded and said hello, then turned back to their meals. When Arta was settled with her sack beside her, Suli went over to the cooking pots and asked the woman in the kerchief, "May I help, Mistress?"

"Yes, if you wouldn't mind, take this bowl and one for your friend. The bread is over there," she nodded toward a basket piled high with loaves. "Master Swift insists we have something hot at midday to keep us going."

Suli carried two bowls, with a chunk of bread balanced on each rim, back to Arta, then sat down and began to eat. Master Swift lowered himself beside her with a grunt. "I'm glad you're stopping with us, Mistress Suli," he said. "I thought you two might need a ride. And I've news you may want to hear."

Arta looked up from her bowl, worry creasing her forehead. "Is something wrong, Master Swift?"

Master Swift waved the idea away with his hand, smiling faintly, but he said no more. When those nearby had finished eating and risen to return their bowls, he spoke softly.

"I hear things on the road. We don't only pay in coin when we stop at an inns or a farmhouse; they expect us to provide the latest gossip, and they repay us in kind. Yesterday I heard something that troubled me."

He paused to gather his thoughts. Suli and Arta leaned closer. "In Winton, a man at the inn told me a story he'd heard from soldier. Soldiers encountered two girls who saw something they shouldn't have. The soldiers let them go, but now they know that was a mistake. Unless they find those two girls, to bring them in for questioning, the soldiers will be punished." He looked away, and leaned back on his hands, staring up at the sky, as though taking his ease. "I thought that was the kind of gossip you'd like to hear."

Arta had turned pale. She opened her mouth but Suli caught her eye and shook her head.

Master Swift gave no sign he'd seen this exchange. "My guess, Mistress Suli, is that you'll need help to continue your journey without being captured. Where are you headed?"

Suli hesitated. He knew they were wanted by soldiers; he could easily turn them in for a reward. But if he'd meant to do that, why bother to warn them? "We're headed for Weatherstone."

"That's lucky. We're headed for the mountains, too."

Arta was frowning. Suli said nothing. Yes, Master Swift had a good heart, but there was more going on here than she understood.

"I don't want to know your secrets," Master Swift continued. "But if you'd like to ride with my caravan, I'd be happy to have you." He added softly, "If we see soldiers coming, there are hiding places in our carts no soldier or Excise man has found yet. We don't want folk poking into everything we carry." He grinned. "You'd just be a different kind of contraband."

"And what do we have to do in return?" Arta asked sharply.

Suli waited for Master Swift's reply.

For the first time, Master Swift looked unhappy. "I don't need you to *do* anything, child! Soldiers chasing children on the road... why wouldn't I help you? Besides, I know about these soldiers; I saw them on our way into town and I know who they work for and why they're here. There's nothing I can do to stop *them*. You, however, I can do something about." His mouth compressed into a grim line. "These men are rebels, and if you aren't afraid of them yet, you should be. If they think you can inform against them, they'll kill you."

Suli inhaled sharply. A chance meeting on the road and now they were in danger of being killed? It didn't make sense.

A man passing on the road called a greeting to Master Swift. Smiling, he raised a hand. "Nice to see you!"

When he turned back, the smile was gone and his eyes were hard.

Suli asked, "What did you mean, 'why they're here'?"

"Let me tell you something else I heard," Master Swift said. "Twice a year we take wool and hides to the coast. We're on our way back from Lofton, returning to our village in the plains.

"While we were there, we heard sad news about Queen Mora. People say she's fallen ill and will see no one but her closest waiting women and advisors. She hasn't been seen in public for months, and everyone says she's dying. King Sito attends his duties, but he also appears ill, pale and thin, as though he's shrinking away. People say it's because he's worried about the queen."

"But you don't think it's that," Suli said quickly.

"No, and neither do many in the town. There are rumors the prime minister is unhappy with the king and queen for limiting his power. He tells the king and queen to enjoy themselves and let him make the decisions. He wants them to be figureheads, not rulers. Some say he'll do anything to become the real ruler of Teveral. And no one has seen their son in months, either."

"Why are you telling us this?" Suli asked. Repeating rumors about the royal family to strangers was foolhardy. *No one has seen their son?* A horrible idea had occurred to her.

"Those soldiers, the ones who let you go—they work for the prime minister," he said.

"You can't know that!" Arta protested. Her face was creased with the stubborn expression Suli was coming to know well.

"I know a great deal," he said. "But I'm only a humble trader, trying to make an honest living on the road, and no one pays me any mind when my caravan stops at an inn or a rest house. I've a free hand buying drinks for soldiers, and they don't mind their tongues when they're in their cups. You saw soldiers chasing a boy, didn't you? I think I know who he is. The prince is missing. No one has seen him at the palace in weeks."

Suli's hands were icy. She said slowly, "You mean the boy we saw running away from the dogs and the soldiers is the son of our king and queen?"

"That's exactly what I mean. The rumors say the prime minister kidnapped him and held him prisoner in the country-side, and now he's escaped."

"But that can't be true!" Suli protested. "If it was, everyone would know! The news would be all over the country."

Master Swift shook his head. "Not if they want him back alive. If they admit the prince is missing, and reveal the prime minister kidnapped him, it will mean civil war. By keeping quiet they hope to get him back before things go too far. So they say nothing. As long as they can't be certain where he is, or whether the prime minister has him, they can't go public with his kidnapping."

Arta stared at him in horror. "That boy was the prince?"

Master Swift glanced over his shoulder. "That's what I fear. And that's what the soldiers think *you've* discovered. Now do you understand the danger you're in?"

6

THE ROAD

WITH THE NEWS that soldiers were looking for them, Suli grate-
fully accepted Master Swift's offer of a ride in the caravan. He led
them to a caravan cottage painted robin's egg blue, with yellow
shutters and red wheels.

"It's my sister's cottage," he explained as he led them up the
steps and knocked on the door. "She'll be good company for you,
and there's a compartment in the floor that no Excise man has
found yet. Now you know *my* secrets." He winked.

The door was opened by a woman with reddish hair, her pale
face sprinkled with freckles, who looked very much like Master
Swift himself. She smiled at Arta and Suli. "Well, Samuel, what
have we here?"

"Molly, may I present Mistress Suli and Mistress Arta? They
need to be safe from prying eyes while we're on the road. Would
you mind keeping 'em in your cottage, and if trouble comes,
hiding them?"

Molly looked the two girls over carefully; she's using her
Seeing, Suli thought, and she did the same. Mistress Molly had a
warm heart, but she was nobody's fool.

"It's kind of you to bring me visitors, Samuel." She bent down and smiled at Arta. "I'm always glad to have company on the road. There's tea brewing in the pot, and we might find some cakes in the cupboards. Could you help me look, Arta?"

Suli glanced at Arta. The wariness on her face a moment before was replaced by curiosity.

"Thank you, Mistress, tea would be welcome," Suli said.

They spent the rest of the day in the caravan cottage with Mistress Molly and her cat, Simmer, whose ginger hair was the same color as that of his Mistress. Suli and Arta had tea and two gingerbread cakes each, and then Molly brought out the games she kept in a neat cupboard over the bed. Suli guessed she often entertained children.

Sheer curtains on the windows let in the light but prevented anyone from seeing in. As long as they stayed away from the windows, Molly said, the girls were safe.

"Do you live like this all the time?" Suli asked. Arta was engrossed in the novelty of a game of hopping stones while Simmer purred happily in her lap.

"No, dear. In winter, when my husband is home, we bide together in a house in Lofton. But in the summer, while Jack is at sea, I travel about with my brother, the same way we did when we were children and my father was the caravan master. I get to see the country and our old friends and hear the news. Lofton is hot and dusty in the summer. I'd rather be out in the country where everything is green."

"Yes!" Arta crowed. She'd won her first game.

"Do you have any children?" Suli asked, scooping the stones from the board with a sigh.

"My two sons are at sea with my husband," Molly said. "They're both nearly grown and will have ships of their own someday."

"What are those, Mistress?" Suli asked, pointing at enormous dolls hanging on the walls.

"That's my paying work," she said proudly. "I make puppets for the shows. That's my latest order for a puppet master in the plains."

"That's where I'm from," Suli said, "the village of Beeshome."

"Is that where we're taking you two?"

Suli shook her head. "No, we're headed for Weatherstone."

"That's all right, then," Molly said. "We'll pass right through Weatherstone, so we can take you all the way."

Suli felt relieved. The less time they spent on foot the safer they'd be from soldiers on horseback.

"Now, Arta, would you like to see if you can make a puppet move and talk?" Molly asked.

Arta nodded, her eyes alight.

THAT NIGHT, they made up the truckle bed that rolled out from beneath Molly's high one, and piled it with colorful quilts. After a dinner of roasted potatoes and a soup of greens, Arta went to bed, falling asleep immediately.

Once the washing up was done and the water tossed from the steps of the moving cart, Molly made nettle tea, and Suli settled at the table again. Molly said she wanted a chat before bed. Suli wondered if she knew about the prince's escape.

"Mistress, your brother warned us that soldiers might come after us, because of something we saw. That drove another danger from my mind. Have you heard of these 'witch camps'? The soldiers we ran into threatened to put us in one."

Molly's face clouded. "You haven't heard this before now? I suppose that means the soldiers haven't reached the mountains yet. It's not a rumor, Mistress Suli, it's a fact. The prime minister says all wise women are witches and a threat to the country. He's ordered his soldiers to find them and take them to 'resettlement camps.' What happens after that no one seems to know." She slumped in her chair, turning her mug of tea round and round to warm her hands.

Suli thought she could trust the Swifts. "I'm the wise woman in Weatherstone, and I've seen Arta use magic. That means we're both at risk. We're putting you in danger, too, by being here."

Molly shrugged. "It makes no difference—we'd help you in any case. And don't worry about us. Caravan folk know how to deal with soldiers, although I admit this sounds worse than what we're used to. But you won't be safe even when you reach your home, not if they're looking for you."

"But why doesn't anyone know what happens to the women in the camps?"

"That's the most frightening thing, isn't it? Only powerful magic could stop wise women from breaking free or sending messages."

Suli glanced at Arta's small form curled beneath the covers in the truckle bed. Her breathing was slow and regular, and she seemed asleep, but Suli lowered her voice.

"But most villagers know magic and witchcraft aren't really the same—"

"Are you certain of that?" Mistress Molly asked gently. "Anyway, the soldiers threaten them and offer gold. That's often enough to change what people 'know.'"

Suli thought of Mistress Parker who lived in Weatherstone. She'd lied at Tala's witch trial, for a bribe of gold. Of course there would be others like her. But wouldn't most of the villagers, and the wise women's families, defend them?

If they'd had enough warning, some wise women would have gone into hiding. She would try to find them. "Were there soldiers in the villages when you traveled through the plains this summer?" She wondered about Beeshome, the village she'd grown up in. Had Hedith, its wise woman, already been captured?

"It was beginning. Soldiers would appear without warning and by the time they left, all the wise women and some of the girls were gone, hauled away in carts."

"How did they know who to take?"

"Informers. There are always informers. Some people resent wise women. People who feel wronged by them, or who resent their power. Young girls can be spiteful. The ones who aren't very good at magic are happy to accuse the ones who are. They can boast about being patriotic, but really they're just envious and mean."

Suli had to admit Molly was right. In her own village most of the girls had called her "witch spawn" because she *was* better at magic than they were, and because she hadn't been able to control it. She wondered if there were others like her, under guard in a camp somewhere, not knowing what would happen to them. "So no one tries to protect them?"

"Of course they do. The husbands and fathers and brothers and sons tried to fight back. But farmers and traders can't win against armed soldiers—and there were too many soldiers together for the wise women to use the Voice. Remember that," Molly said seriously. "Whatever you plan to do to defend your own village, it has to be something that will work on a group of soldiers, not just one man." She sighed and rose to her feet. "We should go to bed. If no one stops us on the road, we'll be in Weatherstone by tomorrow evening."

Suli got into bed beside Arta and burrowed beneath the quilts. Molly put out the lamp and climbed into the high bed.

Suli lay awake thinking. If the soldiers were looking for them, they weren't safe anywhere; soldiers might already be waiting for them in Weatherstone. If they were rounding up *all* wise women, the wise women of the mountain villages would have to go into hiding anyway. Why was the prime minister doing this? Did he really believe they were witches? She doubted it. And where was her teacher while this was happening? She wished Tala would come home and tell her what to do.

All of this was part of something larger and more disturbing, she realized. If there were soldiers still loyal to King Sito and Queen Mora, a quiet civil war was already underway.

She had to get a message to Tala—or to Magda, her sister. They must've heard the rumors about the king and queen, and about the camps for witches, if Arta knew about it in the middle of the marshes…she was struck again by the improbability of that. How had Arta heard the news when she hadn't? She was puzzling over that when she fell asleep.

~

THEY SPENT the next day talking quietly or playing games in the caravan cottage, sometimes walking beside it in the warmth of the autumn sun when the caravan toiled slowly up a steep hill and Molly said it was safe.

When the caravan stopped to rest and water the horses and oxen, Arta would go to the horse pulling their cottage, and lean against it, a contented smile on her face. Suli assumed she was talking silently with the horse, as she had with the dogs.

The day passed peacefully, with no sign of pursuit, but Suli's anxiety grew. She said nothing to Arta about her fears, but Arta watched her nervously.

Molly went outside to check on the horse as they climbed a hill.

Arta crossed the room to ask Suli in a whisper, "Do you think the soldiers will come after us?"

"I don't know. They might."

Arta nodded, apparently satisfied by her honesty.

It was late afternoon when the caravan began to climb the green foothills that surrounded Weatherstone and the high mountains. Looking out the window, Suli's heart lifted as she recognized the hills that meant she was nearly home.

A knock sounded on the caravan door, and Master Swift entered. "We'll be stopping in Weatherstone in half an hour, Mistress Suli. I've seen no sign of soldiers on the road, but that doesn't mean there haven't been other spies watching us. You should be careful and get home as quickly as you can."

Suli said they would, and thanked him over and over again for the gift of a safe journey. "And new friends," she added.

He waved her thanks away. "'Tis no great feat to carry two girls twenty miles to help them get home. Take care of yourselves. My people won't say they've seen you."

After he left, Arta's eyes flicked nervously to the windows. Suli wished she could bring back the relaxed and happy child Arta had been for the last day, but she couldn't pretend they weren't in danger.

Molly caught her eye and winked.

"Arta," Molly said, kneeling down by the girl, "there's something I'd like to give you."

Molly moved the rag rug beneath the table, revealing a trap door in the floor. She pulled the ring handle, and the door lifted silently on oiled hinges. Reaching into the space below, Molly pulled out a small box and placed it beside her, and then lowered the trap door. She shifted the rug to cover it, and handed Arta the small box.

Carefully, Arta lifted the lid and unwrapped the blue tissue paper.

Inside the paper was a small but beautifully carved horse, made of dark wood.

"Do you like it?" Molly asked.

Arta's eyes were wide. "Thank you," she whispered, stroking it, "it's beautiful."

"What will you call it?"

Arta wrinkled her brow. "Her name is Tekka."

"Mistress," Suli said to Molly Swift, "we are truly in your debt. If you ever need to find me, ask for the wise woman or Tala's house in Weatherstone, where I live. I can help with sickness or magic, if your people ever need anything."

Molly nodded. "Thank you. We'll likely come through Weatherstone again on our way back. If so, we'll stop by to see how you and Arta are faring."

Suli smiled. "You'll be very welcome, Mistress."

The light was fading, blurring the shapes around them when Suli and Arta jumped down from the blue cottage and waved farewell to the Swifts. The fear Suli had put aside while they were safe in the cottage now returned, and she felt cold all over, imagining what they might find when they reached the house. Perhaps returning home was folly; it could be a trap. But if Tala had sent her a message, that's where it would come.

Together they climbed the cobbled street that rose steadily through the village until they reached the gate to Tala's house. Three children ran past, playing the last game of twilight. They waved at Suli, and stared at Arta with curiosity.

Suli opened the gate and they climbed the path up the hill. The pond glimmered on their left, but no sound revealed the presence of the flock of shape-shifting geese who lived there. *That's odd,* Suli thought. They should've heard the gate open and come to investigate. Perhaps they're all asleep.

The hill was steep. They arrived in the yard breathless from the climb. The kitchen window facing the yard was dark. No light showed anywhere.

Suli climbed the kitchen steps and Arta followed, clutching Tekka to her chest.

The door was unlocked, which wasn't how Suli had left it. She paused, her heart beating fast, telling herself not to be foolish. Orion had probably forgotten to lock it again after coming by to feed the animals. But what if soldiers had arrived before them?

Suli pushed the door open, turning back to say, "You'll stay in the guest room. I'll tuck you in and then I'm going down to the pond to bathe—"

Arta stared past her, the blood draining from her face.

"What?"

Wordlessly, Arta pointed inside.

7

RUMORS AND SPIES

IN THE DIM gloom of the kitchen, firelight glowed through the latticework pattern on the stove's door, revealing a slumped figure at the table.

"Who's there?" Suli called, her voice shaky.

For an answer, she heard a snort. The figure rose heavily and crossed the room. There was the sound of flint striking steel. When the lamp was lit, the figure turned to face them.

She had salt and pepper dark hair, and the worn face of a middle aged woman. It was Magda, Tala's sister, who had returned from the coast.

Suli exhaled. "Thank the Sisters!"

"Where have you been?" Magda demanded. "The Free Folk sent word you'd be coming home days ago."

For a moment Suli was speechless. It had been almost two years since Tala, her former teacher, and Magda, her sister, had left for the coast. In all that time, Suli had received only a few letters each year to tell her they were still alive. Now Magda demanded an explanation from *her?*

She took a deep breath. "I don't see why I should give an

account of myself to you. I've had no word from you or Tala in months!"

Arta looked nervously from one to the other, hovering near the door.

Magda laughed and sat down, leaning back in her chair. "Fair enough. But I was worried something had happened to you." She grimaced. "My news is urgent, or I wouldn't have come."

Suli noticed Arta was clutching her sack as though she was about to run. "Arta, this is Magda Wing, the sister of my teacher, Tala. After she warms up some food for us, you and Tekka can go to bed." She threw a warning glance at Magda.

Magda nodded. "You both look exhausted. There's plenty left from dinner. *I'm* in the guest room."

"Come, Arta, we'll share my room. It's very pretty and has a fireplace. I hope you and Tekka like it." She lit a candle from the lamp and, shielding it with her hand, led the way down the hall.

Arta followed, glancing over her shoulder. "Are you sure she's safe?" Arta whispered as they entered Suli's room. "She sounds mean."

Suli bit back a smile. "Yes, but that's just her way. She's brave and a good person to have around if there's trouble." She didn't mention that Magda had once been a witch.

Suli knelt to light the fire.

"I think there *will* be trouble, don't you?" Arta said. "Just because they haven't caught up with us yet doesn't mean those soldiers have stopped looking. If they haven't found the boy, they'll be angry."

Suli smiled ruefully. She was still surprised by Arta's cleverness. "You may be right," she said, "but Magda and I can protect you. You shouldn't worry."

"Magda knows something," Arta said in a sleepy voice. "She doesn't want me to hear, but I bet it's about the prince."

"Let's wash before dinner." Suli led her back down the hall

and outside to the pump. When they'd washed their hands and faces, they sat down at the kitchen table.

"Hungry?" Magda asked, filling their bowls with something that gave off the fragrant smell of sage, juniper, and simmering vegetables.. Without replying, Arta began to eat.

Suli eyed Magda over her bowl. "I didn't expect to see you back."

"I didn't expect to be back," Magda said. "And it's years of work gone for nothing if I don't return to Lofton soon." She glanced at Arta, then met Suli's eyes and nodded. *She'll wait until Arta's in bed.*

Suli said nothing more, but concentrated on eating. Arta kept glancing nervously at Magda as she ate.

When they finished, Suli tucked Arta into bed. Arta's eyes were already closed and her breathing slow and steady when Suli blew out the candle and returned to the kitchen.

Suli dropped into a chair and said wearily, "I suppose I'd better hear what's so important."

"Yes, you'd better. I've a message from Tala, and a warning." There were shadows beneath Magda's eyes, and new lines of worry on her forehead. Unexpectedly, Magda grinned. "Can you picture me as a housekeeper in Lofton? Working for a magistrate, no less. He's one of the prime minister's cronies, puffed up, self-important men who think forcing Outsider priests and schools on the country will make them rich and powerful."

Tea was brewing in the old brown pot. Magda poured it into two mugs, handing one to Suli before taking a sip from her own. "While I was attending to my duties," she said, "I overheard the magistrate speaking with an army captain. What do you think they were talking about? Sending soldiers to Weatherstone."

Suli shook her head, trying to make sense of that. "How many days ago was this?"

"Five," Magda said.

Before she and Arta had met the boy. Icy fingertips ran down Suli's spine. "I don't understand. Why here?"

"The heir to the throne was kidnapped by the prime minister's men, but he escaped somehow," Magda said heavily. "Now those soldiers are searching for him. King Sito has men looking for him too, but some of them might be traitors, secretly working for the prime minister. Spies are everywhere, and one of them reported he's coming here."

Suli shook her head impatiently. "But—"

Magda interrupted. "That's the reason the prime minister has ordered his hand-picked thugs here. That's *one* reason I'm here."

"And I'm grateful not to face that alone, believe me," Suli said, smiling at the former witch. "But why would a prince come here?"

"I've no idea," Magda said, "but whether he does or not, if soldiers come here, everyone in the village will be in danger. You'll have to decide what to do."

"He'll never make it—he's only a child. How can he possibly elude soldiers all that way? It's twenty miles from Winton!"

Magda looked surprised. "You sound as though you know where he is."

"I do. I mean I think we saw him, but that was two days ago."

Magda said, "By the Sisters! Where was he?"

"We were on the road to Winton when a pack of dogs crossed our path, chasing a small boy. Arta controlled the dogs so he could get away. But we never even spoke to him. We didn't know who he was, until someone told us later. He never knew our names or where we were headed." She frowned. "We can't be the reason he's coming here—if he is." But maybe someone had reported seeing them eating with the caravan folk, and someone assumed the boy would follow them. She wouldn't believe any of Master Swift's people had betrayed them to the soldiers.

"Well, he might not be coming here because of you. Tala

thought perhaps someone told him to come here; we just don't know why," Magda said.

"What else did Tala say?" Suli's voice rose with hope. She wanted her teacher to return and lighten her responsibilities. It wasn't easy being a fourteen-year-old wise woman. Most people respected her, but some, men especially, couldn't resist mocking her seriousness. Sometimes she considered telling the men who made jokes at her expense to take care of their own colicky babies and see how they liked staying up all night. But she couldn't; it was the mothers who'd suffer if she refused to help, not their sniggering husbands.

Magda smiled as though she knew what Suli was thinking. "Yes. I thought she might return to help you, but she can't leave. You do need help if the prime minister's soldiers are coming here. You'll have to make do with me, I'm afraid."

Suli grinned. "I *am* glad you're here, especially if we're going to be invaded by soldiers. You're a lot scarier than Tala. That should help." There was a time when everyone was afraid of Magda, Suli included, when she'd been the scary witch on the mountain. Magda had been so angry at Tala, who'd only begun to teach Suli magic, that she'd falsely accused her of being a witch. Then a witch investigator arrived and put Tala on trial for her life, forcing Suli to live with Magda. That had turned out to be lucky. She'd discovered Magda didn't really want her sister to die. Suli and Magda together had stopped the witch investigator from hanging Tala, with a lot of help from Coalfeather, her crow teacher.

Tala's relationship with Magda wasn't an easy one; they were always competitive and Suli wondered if that changed while they were in Lofton.

Magda laughed. "I am happy to be scary, if you think that will help."

Suli rubbed her eyes. She was tired and looking forward to

sleeping in her own bed, but her thoughts wouldn't settle. "What other reason could a prince have for coming here?"

Magda sat back in her chair, her eyes on the dancing shadows thrown by the sputtering lamp. "We'll have to ask him when he gets here." She yawned. "I don't see how else we'll find out."

Suli didn't really believe the boy was coming there, but they should make plans just in case. "Tomorrow I'll ask the flock to fly over the roads to the village. The crows could help, too. If the prince does come here, we'll have to hide him. The mountain would be difficult to search."

"Yes," Magda said thoughtfully. "Yes, it would." Magda had lived in the forest on the mountain for years and knew its secret hiding places. But anyone unfamiliar with its rocky valleys was in danger of falling into a hidden pit, or being buried under a rock fall or avalanche. The heavy snows would arrive soon, and the mountain passes would be closed.

"You said Tala sent me a message. What is it?"

Magda hesitated. "Let's wait until tomorrow. You look exhausted. Go to bed."

Suli wanted to insist, but a deep tiredness washed over her. Her eyes kept trying to close on their own. "Maybe the spies are wrong. The prince is probably miles away from here. After all, what's here that could help a boy fight soldiers?"

"You and Arta, perhaps?" Magda said. She rose, lit a candle, and blew out the lamp.

Suli assumed she was joking, but she was too tired to ask. She followed Magda down the hallway to bed.

8

THE SEARCH

WHEN SHE WOKE the next morning Suli realized that she no long had a choice about making Arta her apprentice. Whatever the reason for soldiers coming to Weatherstone, she couldn't simply abandon the girl to another master and hope they wouldn't find her.

When she entered the kitchen, the heat from the stove was an embracing wall of warmth, and porridge was already simmering on a back burner.

A young man with curly dark hair was eating at the table with his back to the doorway.

She touched him on the shoulder, making him jump. "Thanks for making breakfast, Orion," she said.

Orion twisted to see her, his face lighting up. "Magda said you were back, so I made extra." He rose and gave her a crushing hug. He stepped back, examining her. "I'm sorry you didn't get to go on your trip. Are you horribly disappointed?"

Suli sighed. "I was. But it may turn out to be a lucky accident. Sounds like I'm needed here." She ladled porridge into a bowl and sat down across from him. "Why weren't you here when we arrived last night? Magda scared us half to death, sitting here in the dark."

Orion smirked and resumed eating. "I like sleeping with the flock when it's cold. Besides, sounds like you received a warm enough welcome without me." He looked up. "Wait, what do you mean 'us'?"

"Magda frightened my new apprentice," Suli said.

Orion's eyebrows shot up. "*Apprentice*? O wise woman, can I be your apprentice, too?"

"It's not an honor I wanted, believe me. It's a long story, but I should warn you: she can do magic I don't understand. And don't tease her. No witch jokes, please."

Orion made a wry face. "So you don't want me to talk to her at all?"

"Perfect," she reached across the table and batted his shoulder.

Arta came in, sniffing the air. "Is that porridge?" She stopped short when she saw Orion.

"Orion, I'd like you to meet Arta Phos, my new apprentice. Arta, this is Orion. He lives here. He's a shape-shifter, like me."

"Oh." Arta considered him gravely. "Can you do magic, too?"

"No." Orion dropped his spoon in the empty bowl with a clatter and carried it to the sink. He asked Suli, "What will you do on your first day back?"

"Ask the flock for a favor." She grinned. "You can come, too." She pulled out a chair. "Sit down, Arta, and I'll get you some porridge."

Orion opened the door and paused on the threshold. "I'm glad you're back," he said before he left.

Magda came in yawning and wandered over to the stove. She served herself porridge and joined them at the table.

"What will you ask the shape-shifters to do?" Arta asked between mouthfuls. She ate as though she hadn't seen food in weeks.

"Watch the roads from the air. They'll be able to see the boy if he's coming here. And warn us if there are soldiers approaching."

"The boy? Do you mean the prince is coming here?" Arta asked, wrinkling her forehead. "Why would he do that?"

"We don't know for certain," Magda replied, "but soldiers are definitely coming."

Arta stared at her bowl, looking puzzled. "If the boy comes here, and the soldiers find him here, won't they think it's proof we helped him escape?"

"Probably," Magda said.

"When you're finished, would you like to visit the goats in the barn?" Suli asked in a coaxing voice. "Magda and I need to talk."

"We can talk later," Magda said briskly. "Sending the flock out is more important. You should do it now."

Magda was giving her orders? She'd done just fine on her own, thank you very much. And sending the flock to search was her idea, after all. "I thought I might need to know what's in the message."

"It can wait," Magda said again, not meeting her eyes.

"Will Tala's message help us find the boy?" Suli asked pointedly.

Magda shook her head. "No. Let's go to the pond and Arta can meet the flock."

Suli fastened her cloak around her shoulders and handed the old shawl hanging behind the door to Arta. They stepped into a cold and gusting wind that sent their skirts and cloaks flapping. Together they made their way down to the pond.

The pond water was a dull brown, reflecting leaden skies, the wind ruffling the surface. The flock swam toward the bank, calling greetings. Before Suli could say a word, the flock of shape-shifters began to ask excited questions about Suli's trip with the wild geese, interrupting each other, and ignoring Suli's attempts to get them to listen.

Magda put two fingers in her mouth and gave a piercing whistle.

The geese fell silent. "Please," Suli said, "can everyone get out of the water? I have something important to tell you."

There was grumbling about the cold wind, but they did it.

"First, I'd like you to meet my apprentice. Arta. Arta, these are the other shape-shifters."

"Hullo," she said.

"When we've more time," Suli said to the geese, "I'll tell you the story of how we met and introduce everyone. But not now. I'm sorry to ask this on a cold day, but I need a favor that can't wait. A young boy, traveling alone, is running away from soldiers who've been ordered to capture him. They think he's headed here, and if he is, we have to find him before they do. Could you please fly over the roads and fields near the mountain to look for him? Keep an eye out for soldiers or strange men behaving suspiciously. If you see soldiers or the boy, come back and tell me."

Some muttered in goose talk; it looked like snow, after all. Far better to roost at home than to fly over the mountain in a biting wind, but Wilo, the eldest, ignored the grumblers and asked, "What should we do if we find the boy? Should we change and speak with him?"

Suli bit her lip. "Don't let him see you change, but if it seems safe, yes, tell him we are trying to help and offer to hide him. Go in pairs so one of you can fly back while the other stays to keep watch over him."

Orion, in human form, startled Suli by coming up behind her. He asked, "And then what?"

"We hide him from the soldiers until we can get word to his parents."

"Hide him?" Tessa protested. "That's dangerous!"

"I'm guessing getting word to his parents won't be easy, either," Orion said.

Suli raised her eyebrows.

"Magda told me," Orion explained. "But you're searching in the wrong place. If he's come this far, he won't be on the roads. That's the first place soldiers will look."

"So you won't help?"

"Of course I'll help. I'm just saying he won't be on the roads."

"But the soldiers will be—they're on horseback. Besides, for all we know, the boy's already been caught, miles from here. You and Flax are the strongest fliers—you two take the main road. And if we don't find him, we'll search the mountain tomorrow."

Once everyone was partnered, Suli sent them off, asking them to check in every two hours. Orion could well be right—the boy might head for the forest on the mountain as the safest place to hide, *if* he knew about the forest and the mountain, and *if* he knew how to survive outside, which she doubted. How would a prince learn about surviving outdoors, living in a palace?

Flakes of snow began falling, swirling on the gusting wind.

"So what did you tell them to do?" Magda asked. Magda had never learned any animal language.

"They'll look for the boy, and if they find him and it looks safe, they'll change and help hide him." She sighed deeply. "So what about Tala's message? Are you ready to tell me?"

Magda glanced at Arta, who was watching them with a knowing expression. "After I warm up."

The three of them turned and returned up the path to the house.

Every time Magda put off delivering Tala's message, Suli's uneasiness grew.

What was so terrible that Magda didn't want to tell her?

9

COALFEATHER

THEY HADN'T BEEN OUTSIDE LONG, yet Suli's face felt frozen. Impatient to return to the warm kitchen, she led the others up the path.

"*Caw! Caw!*"

The call came from overhead. Suli looked up in time to see a large crow above her before it landed in the silvery dirt.

"Greetings Suli! Welcome home!"

"Hullo, Coalfeather." She was pleased he'd come to find her so soon.

"We thought you'd be gone much longer," he hinted, cocking his head.

She smiled at the implied question. "Something came up. I'd like you to meet my new apprentice, Arta."

Coalfeather gave a little hop. "Apprentice?"

Magda glared at the crow. "I suppose you're telling that busy-body what we talked about last night?"

"He understands every word you say, you know," Suli replied. "Arta, Coalfeather is a very learned teacher of magic; he once taught me."

Arta nodded politely. "Hullo."

Coalfeather said 'Hello' and Suli translated.

"That's Crow?" Arta asked her.

"I'll be teaching Arta basic magic," Suli said to the crow. "And I hope she'll be teaching me. Have you ever heard of humans who can speak to animals in their minds?"

Coalfeather turned and fixed one deep brown eye on Arta, who stared back. He made the purring sound he made when intrigued. "I *have* heard of such magic, but have never seen it. I would like to test her." He bobbed up and down.

"Of course. I'll probably need your help."

"Come with me, Arta," Magda said. "Let them jabber away like starlings, I'm going to get warm." Reluctantly, Arta followed Magda up the path, glancing back.

"But why did you return?" Coalfeather prompted.

How much should she tell him? His flock had a low opinion of humans already. Hearing about the soldiers wouldn't improve it. "A young boy is trying to reach Weatherstone, we're not sure why. Soldiers are chasing him to take him back to prison. Arta used her magic to stop a pack of dogs tracking him—and saved me from being attacked, too.

"We think," she continued, dropped her voice, "that he's the son of the king and queen. Magda came home to warn me that soldiers believe he's coming here. If your flock could send scouts to watch for him near the village that would help. Crows are much less noticeable than geese."

Coalfeather strode up and down, flapping his wings. "My father is right. Humans are crazy! Grown men hunting a fledgling *with dogs*? Why would they do this? What has happened to this land?" He bobbed his head up and down. "I will ask the Council for their approval." He meant the Crow Council that decided how much involvement with humans was wise. "But I have more serious matters to discuss with you, Wise Woman."

That sounds ominous. Suli took a deep breath. "Such as?"

"Something strange is happening to the animals in the plains. We're afraid it will spread here."

Her heart sank. That sounded like the sickness Grisa had mentioned. "What do you mean, strange?"

Coalfeather paced. "My cousin's flock lives a day's flight away; two of their fledglings and a yearling have died. No one knows why."

"Why didn't their wise woman heal them?"

"Their wise woman was kidnapped. Soldiers took her away a few days before this happened."

Maybe there's a connection, Suli thought. First the soldiers take the wise women away, and then the animals get sick. She didn't think it was only because there was no one to heal them. Grisa thought the animals getting sick or forgetting who they were was caused by magic. That would mean the soldiers were using witchcraft. If so, would the sickness happen in Weatherstone, too, when the soldiers came?

"If the soldiers come here, they'll probably take me away, too. They're imprisoning all the wise women."

Coalfeather croaked in dismay. "We can't lose our wise woman now! The flock needs you. We fear the sickness will kill our children. You must find the cause. Other animals are dying, too, not just winged folk."

Coalfeather was right: this was serious. If magic was the cause of the animals' sickness, it might affect everything: crops, people, maybe even the weather.

"Grisa, the leader of the Free Folk, thinks the cause of the sickness is magical. And," she paused, remembering, "on the way home, a flock of crows accused me of murder. They said human magic had killed their children."

Coalfeather gave the alarm call. "This is bad, very bad," he said.

Two crows flew overhead, asking whether Coalfeather

needed help. "No, thank you," he answered. "Just more bad news." The crows dipped their wings and flew away.

"*I* need your help, Coalfeather, if this is caused by magic."

Coalfeather seemed not to be listening. "What? Of course I will help you; I always have. But I must bring your news to the Council." He lifted into the air and was gone.

SULI SAT BEFORE THE FIRE, rubbing her hands. Magda came to sit in the rocking chair across from her

"Where's Arta?" Suli asked.

Magda smiled faintly. "You invited her to meet the goats in the barn, remember? She went to see them, and now we can talk."

"Magda, have you heard stories about animals acting oddly or getting sick?"

Strangely, Magda looked relieved. She leaned forward. "I'm glad you know. Tala and I think it's related to the unnatural storms and wildfires that have been happening lately. Magic isn't flowing correctly. Something is changing—or breaking—it. Tala wants you to find out what's going on."

Suli raised her eyebrows. "*That's* the message?"

"Part of it. Since you'll need the help of other wise women, you need to find the others who are in hiding. *Then* you're to free the ones in the camps. Tala thinks someone is stealing magic."

"You mean the prime minister?"

Magda narrowed her eyes. "Well, obviously."

"But that would mean the prime minister is a witch."

Magda nodded. "Correct. But Tala isn't absolutely certain. She wants you to find out what's going on."

"Why me? Why doesn't she find out herself? What could she be doing that's more important?" Suli rose to her feet, fuming, and paced before the fire. "Find a thief of magic and stop him. Then free all the captured wise women, never mind the soldiers."

She noticed Magda's expression. "*What?* Oh, you're not serious, there's more?"

Magda sat back in her chair staring at the fire. "There's a deadline. I've heard the same rumors; once war is declared, the prime minister will have the king and queen murdered and blame it on Portjean, to whip up support for the war. So if it's perfectly convenient, Tala would like for you to do this before war is declared."

Suli laughed. "I doubt I can do *any* of these things—and certainly not that quickly. Tala should come home." She went to the sink and filled the kettle, then put it on the stove. Taking the teapot and mugs from the shelf, she laid them on the table, spooning leaves into the pot. *This is just like Tala. Asking me to do the impossible with absolutely no guidance as to how to accomplish it.*

"So let's see if I have this right: find out who or what is stealing the magic and stop it. Sneak hundreds of wise women and girls out of the camps, under the noses of their guards. Then, for my next trick—" She stopped, struck by a thought, and turned to stare at Magda. "Does that mean *our* magic is being stolen? Can you still use yours?"

Magda nodded. "The last time I tried, I could See. Try now."

Suli used her Seeing on Magda. It seemed to work; Magda had been telling her the truth, unfortunately. "I wonder why we still have ours when—" Suli became still, lost in thought. "Coalfeather said his cousin's flock got sick *after* the soldiers took their wise woman away. What if it's the soldiers who are stealing the magic? What if they use witchcraft and it disrupts our magic somehow?"

Magda nodded. "That's possible."

Behind her, the kettle began to sing, but Suli ignored it. "That would explain why we still have our magic—the soldiers haven't arrived here yet," Magda said. "And it would explain why we've never heard of any wise women escaping from the camps."

Suli poured the boiling water into the teapot. "Why doesn't

Tala just come home? I don't know what it's like in Lofton, but she's needed here. With her help we could figure this out."

"It's worse than you can imagine in Lofton," Magda said. "Believe me, I tried to get her to come. She says her work there isn't finished and she can't leave until it is. You'd be shocked if you spent a day there. The townspeople believe whatever the prime minister tells them. They really do believe wise women are witches, responsible for everything that goes wrong in their lives. It's as if he controls what they think. Personally, I think everyone in Lofton is bewitched.

"They're eager for war with Portjean. Somehow, he's convinced them that a fleet of fishing boats are a threat. It's absurd." Magda shook her head. "I'm sorry I'm not Tala," she said with a wry smile, "but she knows you can do this."

"Hmph." Suli poured out the tea and handed a mug to Magda.

"Besides," Magda continued, with a nod of thanks, "I plan to return to Lofton before too long. I don't like leaving Tala alone. What she's doing is dangerous and I'm worried about her."

"Sweet Sisters! I can't do this *alone*—you have to help me! If she's in danger, she should come home. What *is* she doing by the way?"

"I can't say," Magda said, looking away. "Not yet. If the soldiers are bewitched, we don't know how the spell works. What if they can force us to betray someone else? They could make you tell what you know. We can't risk it."

"But *you* know!"

"Only because I have to, for the plan to work. I'm sorry. Tala *does* trust you—or she wouldn't expect you to take charge of this."

Suli frowned. "Yes, and that part doesn't make sense. Surely *you'd* be better at—"

"No," Magda said sharply. "Tala said it must be you."

Suli carried her mug to the rocking chair. She sipped her tea slowly, watching the logs shift and settle as the fire consumed them. Suddenly, she laughed. "I can't even find a boy who we think is trying to find *us!*"

Magda was silent.

Suli knew she didn't really have a choice. She sighed. "Of course I'll do as she asks, but I'm going to need help." She took another sip, thinking about Coalfeather's fear that the sickness would come to his flock. She had to find out more about the magical sickness, find out if the connection with the soldiers was true.

For the first time, Suli wondered if Arta's magic was affected. "Don't tell Arta about this. Let me decide what and when to tell her."

"Of course," Magda agreed. "After all, she's *your* apprentice."

"Besides, she'll probably figure it out on her own," Suli said, amused by the idea. "Actually, that's not a bad plan. If we let her work it out for herself, she'll be so busy gloating about her cleverness, she won't remember to be frightened."

10

THE CROWS ARE NOT YOUR NURSEMAIDS

AFTER TWO HOURS had passed since the scouts left, Magda and Suli waited by the pond for their return. The wind whined through the reeds, a lonely sound that added to Suli's gloom. She shivered and rubbed her arms.

Orion coasted down and landed, then became human. With his warm cloak wrapped around him, he leaned against a leafless young tree and said, "I didn't see anything." He made a face, as if to say *I told you so.*

Flax landed, and two others followed. They all shook their heads. No one had seen the boy or the soldiers.

From a distance came the sound of geese calling. Dark silhouettes were flying toward them against the white sky. When they came nearer, Suli recognized Tessa and Wilo. They glided down to the bare dirt where the snow had melted and everyone gathered to hear their report.

"The main road that runs from Grass Village to Weatherstone is swarming with soldiers, and they've put up barricades," Wilo said. "They're questioning every traveler and searching every cart. If the boy is coming here, he'll never make it."

"What about the road *over* the mountain?" Magda asked, after Suli had translated Wilo's words.

"We didn't look there," Wilo said mildly, ruffling her feathers, and glancing at Orion. "We were told not to, remember? Besides, it's more of a cart track than a road. Only the villagers know it's there. How would a stranger know of it?"

Suli translated for Magda.

"We don't know what he knows," Magda replied. "But the soldiers won't know about it, and that's a good reason for the boy to go that way. It's well hidden from below. That's where we should search next."

"I'll go," Suli said.

Magda made an exasperated sound. "*You* can't. We need to make plans. And what about Arta? She'll think you're abandoning her." Magda turned, about to climb the path to the house. "And where has she been all this time?"

"I'll go search the mountain," Orion said. "I've been saying all along that's where he'll be. Someone told him to come here; he might have directions."

He smiled at Suli's sour expression, then gave her a hug, whispering, "Your turn next." He changed and took off, wheeling over them before heading for the flank of the slate-colored mountain.

Suli decided Magda was probably right, that it was too soon to leave Arta alone; the girl didn't even have the ability to See to protect herself.

They heard the sound of wings before they saw Lamisa approaching. She descended, buffeted by the cold wind. When she had landed she said, "Soldiers are cordoning off all the ways into Grass Village on the other side of the mountain. They're interrogating the villagers and asking about magic. Some farmers are stuck at the barricades, unable to return to their farms."

They'll be in Weatherstone soon, then. What could she do? If her theory was right, she was about to lose her magic.

"Weather's changing," Lamisa observed. "There'll be snow tonight. A human child out in the open will freeze to death."

"Thank you, everyone," Suli said. "Now we know where the soldiers are. Get something to eat, and rest. We'll search again later. The mountain next time," Suli said.

It *was* getting colder. She and Magda trudged up the hill to the house.

When she reached the yard, Coalfeather was waiting for her. He floated down from a bare branch. "I have spoken with the Council, Suli, and they reject your request. You cannot use our scouts—the risk is too great. Too many animals have already died. The soldiers and the boy are a human concern. Humans should take care of it."

She was shocked; she'd counted on their help. "But—"

"I am not permitted to say more," Coalfeather said stiffly. "Crows have their own concerns, wise woman, and we do not fight human battles. My father said to tell you that, 'crows are not your nursemaids.' If humans are causing this sickness, it is for you to stop it."

"Does he know that for certain?" Suli asked.

Without replying, Coalfeather rose into the sky and disappeared.

Tears stung her eyes. How could he just leave like that, without an explanation? She felt abandoned. *Which is ridiculous*, she told herself. *I'm a wise woman. I can take care of this myself.* But how would she do that if the soldiers could steal her magic?

Coalfeather's father, Kaark, was powerful on the Crow Council. He constantly warned against close involvement with humans, even with the wise women who were their allies. If Kaark thought humans had caused the disease, of course the crows would refuse to help.

Even if Coalfeather had argued against his father he would never tell her. Humans weren't supposed to know what went on in the Council—they weren't even supposed to know the Council existed.

If Coalfeather's flock blamed humans for the deaths of their relatives, then of course they'd resent her request for help. Almost two years had passed since she'd stopped Magda from harming them. Perhaps they thought the debt was repaid long ago. She couldn't blame them for refusing to help in a magical war. She didn't want to be involved either. But if that was causing the sickness—

Still, the refusal stung. The crows had been her first friends in Weatherstone, and Coalfeather her first teacher. He'd taught her how to survive Magda's attacks when she was a witch bent on kidnapping her. She had no *right* to expect the crows to help, she reminded herself. But without their help the search would be more difficult. Crows could go everywhere and pass unnoticed. The geese were in danger of being shot by hungry soldiers.

She and the flock would simply have to find the boy themselves.

A LONG LINE of wagons loaded with grain and bales of wool crept up the steep mountain road, the oxen straining and sweating against the load. It was more of a rutted track than a road, and the wagons jolted and bounced violently, their lanterns rocking back and forth, throwing menacing shadows on the trees on either side.

Beside the wagons, men on horseback nodded in their saddles.

Hovering above the wool caravan in the evening sky, Orion heard shouts from the lead wagon, and the clash of metal striking metal. He landed in a tree above the lead wagon to see what was happening. The guards at the rear of the caravan woke and urged their horses forward to find the guards around the lead wagon with their hands in the air. Mounted soldiers had their bows drawn, the arrows pointed at the guards.

"Hands up unless you want to be shot!" bellowed a wide-shouldered man wearing sergeant's stripes. He rode toward them, his sword unsheathed. The guards raised their hands.

"Disarm them and search every cursed sack! Use your knives!"

The leader of the guards protested. The sergeant rode over, and without warning, struck him over the head with the hilt of his sword. The guard fell across his horse's neck, unconscious.

The other guards drew back, white faced, while the soldiers stabbed the sacks with their knives and swords, their shadowed faces intent in the lantern light.

"A gold natto if you find him!" the sergeant called. The men worked quickly, pushing the wagon drivers out of the way and stabbing the sacks like mad men. Tufts of wool floated in the air, while streams of barley and oats spilled into the wagon beds.

Someone shouted, "Sergeant! There's something here!"

The sergeant hurried over to look. A terrified child, no more than five years old, lay among the wool sacks. She'd awakened to soldiers stabbing the sacks around her as though attacking an imaginary enemy. She began to cry.

"Mama! Mama there are thieves here!" she wailed.

One of the soldiers took a step back, looking confused.

"Don't worry, little girl," he said, "we won't hurt you."

"I'll do the talking!" barked the sergeant. "Now little girl, tell us what we want to know and you'll be fine. But if you lie—we *will* hurt you! Tell me: is there a boy traveling with you?"

Some of the soldiers looked shocked, but others nodded. "If she knows aught, she should tell," one said.

"Mama!" the girl cried again, then she began to wail loudly.

While the soldiers were distracted, a small shape slipped from the side of a wagon and ran from the light of the lanterns into the darkness beneath the trees, his tracks in the snow disappearing into the forest. Orion landed and followed the trail into the woods.

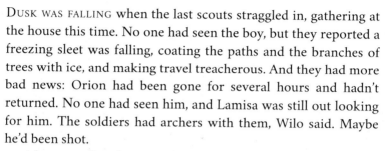

DUSK WAS FALLING when the last scouts straggled in, gathering at the house this time. No one had seen the boy, but they reported a freezing sleet was falling, coating the paths and the branches of trees with ice, and making travel treacherous. And they had more bad news: Orion had been gone for several hours and hadn't returned. No one had seen him, and Lamisa was still out looking for him. The soldiers had archers with them, Wilo said. Maybe he'd been shot.

After spending hours exposed to the bitter wind and sleet, the returning shape-shifters crowded near the fire to get warm. Some changed so rarely they no longer bothered to own clothes and they curled up as geese before the fire. Suli and Magda found blankets for those who changed, and they huddled next to the stove, groaning as feeling returned to numb feet and hands.

Arta made tea, politely asking the shape-shifters if they wanted some, then handed the mugs around. Suli was pleased to see that shape-shifting didn't bother her, and that she'd made herself useful.

Suli counted everyone and realized two others were missing besides Lamisa and Orion. Tessa and Flax were overdue.

Restless, Suli wrapped herself in her cloak and went down to the pond to wait, hoping Orion would return with them. But only two geese appeared in the evening sky. Tessa and Flax called a greeting and landed beside her.

The three of them hurried back to the house together.

Tessa said, "We didn't see the boy or Orion. But soldiers are everywhere now." They fell silent, each busy with their thoughts.

Even after so short a time outside, Suli's fingers were stiff and numb. How would Orion, or a pampered boy, fare out in the open with the world turning to ice around them?

The warmth of the kitchen was almost painful as she came through the door. A swirl of snow and a blast of frigid air entered with them.

"Close the door!" Magda yelled from the table where she was chopping vegetables. She carried handfuls of onions and beets to the stove and dropped them in a simmering pot.

Suli pulled off her cloak and hung it on the back of the door. "I don't suppose there's any tea left?" she asked, looking around.

"Here." Arta brought the teapot over to the table, and filled three more cups. She handed one to Tessa and one to Flax. They had changed and were sitting at the table, shivering.

"I've been keeping it hot for you," Arta said to Suli, handing her another mug. "Are you all right? Your lips are blue."

Suli smiled. "I'll be fine once I warm up." She handled the steaming mug carefully; her hands were still numb.

"You'd better not expect me to do the washing up as well as the cooking," Magda called out grumpily, giving her pots a vigorous stir. Tessa and Flax glanced at each other, smiling.

Suli didn't reply. Her attention was on the warmth spreading through her fingers, and the pain as feeling returned. The warmth of the gingery tea spread through her body.

Orion was smart, she told herself. He wouldn't take foolish chances. But she felt responsible for sending him out when she should have gone herself. And if he heard she was worried about him, he wouldn't even be grateful. He'd say he was nearly a grown man, and didn't need her worrying. He'd been touchy about that lately. "I'm not one of your patients," he'd say.

She sighed and got to her feet, unable to sit still. *Let him resent it.* She was worried. She wrapped the cloak around her again and opened the door.

"Don't be long," Magda called, "dinner will be ready soon."

Suli's skin froze the moment she stepped through the door.

Stars glittered like ice, cold and hard against the darkness. The snow was thicker, no longer melting but piling up where it hit the ground. A gust of wind threatened to knock her off her feet, and there were drifts piling against the barn and the kitchen steps. She took the broom by the door and cleared a path, but by the time she'd reached the barn the snow had sifted over the path behind her. It would have to be done again tomorrow.

She stared up at the starry sky until the sharp wind made tears run down her face, but no dark shape flew across the sky. She went back inside.

The human shape-shifters sat at the table beside Arta, Magda, and Suli to eat Magda's dinner. Lentils simmered with oregano and garlic lay on a bed of turnip greens, with stewed beets and turnips. *Just what's needed on a freezing winter day*, Suli thought. Those in goose form had found a dark corner and were already asleep.

Orion will be all right, Suli told herself. She heard Tessa and Wilo whispering to each other, and heard Orion's name.

The door banged open, sending an icy gust of wind blasting into the room.

Suli turned, smiling in relief, then had to bite back her disappointment. It was Lamisa, in human form. She'd forgotten about Lamisa.

The tall dark-haired woman removed her cloak and shook her head. "I didn't find him, or the boy. He's not at Magda's cottage in the forest. But soldiers are swarming all over the mountain road now. If the boy saw them first, he's probably in hiding. I hope he knows how to survive a winter's night out in the open. It's foul weather."

Whether Orion liked it or not, Suli was really worried now.

11

HIDING ON THE MOUNTAIN

THE NEXT MORNING, just as Suli predicted, the yard was buried in snow and the path to the barn had to be cleared again before the animals could be fed. But as the sun rose the air grew warmer and the shape-shifters returned to the pond before beginning a new search.

Suli was scattering grain for the hens when a loud crow call came from outside.

Leaving the dim light of the barn, Suli had to squint as she stepped into the dazzling sunlight reflecting off the snow.

Coalfeather hung in the air, flapping his wings to stay in one place. "Hurry! You must leave, before they get here!"

"Before who—?"

"The soldiers, of course. They're in the village, with a pack of dogs, and they'll be here soon. You and Arta must hide. Now!"

She was surprised that Coalfeather had come to warn her after yesterday's refusal to help. "Won't your father be angry you're here?"

"I am not a fledgling, Suli," Coalfeather replied with a chuffing sound. "My father does not tell me how to think or what to do.

He is concerned, rightly, about danger to the flock. But I *am* your teacher, and I will help you if I can."

She felt ashamed that she'd doubted him. "Thank you, Coalfeather. I'll need all the help I can get. Tala has asked me to do three impossible things and I don't know how to begin. She wants me to organize the wise women to find out what's happening to the magic."

"The first step is easy," Coalfeather said. "You begin by staying free. If these are the same soldiers you met before, it would be foolish to let them recognize you. Once you're a prisoner, you cannot help anyone. Let Magda handle them." He made a low rumbling chuckle in the back of his throat. "Go hide on the mountain. I will find you. I will inform my father the soldiers are coming." He called a goodbye, already in the air.

Magda stepped out the kitchen door with a bucket. "What was all that squawking about?" She walked over to the pump, hung the bucket over the spout, and began to pump noisily.

"He's saying soldiers will be here soon and we should hide." She felt out of sorts; she was hot from shoveling snow and hadn't slept well the night before, worrying about Orion and the soldiers. Now that the moment had come, she wasn't thrilled about camping on the mountain in the snow while soldiers ransacked her home.

"The crow is right," Magda said. She held a stack of firewood in the crook of one arm, and the full bucket in the other hand. She pushed open the kitchen door with her foot and asked, "Why make it easy for soldiers to find you? Besides, it's time to start on what Tala wants you to do. Find the wise women in hiding."

Suli returned the grain bucket to the barn, and by the time she entered the kitchen, Magda was cooking something on the stove. "Did the crow say anything else?"

"Just that soldiers are in the village. He thinks Arta and I should hide on the mountain."

Magda grunted. "That sounds remarkably like sense."

Suli pulled on her cloak and went outside to speak with the flock.

The snow was melting in the sunlight and the geese were back in the pond, looking oddly peaceful. "Has Orion returned?" Suli asked.

The geese shook their heads and the leaden weight reappeared in her stomach.

"He must be on the mountain; let's search there again. Coalfeather says soldiers and a pack of dogs arrived in Weatherstone last night; they may be the ones Arta and I met before. If you see them, keep an eye on them without drawing attention to yourself. Flax, could you fly to the village to see what they're doing? Arta and I will be at the lean-to in the hidden valley, to avoid them. Send word there."

The geese nodded and flew off in the same pairs as the day before, all except Flax who flew alone to the village.

Suli stared at the reflection of the sky on the surface of the water. Where *was* Orion? She couldn't decide if she was more afraid for him or angry. If he was safe, why hadn't he returned?

Back in the kitchen, bright sunlight poured through the windows, creating pools of warmth. Magda and Arta were eating something that smelled of garlic and ginger. Suli sniffed hungrily.

Arta looked different, Suli thought. Gone were the dark shadows under her eyes and a healthy glow flushed her cheeks. She was still too thin, though. "Good morning. Did you sleep well?"

Arta smiled. "Yes. I like it here. Mistress Magda says I can help take care of your animals. But you don't have any horses," she added sadly.

She looks almost happy, and I have to tell her she's in danger again. Suli smiled nervously. She dreaded having to tell her they'd have to hide, but Coalfeather was right. They couldn't risk the soldiers finding them. "You can take care of the animals later," she said with false cheer. "Today I have a special outing planned. I'd like you to see one of my favorite places on the mountain: a little valley with a waterfall, hidden away. It's so safe, the birds go there to nest."

Arta gave her a skeptical look. "We're going there to hide, aren't we?"

Suli filled her bowl at the stove, deciding what to say. She felt torn; she wanted to look for Orion, but she needed to see what the soldiers were doing in her village. She was supposed to protect her villagers, and she couldn't do that if she was in hiding. But Arta was her responsibility, too, and the soldiers already thought she was a witch. Hiding Arta came first. "Soldiers have arrived in the village. If these are the same ones we met before we don't want them to find us."

Magda cleared her throat. "I'll be here to warn them off." She turned to Arta. "It's nice on the mountain—there are a lot of hiding places." She winked at Suli. Magda had a cottage hidden in the middle of the forest. That might be where they'd end up, if it snowed again.

"Who's keeping an eye on the soldiers?" Magda asked.

"Flax. The others are searching again. I wish Orion would return."

"He can take care of himself," Magda said.

Arta looked uneasy. "You're coming with me, aren't you?"

"Of course!" Suli said cheerfully. "We'll pack enough food for a couple of days, and it will be like a picnic. There's a shelter in the valley. We can sleep under it and watch the stars turn overheard."

Magda met Suli's gaze and nodded. She knew the place and could send a message if needed.

Some of the villagers probably knew about the shelter too, but they'd have to risk it. If the soldiers had a plausible story, say about a lost child, the villagers might even help them search.

Magda found two traveling satchels they could wear across their shoulders, and helped them pack food and warm clothes.

Suli carried most of the food, while Arta carried a blanket and Tekka, the little wooden horse. They trudged across a snowy field, crunching through the icy crust of the snow and soaking their boots, until they arrived at the start of the track up the mountain. Suli sighed as she realized their footprints left a trail anyone could follow. Life was so much easier when you could simply fly.

"Tell me when you get tired and we'll take a break. Once we're out of sight from below, we can stop, but until then let's go as fast as we can."

Arta's face wore a determined look. She nodded, clutching her satchel. Side by side, they climbed the path that snaked up the western flank.

The sun grew warmer. They walked steadily upward for two hours, and grew hot, removing their cloaks. Bright sunlight turned the snow to slush, and the path to mud. Beneath the trees, drifts of snow breathed an icy chill, a reminder that snow would return.

They left the main path to descend into a thickly forested canyon, running west to east. The trail meandered through a copse of birches, tall and pale, still clad in faded yellow leaves. At the bottom of the hill the trail plunged into a rocky defile, where daylight barely reached the ground.

"How much farther is it?" Arta asked.

"Another half hour or so," Suli said. "We can stop and eat if you're hungry."

They were at the bottom of a rocky gorge, its steep sides rising above them. Ahead the path crossed a shallow stream making a chuckling sound as it passed over the stones emerging from the stream bed. Suli looked for a place to stop.

A crow call made them look up. Coalfeather was perched on a branch above them.

"Is there news?" Suli called.

Coalfeather tilted his head to fix one dark brown eye on her.

"Soldiers came to the house right after you left, looking for the village wise woman. Magda threatened them and sent them on their way. It was entertaining." He gave a low rumble, deep in his throat. "They'll be back. They cursed because you weren't there, but the leader laughed and said the dogs would find you." He glanced at Arta as though he thought she could understand his words. "They'll use them to track you."

"What's he saying?" Arta asked.

"Soldiers came to Tala's house and Magda sent them on their way. They've gone to get the dogs to track us. They must be the same men we met before."

Coalfeather flew down to land on the path. "They boasted that wise woman or not, your magic won't work on *them*, because they have protection. You may have to use the third kind of magic to deal with them," he said gravely.

Suli inhaled sharply. Coalfeather had always advised her to avoid using the Voice, or any other form of the third kind of magic, saying the risks outweighed the benefits. If he was telling her to use it, he was truly worried.

"I have a theory about these soldiers," he said. "They do not behave normally. They are too single-minded. Regular soldiers would laugh and joke with the villagers and get drunk. These men are deadly serious."

Suli thought she knew what he was about to say. "I bet I can guess your theory. If they have protection, it must be an object of magical power. Like the story you once told me about Prince Obsidian and his treasures." In the story, a witch broke into Prince Obsidian's castle and stole a magic cap. Later, when Prince Obsidian spied on the witch to discover its powers, he discovered the cap not only transported its owner wherever they wished, but controlled its owner too—they could never take it off.

"Maybe the object of power doesn't just protect them—maybe it controls them," Suli said.

Coalfeather bobbed his head up and down. "Very good," he said, sounding pleased. "That's exactly what I thought. If these men are controlled by a magical talisman, that might be enough to disrupt the flow of magic. But we must know for certain."

"Maybe it's not only being disrupted," Suli said, then hesitated. Should she tell Coalfeather she might not be able to help his flock if one of them got sick? Or at least wait until she knew for certain. But he deserved to know. "Tala thinks something is stealing wise women's magic. It might be this talisman, whatever it is. That might be the cause of the sickness, too."

Coalfeather landed and began to pace thoughtfully. "Yes," he said softly, a low rumble, "that could be it."

Tala had once overheard Suli acting out a story about magic with her dolls; she'd explained that giving magical powers to an object might cause it to do unexpected things—things you had no control over. That could be what was happening. Maybe whatever controlled the soldiers had magical side effects.

"What did he say? Tell me! I want to know too!" Arta demanded.

"That these are the same men we met before," Suli said, "and that—"

"Oh, I knew that," Arta said. "I can hear the dogs."

Suli sat down abruptly on a rock beside the path. "What?"

"They're thinking about me, so I can hear their thoughts."

Coalfeather hopped over to Arta and said carefully, "Ask Arta if she can hear my thoughts too."

Suli translated his question.

"No—why would I?" Arta looked frightened, as though she'd been accused of misbehaving. "I know what the dogs are thinking, because I was afraid when I spoke to them before. They remember me and think about me. That's how I know what they think now. It upsets them to hunt me. They like me!" She smiled for a moment, then her expression grew serious. "It confuses them to track me, when they know I want them to stop. They don't know what to do."

Coalfeather bobbed his head and Suli thought he looked irritatingly smug. He seemed to understand Arta's abilities, when she didn't.

"Where are the dogs now, Arta?" she asked.

She wrinkled her forehead. "I'm not sure. The place smells like streets, and privies—no fields or animals. It smells like a village," she said.

"I'll find them," Coalfeather said. "Go to the hiding place and I'll bring news when I can. Be ready to leave if the dogs find your trail." He rose into the air and disappeared from sight.

Suli and Arta hurried down the path, all thought of eating forgotten. "Did you leave anything at the house they can use to follow your scent?" Suli asked.

"No. But they might recognize my scent anyway. They remember me. And that's your house isn't it? They'll be able to track *you*, if the soldiers realize it."

"I could fly away to confuse them." But if the dogs remembered Arta, they'd track her anyway.

"I'll tell the dogs not to follow us. They don't like that bad man who beats them and doesn't feed them enough. They'll follow a false trail, even though they know they'll be beaten." She looked up at Suli, her eyes solemn. "They're brave and loyal. I wish I could protect them. Can't you do anything?"

"I'll try to think of something," Suli said. She didn't say aloud that she thought it was hopeless.

Arta was asking for her help and she had none to give. Sooner or later the dogs would be forced to obey, and the soldiers would find them.

12

ROASTED FISH

"I SMELL SMOKE," Arta said.

Instantly alert, Suli searched the forest around them for anyone using an invisibility spell, although it was unlikely the soldiers knew such magic. As far as she could tell, no one was hiding nearby.

They walked warily into a sheltered canyon. Twisted trees struggled to grow on the steep defile, their roots clinging to the rocky walls. The sound of a waterfall came from somewhere out of sight.

"Wait here," Suli whispered. She crept forward through a tangle of vines and dead stalks of hemlock until she saw the clearing. Smoke rose over the roof of a small lean-to built against a granite boulder twice her height. Suli traced the smoke to where a young man squatted beside a pot hung over a fire. He must've sensed her watching, for he rose and turned.

Relief flooded through her. Suli stepped into the clearing and Orion grinned, shielding his eyes against the sun.

"I wondered when you'd finally get here," Orion said. "Where's your apprentice?"

Suli ran across the clearing to hug him, then took a step back and scowled fiercely. "Where have you been? Everyone's been searching for you. We thought you were dead, but of course you're here lazing in the sun. You might've told one of the flock where you were."

"No one else was around. And *you're welcome*, by the way."

Suli blinked. "You found him?" She looked around the dell, but no one else was there. "Where is he? What if the soldiers see your smoke?"

Orion shook his head. "The soldiers never came this far. I saw the prince slip away from a wool caravan last night, while the soldiers were searching it. They never saw him. It was pure luck that I did."

"Why didn't you tell Flax?"

"Flax was already gone."

Suli looked around the clearing. A waterfall splashed down one rocky wall. A breeze rustled the boughs of the pines. No one else was in sight. "Should a prince be wandering around unguarded?"

Orion waved an arm casually. "He's fine—he's upstream where it's deeper. He wanted to try fishing." He saw her expression. "He can't get lost with the stream right there, and there's not much here to amuse a prince."

"Are you sure it's him?"

"Who else could he be? He says his name is Benno and he's running away from soldiers. He hid with the caravan, and when the soldiers came, he slipped away and I followed him. He wants to find the wise woman of Weatherstone."

"I need to find him."

"He's fine." Orion stood up and stretched. "Where's *your* charge?"

"I'd better get her. I left her behind to investigate your fire."

But Arta was coming toward them, hand-in-hand with a dark-haired boy Suli recognized as the one Arta had saved from the dogs. The two children stopped beside the fire. Arta smiled. "Benno, this is Suli. She's the wise woman here."

"I remember," he said to Suli. "You saved me from the dogs."

Suli shook her head. "Arta did that. How on earth did you come all this way without the soldiers capturing you?"

Benno's gaze slipped away from hers. "I had help. And when the traitors came, I ran." He glanced from Suli to Orion. "So what he told me is true? You were looking for me?"

"We got word you might come to Weatherstone, although I don't know why. Are you all right? We're glad you're safe." She hoped Orion had been careful and hadn't changed in front of him.

"The traitors, as you call them, won't find this place easily," Orion said. "You're safe here for now."

Suli shook her head. "Except the soldiers have hunting dogs." She asked Arta, "Can you tell where they are?"

Arta frowned, concentrating. "I'm not sure. But they aren't following our trail, they're only pretending to. Maybe they can pretend for a day. It depends."

Orion looked surprised.

Benno said gravely, "I wish to thank you for your help. I will remember."

"Benno—is that what you want us to call you?" Suli asked.

He nodded, his eyes wary. So he didn't trust them completely. She didn't blame him.

"I'm starving, let's eat," Suli said. "Then we can decide what to do."

They sat on the grass by the stream and ate Orion's fish soup with the bread and cheese Suli had brought. Then they put out the fire so the smoke wouldn't reveal their hiding place.

"Benno," Suli asked cautiously, "Why come *here*?" She handed everyone a withered apple from her pack, then bit into her own. It made a satisfying crunch. "Weatherstone is crawling with soldiers—um, traitors—so if that's where you were going, you'll have to change your plans. What did you expect to find there?"

He was watching her. "Is what Arta said true? You're the wise woman here?"

"Yes, while my teacher is away."

Orion stood and stretched, raising his arms over his head. He stepped a few paces away from the fire's ashes. "I think we should talk about shape-shifting."

Suli inhaled sharply. "What?"

Benno's face was pale and he stared at Orion. "Why would you say that?"

"I think we all need to trust each other," Orion said, waving his hand. "Keeping secrets doesn't help."

Benno stared at the ground, stony-faced. "Don't know what you mean," he mumbled.

"I think you do, Benno," Orion said, "but I'll go first." Then he changed. One minute a youth of fifteen stood there, the next a pale grey goose with dark feathers on his wings and head. He watched Benno's face.

Arta gasped.

Benno's face registered shock and then wonder. Finally he gave Orion a timid, hopeful smile. "You can change!"

The grey goose nodded. Then its figure blurred and human Orion stood there once more. "And you can too, can't you?"

Benno nodded. "Mama said I must never do it where anyone can see me." He closed his eyes and became a young goose, his dappled feathers grey and brown.

Suli began to laugh. Arta stared, wide-eyed.

Benno quickly changed back. "What's so funny?" he asked suspiciously.

"We are!" Suli said. "You, Orion, and me: we all have the same secret. How did you know, Orion?"

Orion sat down, looking pleased with himself. "You're not the only one who notices things, O Wise Woman. He has the signs. Besides, it explains how he evaded the soldiers for so long."

Benno smiled. "You must've guessed how I got here. I only joined the caravan at the foot of the mountain. Before that, I flew."

"But why here? Why not fly home?" Suli asked.

Benno straightened his shoulders and raised his chin, as though making a decision. "Mama said I had to get away, that it wasn't safe. She told me to find the wise woman of Weatherstone. She said the wise woman here knew all about changing. But the traitors caught me and locked me up in a farmhouse. I had to hurt one to escape, and then I flew away. The dogs tracked me and the soldiers would have caught me again if Arta hadn't helped me.

"At the foot of the mountain, I hid among the sacks in the wool caravan." He frowned. "Are you the wise woman Mama told me about? You're awfully young."

Orion turned away so Suli couldn't see his face, but she was sure he was grinning.

She replied seriously, "Your mother probably meant for you to find Tala, my teacher. She isn't here now, but I'll help you any way I can. There's a whole flock of shape-shifters here. You can stay with them if you need to hide."

Benno looked intrigued by that idea. "Then you can help me, like my Mama said?" he asked uncertainly.

"What exactly do you want us to do, Benno? You already know how to change." Suli saw Arta was scowling at her.

Benno took a deep breath. "Mama says I must find people to help me free her and Father from the prime minister and his soldiers."

For a moment words failed her. "But—and I mean no offense, but you're a child. How can you rescue the king and queen if your soldiers can't?"

"Not by myself, of course. Mama says we need the wise

women to use their magic together. It's the only way to stop him. The loyal soldiers can't do it alone, they need help. They can't fight magic—but *you* can. She says a wise woman told her I should come to the lake on the mountain above Weatherstone."

Did Benno mean Tala? And what did the *lake* have to do with it? Suli and Orion exchanged a glance.

Arta patted Benno's arm. "All of us will help." Then she led Benno away, heading upstream, whispering something Suli couldn't hear.

The queen wanted the wise women to fight magic with magic. Well, that made sense.

If her theory was correct (and since Coalfeather agreed, it probably was) the magic protecting and controlling the soldiers was disrupting the flow of magic, maybe stealing it. Either way, the wise women might not have the magic they needed to stop them.

She didn't know about wars or prime ministers. But the prime minister considered the wise women his enemies. He used *his* magic to change the flow of magic.

The prime minister, who accused wise women of being witches, was the real witch.

Wise women were supposed to protect everything in their community: the plants, the people, the animals. But if their magic was being stolen, they'd have to find another way. Without magic, the wise women couldn't even protect themselves.

A crow called from somewhere nearby, a simple "I am here."

It wasn't anyone she knew, but the sound flared in her head, reminding her of her allies. They had their own wisdom, their own power. She didn't have to find the answers by herself.

Wise women were responsible for more than the human community; all living things were included in their care. She doubted the prime minister knew anything about the way the wise women had always helped the animal nations.

Suli could talk to her animal allies and ask for their help. It would be more difficult, now that the crows had refused to become involved, but she hoped others would. Maybe this was the reason why Tala wanted Suli to be in charge of the resistance instead of Magda.

The thought gave her hope.

13

WEATHERSTONE

SULI PACED BESIDE THE STREAM, watching white clouds skim swiftly across the sky. Benno, Arta, and Orion were safe here; she could leave them for an hour or two and see what the soldiers were doing to her village. Magical threats were here responsibility; she should be there.

At the sound of giggling, she turned to look.

Benno and Arta were wading in the stream, splashing each other and plunging their hands below the surface to grab fish. Benno's foot slipped and he fell in. Arta was laughing so hard her eyes were squeezed shut.

That's the first time I've seen her laugh like that, Suli thought. The wary, mistrustful child was playing. She sounded happy.

They wouldn't notice if she left; they were having too much fun.

Orion wandered over and sat down on the grass beside her, leaning back on his hands. He squinted sideways at her. "Go check on things," he said quietly. "I'll watch them."

Arta ran up to her. "I caught one!" she cried. She held out her dripping hands. A silvery fingerling looked up from the tiny pool in her cupped palms, kissing the surface of the water.

Suli smiled. "Wonderful! But shouldn't you put her back now so she can grow up?"

Arta's smile disappeared. "I didn't think of that." She turned and shouted, "Benno! Put the fish back!"

Benno looked surprised, but waved and bent over, his hands beneath the water. Arta ran back to crouch beside him, releasing the young fish into the stream. She waved.

Arta returned, out of breath, face flushed and eyes bright. "No baby fish will be harmed today."

"Do you mind if I leave you with Orion for a little while?" Suli asked. "I need to see what's happening in the village."

Arta nodded. "Don't worry, I can protect Orion, and Benno too. The dogs will tell me if they have to find us. We'll be fine." She gave Orion a stern look. "You *are* going to help Benno, aren't you?"

"Yes, Arta," Orion said meekly.

She turned to Suli. "He came all this way to find you, and you haven't even said you'd help."

As if I had a choice. "Of course we'll all help him. But no one knows what magic these soldiers have. I may not be able to stop them."

"Once you find out, you'll use your magic, Orion can fly, and I can—" she broke off suddenly, looking thoughtful.

"And what will you do?" Suli asked curiously. Arta looked like she was about to reveal a secret. Then Suli remembered something. "How did you know soldiers were capturing wise women? You were in the middle of nowhere, yet somehow you heard about it. How?"

"I don't remember."

Suli gave her a skeptical look. "Yes, you do. Do you know magic after all?"

"I don't know any magic," Arta said, looking worried. "But sometimes I would know things without knowing how. I thought

I was going crazy until I figured it out. The animals on the farm were telling me things—warning me, mostly."

"They spoke to you?"

"In my mind. If that's magic, I wasn't trying to do it. It happened by itself." Arta sounded worried. "Is it the bad kind of magic?"

Suli thought before she spoke. "It doesn't sound like it. It sounds like a different kind of magic altogether. You told Coalfeather you couldn't read his mind. Are you saying that maybe you can?"

Arta looked at her feet. "I never tried. I don't know."

Hmm. Suli used her Seeing; Arta wasn't being completely honest with her. Suli guessed Arta could listen to any animal's mind she wanted to—and Coalfeather suspected it. Arta hadn't told Coalfeather the truth. Then a new worry struck her: *Does her mind reading include humans?*

"How would farm animals know about the soldiers imprisoning wise women?" Orion asked Arta.

"The cats were arguing about it in the barn, and I overheard them," Arta said. "They said Marietta told them, so I asked her and she said 'twas true."

"Who's Marietta?"

"Mr. Munro's horse. She went to Winton every week for market day and heard things from the other horses. I'm going to miss her," she said with a sigh.

That sounded plausible, at least. "Don't worry, Arta, you did nothing wrong," Suli said.

"So it wasn't the bad kind of magic?" Arta asked again.

"No. The bad kind forces you to do things against your will. You didn't hurt anyone, and you didn't force Marietta to tell you anything, did you? But let's ask Coalfeather about it. He knows about all kinds of magic."

"I like him. He's so serious, he's funny," Arta said.

Orion snorted, his hand over his mouth.

Suli hoped her dignified teacher never heard this opinion.

"You'd better go if you're going," Orion said. "We'll be fine. Hurry back, and don't take foolish chances. Stay away from the house—that's the first place they'll look."

Why did everyone feel she needed advice? "But the flock will want to know you and Benno are safe so they don't keep searching—"

"Be sensible. Promise you'll go straight to Weatherstone and then come back."

It wasn't like him to be so serious. She sighed. "All right."

She closed her eyes and silently chanted the spell before she changed. She'd never broken the habit of closing her eyes, a habit from when she'd first learned. Orion kidded her about it.

In the air, in spite of the danger surrounding them, she felt the floating sense of happiness she always did when the weight of the earth fell away and the wind lifted her into the sky. She flew above the path that crisscrossed the western flank of the mountain, keeping an eye out for movement. If the dogs were tracking them, that was the way they'd come.

Her wings beating steadily as she skimmed over the stubbled fields with unmelted snow lying in the empty furrows.

She glided over the central square of the village and landed on the high ridgepole of the Grain Exchange's roof. From there she could see most of the village.

A wain was parked on the village green, piled high with bales of hay. Next to it, poles had been driven into the grass with ropes strung between them, where twenty-odd horses had been picketed. The duck pond was deserted. Here were the soldiers' horses, but where were they?

At first glance it seemed the market stalls were doing brisk business, but Suli soon realized no one was buying anything. Instead, the women of the village had gathered to talk to each other in low voices, their faces shadowed by the canvas awnings. They kept glancing over their shoulders.

One of the women said something to the others and pointed.

Four soldiers stood on a doorstep, their swords drawn. A woman answered the door and a soldier thrust a piece of paper at her before the men pushed their way inside.

~

COALFEATHER WATCHED in silence from a sycamore tree, concealed within its branches by withered brown leaves. He couldn't put off his decision any longer.

The soldiers were back on the doorstep, leading two young girls by the hand. A woman followed, crying, and the soldiers shoved her back inside. One of the girls started to cry, but the other remained silent and grim. They were dragged into the street and lifted into a waiting wagon.

This was not their fight, his father had said, but the wise women had always helped *them*. Surely he could do more than watch human fledglings be stolen from weeping and cursing parents, to be taken who knew where.

He didn't know what to do. And that girl Suli had brought back with her worried him. He'd heard stories of humans born with the ability to speak with animals in their minds, but he'd never seen such a thing himself. Yet here she was, with a power that might help them fight the soldiers. Too conveniently, perhaps. That worried him, also.

He shook his head. It was sheer chance that Suli had flown by when she did and taken the girl away. Suli knew nothing about such magic; after all, he'd been her teacher, and he'd never mentioned it. Most wise women knew nothing about it. But Arta could use it, even without training. He hadn't dared to mention *that* to the Council. If he taught Arta secret animal magic, he wouldn't just be disobeying the Council, he'd be breaking the Law. The flock could expel him.

But if he didn't teach Arta how to use her power, no one

would. The girl would be a danger to them all if she fell into the hands of the prime minister, and *he* used her to control the minds of others. That was too much power in the hands of a child. The girl couldn't even See to protect herself.

And it was possible she'd be overwhelmed by the minds she listened to; she might become a gibbering idiot, prey to every thought around her. She'd be useless then, her own life wasted.

With Tala gone, there was no one else he could trust to watch the girl—both to help her and to control her. He had no choice. He had to defy his father and the Council. They refused to understand the danger, saying it was a human problem and none of their affair. Eventually they'd understand that decision was a dangerous mistake, but by then it would be too late.

He had to risk it. He told himself he'd decided, but he hesitated. Now that it came to it, he realized he was afraid. What if he failed? What if the girl was already uncontrollable? What if she were able to control *him*?

There was something he could do right now to help the wise women. And, he admitted to himself, it would allow him to put off the moment when he became a traitor to his people, or a hero, depending on your point of view. He didn't want to be either.

He plunged from the sycamore branch and rose in the air, following the wagon.

~

SULI LANDED beside the horses cropping grass on the village green, stretching the picket ropes to their limit. She sidled up to a bay mare, and said in pidgin, "Excuse me, but have you seen a pack of hunting dogs?"

The mare looked down her nose with a disapproving snort. "I'm one of the king's troops, and so are the dogs," she said. "Neither of us waste time in idle chat with silly geese."

Suli felt the urge to transform so she could startle the mare, but controlled herself. "I doubt these dogs could track anything," she said. "They looked lazy and flea-bitten to me. And what's there to find in our village, anyway? You lot are trampling our grass and muddying our water for nothing."

The mare fixed an unfriendly eye on her. "That's all you know. The dogs are searching for a *traitor*, and his trail led to your dirty little village. Better them than me, that's all I can say, breathing the stink of traitors. I know you're ignorant of the world, goose, but I assure you king's horses are used to better fare than this poor grass and muddy pond water." She snorted again and swung her head away, ending the conversation.

"Feel free to leave," Suli muttered. She walked over to look at the wagons and equipment the soldiers had brought. No one paid her any attention because *of course* there would be geese on the village green. There were far more soldiers in Weatherstone than were needed to capture one boy. They were there to imprison the wise women and the girls of the village.

She flew from rooftop to rooftop, following groups of soldiers. They searched each house and dragged away the girls old enough to start magical training.

On the benches outside the local tavern, two soldiers were buying drinks for the village men, hoping for information. Suli doubted they'd be fooled by false generosity from their daughters' kidnappers.

The dogs were nowhere to be seen.

Suli flew back the way she'd come. A few women were out working in the fields in spite of the invasion of strangers. She flew up the hill to Tala's house, following the main path. No dogs here, either.

She'd promised Orion that she wouldn't go home, but it all looked peaceful enough. It didn't seem much of a risk, and she wanted to tell the flock they could call off the search; Orion and the boy were safe.

She landed in the yard and waited, listening. Everything

looked normal, but a prickly feeling on the back of her neck made her uneasy.

She was safer in winged form, but she could only use her Seeing and her magic when she was human. She made a quick decision and changed shape, immediately using her side-Seeing to check for anyone using an invisibility spell. But no one was there.

Now that she was human, she thought the air smelled wrong. She searched the yard for the reason, and finally looked up.

No smoke rose from the chimney, in spite of the cold day.

She climbed the kitchen steps and pushed open the door. "Magda?"

Silence. She crossed to the stove and touched the side. The black metal was warm, but when she opened the door to the firebox, the fire was out. Worried now, she glanced out the window. There was no reason for Magda to let the fire go out.

She walked down the path to the pond. No birds called from the trees. The silence was unnatural.

She was relieved to see part of the flock was there, swimming.

"Good morning," she called, as she drew near. "I found Orion, you'll be glad to hear."

As one, the flock turned their heads and raised their wings in alarm. "Fly away! It's a trap!"

But it was already too late.

14

THE AMULET

BEFORE SULI COULD MOVE, two soldiers rushed from where they'd hidden in the trees. The first one, his surly face marked by a broken nose, grabbed her arms and pulled them behind her back. "She's one of the witches who helped the boy," he crowed to his companion. "He must be here somewhere!"

"We've already searched the place." The other soldier sounded bored. "He isn't here. Just one more witch to send to the camps. It doesn't help us find the boy."

Suli squirmed to look over her shoulder at the man who had her pinned and recognized him. Broken-nose had been with Tanner and the dogs.

"Wrong. She knows something." Broken-nose was smiling. "I bet you three squals she knows exactly where he is. Why else would he come here, if not to get her help? There's now't else in this flea-bitten village." He leaned over and spat near Suli's foot.

"Let me go! This is private property and we deal harshly with criminals here," Suli said, trying to sound outraged.

Broken-nose leaned close and spoke in her ear, "Criminals, eh? Well, we deal harshly with traitors to the Crown, so you'd best stop pretending you don't know what this is about by the time Sergeant Lito arrives." He yanked her arms tightly behind her, and bound them together with a piece of rope.

Without turning, Suli called loudly in pidgin, "Tell Orion at the hiding place in the valley, but warn him to stay there!" A flapping sound told her one of the geese had taken flight.

The broken-nosed soldier shook her, and the other one slapped her, hard. "Be quiet! Signaling your confederate in witch talk? She's tied up and can't help you."

Suli staggered from the blow, tasting blood in her mouth. She would have fallen if the soldier hadn't jerked her upright using the rope. He shoved her up the path, the rope biting into her arms.

When they reached the top of the hill, the soldiers pushed her toward the dairy, a small shack of weathered grey boards. The second soldier opened the door and the broken-nosed soldier behind her placed his foot on her back and shoved her into the darkness. She stumbled but caught herself before she fell against the shelves where the aging cheeses were stacked. In that brief moment of daylight, she'd seen Magda sitting on the dirt floor, her hands bound in front of her.

The soldier who'd hit her laughed. "Now you can tell her anything you like. It'll be good practice. Once the sergeant gets here, you'll talk your head off." He slammed the door, leaving them in darkness.

A LARGE GREY goose and a smaller brown one floated on the surface of the stream. "Watch what I do," the grey goose said. He dived head first beneath the water. Benno imitated him, trying to master the darting motion. He emerged from the water with a silver fingerling in his beak. Orion surfaced and splashed him, and Benno laughed, dropping the fish, and splashed him back.

"Well done," Orion said. "You're getting the hang of it."

Arta watched them with an envious expression, then raised her eyes to scan the sky. Already the sun was sinking toward the treetops. Clouds were moving in and the light was fading. Several crows flew past, heading east, and she wondered if they knew Coalfeather. Their wings reflected the late afternoon sun, flashing silver white. They called to each other but she didn't understand them.

She walked over to the small waterfall, which bubbled cheerfully, its rivulets of lace plunging down a rocky cliff. Arta frowned in concentration, ignoring the soothing sounds of the water, and then went to find Benno and Orion, who were diving in the stream.

"Orion? They're coming."

The grey goose stared at her a moment as though he'd forgotten who she was, before he climbed out. A shadow seemed to pass over the sun, and then human Orion was there, his breeches and shirt dripping on the grass. "You mean the soldiers are coming here? I thought you told the dogs to follow a false scent."

"The soldiers beat the dogs," she explained. "They had to obey to stop the beatings. Where else can we hide?"

Benno climbed out of the water and changed, looking solemn. "If I go away from here, they'll follow me and you'll be safe."

"That's true," Orion said thoughtfully.

Arta looked shocked. "You can't abandon him!"

"I'm not. You have to trust me, Arta. Benno's safe as long as he's in winged form. You won't be if the soldiers find you. So you're the one who has to hide. But if it will make you happy, I'll take Benno to hide with the geese on the lake first, then come back for you. He'll be quite safe with the other geese. Will you be all right alone here for a few minutes?"

"But where can we go?"

"Magda has a cottage here we can stay in; it's not far, but it's well hidden."

"The soldiers will find us there, too!" Her voice caught, and she looked about to cry.

Orion knelt beside her. "Not if the dogs are following Benno's scent. They'll lose the trail as soon as we fly away. It will be okay, I promise."

Arta said, "Go. I'll be fine. The dogs won't hurt me."

"I'll be as quick as I can. If you see or hear the soldiers, hide—climb a tree if you have to. Can you tell how long before they reach here?"

Arta concentrated, frowning. "I'm not sure, but not long. The dogs smell water. They may have gone to the lake first, if that's where the main path goes."

"Can you make the dogs pretend they can't smell you, if you hide from the soldiers?"

"I don't know," Arta said. "I'll try."

"Good. Let's go, Benno." Orion and Benno changed and rose into the air, their wings flashing silver in the sunlight for a moment before they passed out of sight.

SULI TURNED toward the darker shape in the gloom. "Have you tried the Voice on them?"

Magda shifted and sighed. "No. I couldn't get one alone. Besides, I'm not sure it would work. They're controlled by a spell, and dumb as dirt besides. I've tried to act helpless, so they don't suspect what we can do. The longer we keep that hidden, the better. They're from the coast, remember. They don't understand about magic."

Yet they talk about witches all the time. "Can they hear us from outside?"

"I don't know. Best keep your voice down."

"Benno and Orion are at the hiding place with Arta," Suli whispered softly.

"Benno? Who—you mean the prince? So he *was* coming here. Then we have to move soon. But there are so many of them, I'm not sure—"

"Benno can change shape," Suli whispered. "His mother told him to find the wise woman of Weatherstone and ask for help. She wants him to ask the wise women to defeat the prime minister with magic." Suli's voice rose. "She must've meant for him to find Tala. Can we get a message to her?"

"Yes," Magda said, without explaining.

They heard the sound of horses arriving in the yard, and voices coming toward them. When the door opened, Broken-nose leaned in, grinning. "All ready to confess? Sergeant's here and wants to see you. On your feet!" He grabbed the rope around Suli's arms and yanked her to her feet, backward. "You first, witch!" He pushed her and she tottered outside, blinking in the daylight. She heard a scuffle behind her, and a grunt from Magda, who emerged from the dairy rumpled and angry.

Three more soldiers waited near their horses. Suli immediately recognized the leader, Sergeant Lito.

He nodded with satisfaction. "So it wasn't chance that threw my dogs off the scent after all," he said. "I like having someone to blame, and here you are." His eyes narrowed. "Where's the boy?"

The broken-nosed soldier dragged Magda by the rope to stand beside her. Suli wished they'd had time to think of a story. She'd have to stick close to the truth.

"I told you before," she said. "I don't know anything about a boy. Why are you doing this? What do you want? We don't have anything worth stealing, if that's what you're after."

The sergeant's face reddened and his eyes glittered. "We're not thieves but king's men, hunting a traitor—the same traitor you helped before. Word is he's coming here, and you must be the reason, so you'd best speak civil. My men have done much worse than beat a girl until she talks."

He counted on fear to make her talk. She *was* afraid, but that made her angry, too. She opened her mouth, but Magda stepped forward and said politely, "Sir, could you explain about this boy? I don't understand how a boy could be a traitor, or if he is, why so many men are needed to capture him." Her expression was blandly curious.

Sergeant Lito kept his eyes on Suli. "Well, Mistress, I was hoping you'd answer that question for me. It pains me that you claim ignorance, it really does." He nodded to the broken-nosed soldier. The man stepped forward and backhanded Suli, knocking her to the ground.

Stunned, Suli lay without moving, her face in the dirt. They hadn't even given her a chance. She didn't want to be beaten bloody, but that seemed likely. Her thoughts swam thickly. When she raised her head the pain grew worse.

"Sergeant!" Magda barked. "That was uncalled for! We're innocent and you're treating us like criminals!" She took another step forward. "Tell me why this child is so important. Perhaps I can help."

Suli raised her head. The soldier, whose job seemed to be hitting people, moved toward Magda.

Sergeant Lito caught his eye and shook his head. The soldier stepped back, looking disappointed.

"I hope you can, Mistress, because telling me about the boy is the only thing that will save this girl a beating. Is she related to you? Is this your house?"

Magda nodded. "This is my house, yes, and she's my cousin. She's here to help me while I teach her how to manage a house."

Sergeant Lito smiled skeptically. "If she's supposed to be helping you, why was she on the Winton road a few days ago with a girl who acts like a witch? I've no doubt you're all witches together here. I wonder where that girl is now. Hiding with the boy, perhaps?"

"What boy?" Magda asked. "You haven't explained why you're looking for a child."

"Eight years old, with dark eyes and hair. Have you seen him? Surely a stranger in your small village would be hard to miss."

"I've seen no one like that in the village," Magda said. "But then, I don't go into the village that often. Have you looked there?" she asked innocently.

The sergeant ignored Magda and stood over Suli. "Why were you on the road, girl?" He lifted her by the rope, turning her over. "Were you looking for the boy to help him? Who else knows about him? Who else is helping you? Answer me!" He raised his foot over her face. "I'll break your nose if you don't," he said softly.

Suli stared up at the foot inches from her face. What could she say to stop him? "If there was a boy those dogs were chasing, I never saw him! Your dogs attacked *us*—that's all I can tell you. We thought they'd kill us!"

Sergeant Lito lowered his foot. "Well now, that's better. At least you admit you were there. Not the whole truth, I'm sure, but better. You see? I can be reasonable. But if you don't tell me what I need to know soon, my friend here"— he gestured to the other soldier—"will start work on your face."

He pulled her to a sitting position, and paced slowly around her. "Let's start again. What were you doing on the road?"

Magda said, "Sir, if I may? I sent her to collect a child from our cousin's house. She's only a little girl and couldn't travel by herself all the way to Weatherstone. They would've passed through Winton, right enough, where you saw them, evidently. But I never heard about any soldiers." She turned to Suli. "Why didn't you tell me about this?"

"Didn't know it was important," Suli mumbled.

Magda glanced at the soldiers by the horses and then at the other two, who had moved away to talk softly.

She's deciding whether to risk the Voice, Suli thought.

"That was naughty of you. You must be tired and sleepy now. Yes, you should have told me. A nice lie down is what you need.

So sleepy, and the sun is warm. Feeling drowsy." Magda continued to speak in a soft murmuring voice. Suli had to fight to stay awake.

She watched Sergeant Lito out of the corner of her eye; he hadn't noticed anything, but he didn't look sleepy, either. *It isn't working.*

Suli had an idea. "I could tell you more," she whispered. The sergeant kept glancing at his men, as though he didn't trust them. "But it must stay between us. I don't want your men to overhear."

"Why not?" the sergeant asked suspiciously.

"Do you want to share the reward?" Suli asked. "Let's go inside. I need to get warm."

The sergeant frowned, but they'd caught his attention and his eyes glinted with greed. "Fine. If you witches are planning something and think this is your chance, I assure you it won't make any difference. You'll get the same beating for a lie whether it's here or inside."

He turned to the two men who waited. "You two," he said, "get your horses and join the others."

"But Sarge, our orders say not to be alone with—"

"Do you think I can't handle a girl and an old woman?"

"No, Sarge." The broken-nosed fellow looked disappointed.

"Then do as I say."

Magda managed to fumble the door open with her bound hands. She stepped inside.

The other soldier gave the sergeant a resentful look and grumbled quietly to the broken-nosed soldier as they walked slowly toward the horses. The broken-nosed soldier laughed.

Suli struggled to stay upright, still dizzy from the blow. She was about to climb the steps, when Sergeant Lito came down them, pushing past her. She tottered and almost fell.

The sergeant bellowed at the two men, "I'll have no insubordination under my command, soldiers!"

The men's faces became carefully blank. "Sir!" they both said, saluting.

"That's better," the sergeant said in a threatening tone. He turned and climbed the steps. Suli followed slowly, and was on the top step when she heard a dull *thwack!*

In the kitchen, Magda was holding a cast-iron skillet in both hands and breathing hard. The sergeant was unconscious, splayed out on the floor.

Suli pushed the door shut. "You've killed him." Her body was icy cold.

"I don't think so. Help me search him."

"Unlike you, my hands are tied *behind* me," Suli reminded her.

"Then find a knife!" Magda said crossly, kneeling beside the sergeant. She began to search his pockets. "Whatever this thing is that protects him from the Voice, we have to find it."

Suli bit back a retort. She opened the drawer where the knives were kept and pulled one out, twisting to see over her shoulder. Holding it carefully, she returned to kneel beside Magda.

Magda, meanwhile, had emptied the sergeant's pocketbook and coat pockets. Now she rolled him over and sat back on her heels, gazing at him thoughtfully.

"Did you find it?"

"No."

"Then help me get these ropes off!"

Magda grunted. She took Suli's knife and sawed at the ropes around her wrists. When they finally parted, Suli exhaled in relief, and began to rub her arms, wincing at the pain.

She waited until the feeling returned to her numbed fingers before she took the knife and hacked at the rope coiled tightly around Magda's wrists. There were angry burns where the rope had twisted and cut into her skin.

"Hold onto that knife—tuck it in your waistband. I've a

feeling we're going to need it again." They were kneeling beside the sergeant.

"What exactly are you looking for?" Suli asked.

"Something they could give to every soldier," Magda said. "Shh! He's coming to."

"Sergeant, can you hear me? You're feeling relaxed and happy. In fact, you're dozing, happy as a cat, with your eyes closed."

"If he's protected, that won't work!" Suli whispered.

"Shut up and help me get him up and in a chair, it'll be easier," Magda said.

"You're joking! He's three times my weight!"

"Shut up and help," Magda said.

Someone outside called, "Hey, Sergeant! Are you all right, or do we have to come rescue you from the witches?" There was the sound of laughter.

"Hurry," Magda said. "Take that arm and I'll take this one." Together they dragged him across the floor and somehow lifted him onto a chair, resting his head on the table. Magda chewed her lip thoughtfully. "The Voice almost worked. We need to find what's blocking it before his men interrupt us."

"So do something," Suli said. "Hurry."

Magda shook Sergeant Lito's shoulder. "You're sleepy, but you want to answer my questions. It's important to you."

Sergeant Lito sat up straighter and nodded, breathing deeply, his eyes shut. It did look like the Voice was working.

"Why are you searching for this boy? What's he done?" Magda asked softly.

Sergeant Lito frowned. "He's a threat to the prime minster, and a traitor to our country."

"How can a little boy be a threat to the country?"

"I'm not allowed to say." He shook his head. "Folk would get upset if they knew it was the prince. They're loyal to the king and queen. The fools don't realize they're traitors."

"I see," Magda said. "The boy is the prince, and the prime

minister is afraid of him. Because the prime minister wants the throne himself?"

A confused look passed over the sergeant's face. "That can't be right." He straightened up and said in a singsong voice, "The prime minister cares about the soldiers and the people, and the king doesn't. If we catch the boy, the prime minister will reward us; he'll take care of the army." His arms began to flail wildly, almost knocking Magda down, and his head twitched from side to side.

He's fighting the control of the Voice. Or something is, Suli thought.

Magda nodded as though she'd expected this.

"Aren't you being disloyal to the king?" Suli asked him gently. "If you kill his son, doesn't that make *you* the traitor, and a murderer as well?"

Sergeant Lito's eyelids fluttered and his mouth worked, but he was unable to speak.

Magda said quickly, "You feel drowsy and peaceful. You can say anything you wish."

The sergeant grimaced. "I can't!" he gasped. "No!" He face blanched and his eyes rolled up into his head, with only the whites showing. He fell forward onto the table.

"What was that?" Suli whispered.

"The spell," Magda said grimly. "It must be under his clothes."

"Eew," Suli said under her breath.

They lifted his arms and took off his coat, going through the pockets again. Suli unclipped the moneybag at his belt, and spilled it on the table, but it held only a few coins.

"His dagger?" Suli asked doubtfully. Magda pulled it from its sheath and examined it. She shook her head. "Open his shirt," she said.

Suli leaned forward to pull open his shirt, wrinkling her nose at the pungent smell. A metal disc hung on a cord around his neck. She lifted it, about to pull it free, when the sergeant snapped awake and grabbed her hand with a look of fury. "I'll kill you!" he roared.

"Sleep!" Magda commanded, using the Voice.

The sergeant swung around in a rage. While he was distracted, Suli quickly sliced the cord with her knife. The disc fell on the table and the sergeant collapsed.

"This must be it," Suli said, reaching for it.

"Don't touch it—leave it there!"

Suli obeyed, stepping back in surprise. It was round, silver-colored, with a raised design of interlocking squares etched on the curved front. She'd never seen anything like it before. "How do we neutralize it?"

"I'm not sure it *can* be neutralized," Magda said grimly.

15

STOLEN MAGIC

SULI STOOD BESIDE THE WINDOW, careful not to let herself be seen by the soldiers waiting beside their horses. They weren't approaching the house. Yet.

But if Sergeant Lito didn't come out soon, they'd come to investigate. Above them, the sky was fading to the grey blue of early evening and they'd want to return for their evening meal.

Magda was watching the sergeant, her eyes shadowed. "There's a powerful spell on this amulet," she said in a low voice. "More powerful than anything I've seen before. He may remember I tried to use the Voice on him. All we can do is hope he'll recover his wits and his will if we take the thing away." She shook her head. "But it may make no difference; he may search for the boy and lock us up as witches anyway."

"We could put the disc in a jar and bury it," Suli suggested.

Magda waved a hand dismissively. "No. The spell has to be neutralized, or it will control anyone who finds it. We'll have to try lake water."

Suli frowned. *Lake water?* That sounded like something the old Magda would say, the angry witch who thought lake water and the right incantation would turn her into a shape-shifter.

Tala had laughed about Magda's naive hope; she'd told Magda over and over again that shape-shifting was inherited, and you either had it or you didn't, but Magda had refused to believe her. Suli had assumed there was no magical power in the lake water—but there was the fact that the villagers avoided the lake, and she'd never discovered why.

"Are you sure?" Suli asked doubtfully.

"Hmph," Magda grunted. "The wise woman of Weatherstone doesn't know everything. I thought Orion or someone would have told you by now. Tala never explained about the magic in the lake?"

Suli frowned. She didn't like feeling ignorant. "She never told me about any magic in the lake. Tell me now," Suli said, "before he wakes up."

"I suppose I'd better," Magda said with a sigh. "We may need the lake water, and not just to neutralize these cursed amulets. The lake water has magical power of its own. It's a kind of well or reservoir of magic. That's why it can destroy the third kind of magic, like the spell on these amulets."

Suli frowned. "Why didn't Tala tell me this?"

"She was trying to protect you."

"From what?" Suli asked.

"You're still very young," Magda said in an uncharacteristically gentle voice. "Tala thought you didn't need to know about such things at a young age. The lake holds powerful magic for the same reason the villagers never go near it."

"Which is?"

Magda sighed again. "A group of villagers from Weatherstone murdered two wise women and threw their bodies in the lake near the waterfall. The wise women's power collected there. It absorbs the third kind of magic, maybe even uses it, I don't know. The villagers are afraid the women's spirits will punish them for what their ancestors did. They're afraid of the magic there.

"And that could be lucky for us," Magda said. "Tala thought we could use the power of the lake water for our magic if something happened to ours. We never tried it because we never needed to."

Suli sat down at the table and considered that.

Magic had always seemed a thing of sunlight, rushing water, and growing things. She used it to help plants, people, and animals stay healthy so they could go about their business. But this was something darker. She thought of the water mirroring the sky, its magical power waiting to be used, not far from where they sat in the warm kitchen.

"So even if we lose our magic, we could use the lake water?" Suli asked. "*Are* we losing our magic?"

Sergeant Lito stirred and moaned softly. Magda put a finger over her lips.

"What do we do with him?" Suli asked. "Those soldiers won't wait forever. Will he help us, do you think?"

Magda shrugged and went to the window. "We need to know how he behaves without the spell. But you're right; let's get rid of the others. That's a good first test."

"Wake up, Sergeant Lito," Magda said softly in his ear.

His eyelids fluttered before his eyes opened. He sat up with a grunt and looked around him. "What in blazes am I doing here?"

"You don't remember?"

"Who in blazes are you?" he shouted, his eyes darting around the room.

"My name is Magda and you're in my house," she said calmly.

He stared at Suli. "I know you," he said uncertainly, "don't I?"

"We've met."

The sergeant looked bewildered. "I don't know what I'm doing here, but you two look like witches to me. You'd better start explaining things, or I'll—" His hand went to the sheath on his belt, searching for the missing knife. "Where's my knife?"

"Over there by the door," Magda said smoothly.

He kept his eyes on her as he collected the knife and stuck it back in its sheath.

"Sergeant, do you remember searching for a boy?"

Slowly a look of comprehension appeared on his face. "Yes. The prime minister wants the boy."

"Shouldn't you be looking for him?"

He narrowed his eyes. "I don't work for the prime minister. I swore an oath to the *king.*"

"But you *were* working for the prime minister. Do you remember that?"

He glared at her, and shook his head. "That can't be. I would never turn traitor—"

"You were bewitched, Sergeant," Magda said. "The prime minister put a spell on you and your men."

He looked stunned, as though he'd been slapped.

"Your men are here, waiting for you, Sergeant. We should talk about the prime minister's spell, but perhaps your men should ride back to town first. They're still bewitched," Magda said.

"My men?" he said, looking dazed.

"They're waiting in the yard." Magda waved toward the door.

She didn't even use the Voice, Suli thought.

Sergeant Lito rose and walked unsteadily to the window. He stared at the soldiers as though trying to remember something, then opened the door and stepped out.

He could still turn around and arrest them, Suli thought. She moved quietly to the draining board beside the sink to pick up the skillet. She could hardly lift it, but held it with both hands, waiting.

Sergeant Lito yelled, "You men! Go back to town. I'll finish here."

The broken-nosed man protested, "But sir—"

"Now! I said go!"

The soldiers stared curiously, but they mounted their horses and rode off, leaving a cloud of dust hanging in the air behind them. The sergeant's horse stared after him, mournfully.

He came back inside, looking wary, but curious. "All right, witch. I've done as you asked. Now you have some explaining to do."

Magda nodded. "That's fair. But first, my cousin has an errand to perform. Suli? Come with me."

While the sergeant was outside, Magda had dropped a napkin over the amulet and tied off the corners. She scooped it up and walked past him to the door. "I'll only be a moment," she said.

"No magic, witch," he warned. He rubbed the back of his head. "Why does my head hurt?" he asked suspiciously.

Suli followed Magda into the garden.

"Take this to the lake and drop it beneath the waterfall," Magda said. "Then you'd better take the children to sleep in my cottage tonight." Magda handed her the amulet by the knotted loop of the napkin.

"Wait. I want to test the Voice on you. Then you test it on me."

Magda inhaled deeply, then nodded. "Go ahead."

Suli began to chant in a singsong way, now high, now low. She told Magda to stand on one foot with her arms in the air.

Magda didn't move. "I'm not resisting at all," she said heavily. "It doesn't work. Probably pointless, but I'll try."

Magda told Suli to whirl in a circle.

Nothing happened. They stared at each other for a moment.

"So…" Magda said heavily. "The amulet *is* responsible for stealing wise women's magic. Hurry to the lake before it gets dark. I have things to discuss with the sergeant."

"Be careful," Suli said, "even without an amulet he's dangerous."

"Same to you," Magda whispered. "Fly safe."

Suli nodded, but when Magda turned the corner of the house, Suli didn't change. Instead, she found an old sack and knelt beside a plot of winter vegetables, laying the amulet beside her on the ground.

Coalfeather was afraid the sickness would come here and Suli thought he was right. She had to test it. If the amulets the soldiers wore stole magic, had the sickness arrived with them?

She held a cabbage leaf between her thumb and forefinger, careful not to disturb the bed of straw around it. She closed her eyes and Saw the energy rising from the ground, the energy from the soil, sun, water, and air that enabled the plant to grow and breathe. She Saw the magic flowing to it, and felt weak with relief. At least she could still See.

But something wasn't right. The magical flow, which should've been straight and easy, was blocked by dark, jagged scars cutting across it. There were dark spots, too, as though something had burnt the plant, leaving wounds. She opened her eyes and stared at the leaf. Nothing visible explained those wounds—the leaf seemed healthy and whole. Whatever had savagely torn the plant was more subtle than insect or frost damage. The *spirit* of the plant had been damaged by magic, and if it wasn't healed, the plant would sicken and die.

What about the rest of the garden? She shifted on the sack, the cold from the ground stabbing up into her body, and reached for a leaf of winter chard.

The sickness was here, too. She could See tiny black spots where it was beginning to eat away at the plant. Concentrating on the spots, she tried to push the flow back along the plant's veins and capillaries, using her magic burn away the sickness.

Only it didn't work. She couldn't move the energy at all.

Shocked, she opened her eyes, still holding the leaf. This had never happened before. Healing had always been easy for her. But it depended on magic to flow normally. The amulet had changed that.

She tried again with another plant, searching for the energy she normally used to Heal.

It wasn't there. The energy that should have flowed from the plant itself was missing. Magic wasn't rising from the ground or flowing through the air. The magic she needed to Heal was gone. *She couldn't Heal.*

She followed the root system into the ground. The roots, too, were diseased. Soon the garden would be completely infected by these spots, and the plants would wither and die. If the rest of the country was like this, there would be nothing to eat when spring came. Everyone would starve.

The same thing was happening to the animals, she realized; this was why they became forgetful and sick.

She felt a cold gust of wind and looked up. The sun was hidden behind clouds, but it was time to feed the goats and chickens. She'd do that now, and check on them at the same time.

She rose stiffly, rubbing her hands to warm them.

In the barn, she scattered grain for the hens in their small enclosure. They pecked and scolded at her feet, apparently normal.

But the goats were listless, not even raising their heads when she entered. Instead of following her with their golden eyes as they usually did, they stared into space, not even noticing when their piles of food appeared.

Suli laid her hand on the head of the goat who had a notch in one of her floppy ears. Silky was Suli's favorite; she loved to follow Suli around, butting her hand (or her leg, or her hip) affectionately. Suli closed her eyes and concentrated on Seeing Silky.

She gasped and when she opened her eyes, they stung with tears.

Silky didn't recognize her.

The goat's mind was a cloud of confusion; she didn't even remember what eating was.

And Suli couldn't Heal her. The amulets had brought the sickness here while simultaneously stealing the energy she needed to Heal or to protect against witchcraft.

Feeling hopeless, Suli changed shape, and slid the knot of the napkin over her beak.

She could neutralize one amulet by dropping it in the lake. But there were many more across the country; how could she stop the amulets from stealing the magic wise women needed?

16

A WILD GOOSE CHASE

SULI'S WINGS floated on the updraft of warm air, her body carried by the current. Without her Healing, she felt hollow and empty. She wanted to cry, but there were no tears. Geese couldn't cry.

Whatever had happened to her magic, she could still fly. Her wings beat steadily and she flew swiftly above the village's fields until she was rising above the rocky, tree-covered slopes of the mountain. *You can fly*, she told herself. *You can See. You can change shape. You aren't helpless.* The reminder was silly and obvious, but it *did* make her feel better.

Then she heard it: the sound she'd been dreading for days.

She dropped lower, scanning the trails, searching for movement.

There they are.

A pack of dogs was running up the path, followed by three soldiers on horseback, with Tanner in the lead. He must have decided to go ahead without Sergeant Lito. That might work in their favor. Tanner was brutal, but he'd be easier to fool. She'd thought of a way to do that, even without her magic.

First, though, she had to get rid of the amulet.

The sun escaped the clouds as she reached the lake, bathing

tree trunks and branches with orange light. She skimmed over the dark surface of the lake and approached the waterfall. As she passed, a few of the wild geese who lived there called a greeting. She hoped Magda was right and that the lake water would render the amulet harmless. She didn't want to harm anyone who lived there.

She flew as close to the thundering wall of water as she dared and dropped her bundle into the churning white froth below. She banked and turned, searching for familiar faces. A few of Sigur's folk were there, but Orion was not. Then she saw the small brown goose, floating on the water with Timber's family.

Benno.

She glided down, using her feet to brake, and settled on the water, wings folded. She swam slowly toward them to give Timber and his family time to recognize her. She'd healed his daughter once, and he'd helped her in turn.

When she reached them she greeted them and said, "I hope everyone is well, Timber. Thank you for looking after Benno. I need his help with something."

Timber bowed his graceful neck, and then he and his family tactfully swam away.

"How are you, Benno? Where are Orion and Arta?"

"They've gone to Magda's cottage in the forest. Orion said I should stay here so I don't lead the dogs there. I don't know for how long." His head drooped.

Suli felt sorry for him. He was new to being a goose, and was in a strange place with strange people. "Don't worry—we'll join them tonight." She smiled to reassure him. "First there's something you can help me with. The dogs are coming up the main path, and you're the only one who can help me lead them away. After we do that, it will be safe to join the others."

"I'm ready," he said, straightening his long neck.

"We'll have to risk getting close to them, but we're going to lead them on a wild-goose chase." It was a feeble joke, but he rewarded her with a chuckle.

Benno followed Suli into the air, his takeoff a little unsteady, but he quickly righted himself. The final rays of the setting sun lit their wings as they flew through the forest. Suli landed beside the boulder that marked the path to the lake and Benno floated down beside her.

"I think they'll come at least this far. From here we'll go somewhere they don't expect. There's a foot path that switches back and forth across the eastern side of the mountain, before heading into the valley on the other side."

"Do I have to walk the whole way?"

"No. We'll fly and then become human to leave a trail."

They changed. Benno walked around, touching the boulder and the moss below the pine trees.

"Now we'll fly to the start of the path and do the same."

They stopped every now and then so human Benno could touch whatever they found. They did this over and over, until they reached the end of the trail on the other side of the mountain.

"That's the best I can think of for now," Suli said. "Let's go back to the cottage. If the dogs follow your scent, they should end up in Grass Village."

It was dark when they landed in what was once a clearing around Magda's cottage. Now it was choked with weeds as tall as Suli, and and saplings of ash and hemlock. No one had lived there since Magda left two years before.

Suli expected to see a light in the window, or smell smoke from the fireplace, but the cottage was dark and forbidding. No light shone from any window, and there was no sound except the rustling of leaves in the dark trees around them.

"Don't change, until we know it's safe," she said. "Let me check the cottage. If anything happens to me, fly to the lake and stay with Timber's family."

Benno nodded.

She gazed around the clearing carefully, using her side-Seeing. It was animal magic and she thought it would work. But nothing human or animal was hidden in the darkness.

She approached the door quietly. The place seemed deserted. She could smell the rank, earthy smell of wet dirt and rotting plants; there was no smoke, no smell of food cooking, not even the smell of lamp oil or candles. Without knocking she lifted the latch and stepped inside.

Feeling her way through the darkness, she banged her knee painfully against the stove, maneuvering around it with her hands, until she found the shelf where the candle stubs were kept. She groped for flint and steel, but there were matches in the drawer below.

She struck a match and lit a candle stub. Hearing a sound behind her, she turned quickly, her heart beating fast.

Benno stood in the doorway. "Stay right there," she said. She held up the candle and examined the room.

Everything was the same as it had been two years ago, from the threadbare cushions on the chairs by the hearth to the bare wooden table, except now all was coated with a layer of dust. The cottage smelled of mildew and mouse droppings.

"Orion? Arta?" Her voice sounded dead in the stillness of the kitchen.

She thought she heard a *thump*, the sound of a door closing in the distance. She started down the hallway that led to the bedrooms, listening. Why did no one answer?

"Arta? Orion?" she called. "It's me."

She opened the first door on her right, Magda's bedroom. Dust filmed the chest and bedside table and it smelled strongly of damp. Back in the passage, she opened the next door, the one that had been the workroom. It too looked undisturbed. She was about to open the door at the end, when she heard Benno honking. She ran back to the main room. The doorway was empty.

She ran outside. "Benno! Where are you?"

A light held by a tall dark shape approached through the forest of weeds. When it grew closer, she recognized Orion, holding a safety lantern. He recognized her at the same moment, and smiled. "Finally!" Orion said. "Arta said it was you."

"Where's Benno?"

"He went to find Arta in the shed. She likes the hammock and wants to stay there tonight. It might be safer than the house since that's the first place they'll look. It would give us some warning."

Suli shivered. "You're joking! The cottage has a *stove* and a *fireplace* and a *bed*. I'm sleeping beside a fire tonight. You don't know how cold it gets in that shed, but I do."

They picked their way through the forest of weeds to the shed, the smell of crushed plants and sap rising in the air.

It felt as though there were a hundred eyes watched them from the trees. *And maybe there are,* she thought, maybe the animals of the forest are wondering why humans have returned to the witch's cottage.

Suli had been forced to sleep in the shed when Magda offered to "look after her" when Tala was locked up as a suspected witch. It was even more weathered and dilapidated now, with the roof slumping to one side.

Orion scratched lightly on the door three times. The door opened a crack and a brown eye appeared. Arta opened the door and motioned them inside.

A second lantern hung from a roof beam, bathing the dusty shed in a warm yellow light. Benno was sitting in the hammock that had been Suli's bed two years ago. Arta climbed up beside him and began to swing back and forth, looking pleased.

Suli said, "I saw the dogs on the mountain path, heading for the lake, but Benno and I laid a false trail. Can you tell if they're following it, Arta?"

Arta stopped swinging. A distant expression came over her face. "I think so. They're hungry and cold and want to rest by a fire, but that bad man is making them run to the other side of the mountain! I'll tell them they're helping me."

Orion asked, "Anyone hungry?"

"There's food?" Suli looked around hopefully.

Orion pointed toward the row of sacks that lined one wall. Mice had gnawed holes in many of them, spilling oats or barley on the floor, but there were also shelves holding jars of apple and blackberry jam, and pickled vegetables.

Suli selected an apple from a sack and bit into it; it had stayed sweet. "Looks like Andragora's people are using this shed as their private larder. I'm glad they left some for us."

"Who's Andragora?" Arta asked.

"The queen of the mice on the mountain. She helped me when I lived here before. You haven't seen any mice?"

Orion shook his head. "Not yet. Where have you been all day?"

Suli sat down cross-legged on an old crate. "I have a lot to tell you."

Orion raised a hand to stop her. "I've changed my mind. I'd feel better behind a locked door. The lock on the shed door is broken and the wood's practically rotted through."

Arta looked as if she was about to object.

Suli said quickly, "I'm freezing. I'd like to sit beside a fire."

"I wouldn't mind sleeping by a fire," Orion observed. "Arta, are you sure the dogs are on the other side of the mountain? They're not coming here?"

"I'm sure," she said.

"Come on," Orion said, getting to his feet, "bring anything you want with you."

They trooped into the house, and while Benno and Arta went exploring, Orion cornered Suli in the kitchen. "So where have you been? You went to the house, didn't you?"

She sighed. He was going to say, *I told you so.* "Yes, you were right. I was ambushed by soldiers. But we know for certain now that the soldiers are controlled by magic. Magda used the Voice on one, but he was able to resist it until we removed the amulet they wear around their necks. That's why they believe Benno and the royal family are traitors and the prime minister's a hero. After we removed it, from this sergeant was angry that the prime minister had bewitched him."

Orion gave a low whistle. "So that's how he does it. Not persuasion or bribes, but magic. I bet that's why Tala is still in Lofton. She's trying to find a way to stop it."

"But that's not the worst part." The way her voice trembled was embarrassing. It was time to accept that all her magic was gone. "The amulets steal magic, too. After being near it, I can still See, but I can't Heal or use the Voice. Neither can Magda. We tried."

Orion met her eyes. "I'm sorry."

She didn't need her Seeing to tell he meant it. "Thanks."

He said thoughtfully, "But now we know *why* the wise women can't escape—the amulets have stolen their magic. And if they can steal magic," he paused, considering, "I bet they're the cause of the animals' sickness."

She nodded. "I agree. The animal deaths began in the places where the soldiers first arrived. And after the soldiers arrived in Weatherstone, my goats became sick, and the plants in the garden have some kind of disease. But I can't heal them."

Arta and Benno came running down the hall, smiling at each other.

"It doesn't seem any warmer here," Arta observed. "Also, Benno and I want to sleep in the bed."

Suli sighed. "Arta, please help Orion start a fire in the fireplace. Benno, I'll teach you how to start one in the stove. I bet you never learned that."

Benno looked interested. "It's much colder, when you're human, isn't it?" He had wrapped his arms around his body.

Orion laughed. "I'm afraid so. There's firewood in the lean-to.

You two, come with me and help me carry the wood. We'll get a fire going quickly. Let's just hope the chimney's not blocked."

Left alone, Suli poked through the jars and sacks Orion had brought, shivering. She was too tired to think anymore. She had to hope her false trail would keep them safe, at least for the night, but it wouldn't protect them forever.

Tomorrow she had to come up with a better plan. She had to find other ways to protect them all, now that her magic was gone.

17

THE SPY HOLE

THE CLOCK on the mantelpiece of the prime minister's house ticked loudly, a seemingly predictable sound that fell half a second later than expected every now and then.

Tala Wing, Suli's former teacher, ran a feather duster over the clock and the pictures propped beside it.

If that's the heartbeat of this house, this house is sick, Tala thought, *but I'll not fix it.* She looked at the people in the old-fashioned sepia photographs. Old people in stiff formal clothes and stiffer expressions stared back; children dressed in frills and lace, looking surprised to be caught wearing their best clothes. None of them resembled the people who lived in the house now.

When the prime minister appropriated the former prime minister's house, he must have taken the previous prime minister's possessions as well. *That would be typical of him,* Tala thought. After she'd worked there a few months she'd told Magda, "He's an actor. He looks for settings to reinforce the illusion he wants to create." The previous prime minister had been thrown into prison on charges of corruption. Conveniently, he'd died soon after.

Magda had asked, "And how do you plan to destroy these illusions, Sister?" Tala pursed her lips, remembering. She didn't know the answer to that question yet. But destroying the prime minister's lies was what she was here to do.

She opened the curtains wide and raised the window sash to let in the morning air. The sound of horses and carriages on the cobbled streets entered the room from the street below. A carriage pulled up to the front steps and two men in black frock coats, carrying slim leather boxes, got out and climbed the steps. She heard the distant peal of the bell and the men disappeared inside. The carriage remained in front of the house, the brightly colored heraldic shield on its doors attracting curious glances from the people in the street.

She hurried down the long carpeted hallway to the servants' staircase. The prime minister and his visitors would be in the morning room at the front of the house. Tala descended the staircase quietly, and made a sharp left when she reached the bottom, treading softly down a dark, uncarpeted passage that smelled of boiled cabbage and tallow candles. Checking there was no one in sight, she pushed a wooden panel that looked the same as the others, and stepped inside a dimly-lit hallway, closing the panel behind her.

The narrow passage ran behind the public rooms at the front of the house. Circles of faint light outlined the spy holes; the plugs fit loosely so they could be removed without making a sound. Moving carefully, she made her way to the spy hole for the morning room and removed the cork plug. Whoever had made the spy holes had also created an ingenious way of amplifying sounds. A small metal cup was fixed into the wall beside the peephole. A flexible tube of leather dangled from it, with another cup at the end. Tala bent over to put her eye to the hole and placed the cup over her ear. Now she could both see and hear what was happening in the room.

"The matter is urgent, Prime Minister," one of the men was

saying. He fingered the metal pin on his coat. The brightly colored enamel pin of the country's flag was a sign of patriotism in support of the coming war. "The delegation from Portjean requires an immediate answer. They are threatening military action if we don't respond satisfactorily."

The prime minister didn't look at the man who spoke, but stared at the document before him on the dark mahogany desk. He appeared to be admiring the patterns of gold and ivory inlaid on its surface, tracing each swirl with a finger. "Is there a deadline?" he asked, without raising his eyes.

The second man stepped closer to the desk and Tala recognized the grey bearded face—Hallard, one of the king's senior advisors. "They demand our ships return to Lofton immediately and that we send a formal agreement that we will pay their tax, the same amount as always—no reductions. Their position is the same: blockading the ships is an act of war. If our ships aren't removed by the day after tomorrow, they'll attack them."

The prime minister raised his eyes and stared at him, his pale face expressionless. "What is your recommendation, Master Hallard?" His eyes flicked to the plain coat the older man wore, unadorned by any jewelry, then back to Hallard's face.

"We should recall our ships at once, sir. No one wants a war."

"True, very true," said the prime minister, tapping his finger on the paper. "But isn't it possible that they're bluffing?"

Hallard blinked in surprise but said evenly, "I don't think so, sir. The fishing fleet is the mainstay of their economy. They are correct when they say that by preventing their fleet from leaving port, we threaten them with economic ruin. I don't understand why we insist on reducing the tax in the first place."

"Don't you?" The prime minister's eyes flashed coldly. "I'm surprised you take their side."

Hallard frowned. "It's not a matter of sides, sir. You asked my opinion. In all my years as an advisor to the king—"

"Quite so, yes," the prime minister said in a soothing tone.

"I'm sure we are all grateful for your long service. Indeed, I believe you may have earned a rest."

Hallard glanced at him sharply.

The prime minister turned to the second man. "What do you think, Merrill?"

Merrill's glanced uncertainly from Hallard to the prime minister. "I think we should reassure the Portjean government that we have no wish to harm their fishing trade," he said. With a distracted air, he fingered the flag pin on his lapel. "But we have to show that we can't be bullied."

The prime minister nodded. "Diplomacy. Yes. That sounds well. And the ships?" He looked at Merrill with eyes like chips of ice.

"They should stay where they are while the diplomatic courier delivers—" Merrill began.

"But this is madness!" Hallard broke in. "They will see our ships as an occupying force and will feel compelled to defend themselves."

The prime minister stared at Hallard for a long time.

The older man grew pale. Beads of sweat appeared on his forehead. "I have told you what I think, sir. I cannot stand by and watch my country slide into war for no good reason."

"Thank you for stating your views so clearly," the prime minister said, his eyes never leaving Hallard's face. "But in this case, I fear you and I disagree. I think Portjean is bluffing, and to give in to their demands would look like weakness. For too long we have danced to the tune of other nations, even though we are stronger than our neighbors. It's time we demonstrate that strength."

Merrill nodded and smiled, reassured.

"Good." The prime minister gave Merrill the smile of a man who has seen his opposition crumble. "I will have a message for you to send within the hour. Have a courier standing by."

"But, sir," Hallard said, moving closer to the desk, "surely the king must be consulted first? Before we go to war?"

"Rest easy, Hallard," the prime minister said, leaning back in his chair. His large white teeth flashed unexpectedly from the concealment of his dark beard, but his eyes narrowed. "The king has complete confidence in me." He waved his hand. "You may go."

Merrill and Hallard exchanged looks, then turned and left the room. The prime minister didn't notice; he'd already forgotten them.

~

Tala crept back along the passage and stopped to listen before she stepped into the servants' hallway. Closing the panel behind her, she walked to the kitchen. The crisis was here and she still hadn't learned how the prime minister controlled the men around him. Hallard was the key. So far, he was the only one who had been able to stand up to him.

In the kitchen she put on a clean, well-starched apron and began her rounds. She checked that the maids and footmen had restocked the fires and finished their cleaning. She surveyed the preparations for dinner laid out on the table, and nodded approval to the cook, while considering what to tell Magda in her message.

Things were moving quickly; they wouldn't make the deadline now. In two days' time they would be at war and her task would be much more dangerous; any opposition to the prime minister once war was declared could be called treason. It might be too late to save the king and queen, although the boy had a chance.

Tala was certain the prime minister used magic to control his soldiers and the people in Lofton, but she still didn't know how. If she were caught, Suli and Magda would have to find out.

She wondered if the wise women in the camps already knew the answer.

18

FIRE MESSAGES

THE WAGONS HAD ARRIVED at their destination.

Coalfeather had followed them all the way from Weatherstone. Darkness had fallen before the wagons loaded with wise women and girls arrived at a high palisaded fence, with sentries patrolling behind it. One of the soldiers accompanying the wagons on horseback called for someone to open the gate.

A head appeared above the fence. "Password?"

"Death to Portjean!"

The gates swung open and the wagons rumbled inside.

Coalfeather flew over the palisaded wall. Behind it, dirt-colored tents were pitched in rows on a muddy field. To the far right was a barracks hastily nailed together of raw wooden planks. It resembled a military camp, but instead of soldiers, women and girls huddled around small fires in the lanes between the tents. The prisoners shivered in the bitter wind, pulling their shawls and cloaks tighter.

Sentries stood on the platform that ran around the inside of the palisade. The archers held their bows with arrows already nocked on the bowstring, waiting for an excuse to shoot. They watched the women as though they were dangerous animals.

That can't last, Coalfeather thought. The soldiers will get bored and try to start something, try to provoke a fight. These women are in danger.

He scanned the faces of the wise women until he found one he recognized. She seemed healthier than the others and Coalfeather guessed she'd arrived more recently, from a mountain village near Weatherstone.

"I am here!" he called. She looked up. He flew behind an outbuilding. The woman glanced at the guards above her, then hurried to join him.

THE PRIME MINISTER sat at his desk, turning a metal disc between his fingers. From where she watched behind the spy hole, Tala saw an odd purplish light glinting off its edges.

No matter how she shifted, she couldn't see it clearly. After months of searching, this had to be it, the way he controlled the amulets he used to command the soldiers. She'd seen no other magical object near him, besides the desk itself, and the webs of protection surrounding it that prevented her from getting too close.

She ached to get a closer look. Biting her lip, she forced herself to remain still, waiting to see what he would do. After ten minutes of turning the disc in his hands counter clockwise, he opened the top drawer of the desk and dropped it inside, locking the drawer with a silver key. Then he slipped the key on its silver chain over his head and beneath his shirt. Tala's nails dug into the wall beside the spy hole.

That disc *had* to be the way he controlled the soldiers—why else fondle a piece of metal for so long? Faint lines of green vibrated in the air around the desk, lines of protection visible only to those who could See. To evade them, she had to know more about the kind of magic he was using. She suspected the desk itself was magical, too, but she couldn't get past the protection spell to find out, not without warning the prime minister that someone had breached his defenses.

A knock sounded on the door. She shifted quietly to another spy hole.

"Enter," the prime minister called.

A messenger came to the desk, bowed, and handed him a letter affixed with a red seal. The spell didn't prevent everyone from approaching the desk, only those with magic. She was impressed by the prime minister's cleverness. And afraid of it.

The prime minister took a silver knife from the desk to break the seal. He read silently for a moment. "No answer."

The messenger bowed and left, closing the door softly behind him.

Tala watched, her frustration growing. She could think of no plausible excuse to go into the study to read it "accidentally," and unless he left it somewhere other than the desk, she couldn't approach it anyway. That was the difficulty of her role here. She didn't dare become invisible using Coalfeather's invisibility spell, not without knowing more about the prime minister's magic—for all she knew, he might be able to see through it. The danger of being caught was too great. Patience, that was the key.

No word had come from Magda, and that worried her. It was up to her to send a message now; Magda and Suli needed to know the war would start soon and the amulets were important. They'd have to figure out what to do. She could be caught at any moment.

She slipped into the servants' corridor, and hurried to her own room off the kitchen pantry. She'd insisted on this smaller room, rather than the more imposing one on the third floor, because it had a fireplace and a door that locked. She locked it now, and bent to stir the fire so that it blazed up. She placed another log on the fire, then sat at her small desk. Pushing aside the household accounts, she took a fresh sheet of paper from a stack in a tray. She removed a blue bottle from a locked drawer, uncapped it, and dipped her pen into the ink inside. Swiftly she wrote a message in her flowing hand; the letters flared green for a moment, then dried the color of old ink. Kneeling before the fire, Tala fed the paper slowly and carefully into the flames.

SULI GLANCED out of the now sparkling-clean window in the main room of Magda's cottage. Clouds were rolling in and the pale blue of a winter sky was turning grey. It looked cold outside; she was glad to be in a warm room instead.

She lowered herself into the rocking chair near the fire with a sigh of relief. She'd cleaned all morning, with Benno and Arta's help. They'd knocked down cobwebs with a broom, removed a bird's nest from the chimney, and scrubbed the dust and dirt from every surface of the cottage while the bedding aired before the fire.

Now a roaring fire warmed the room, and the kitchen gleamed. Arta was asleep in Magda's room; she hadn't slept the night before, she said, because the dogs' thoughts kept her awake. Benno was outside with Orion, learning to clean the fish they'd eat for lunch, a useful skill for a prince to know, she thought, smiling to herself.

She stared drowsily into the flames. She could finally relax.

A flicker of green made her sit up. She rubbed her eyes, and stared harder at the blue and yellow flames in the center of the fire. There it was again, wavering green letters, words inside the fire. She fell to her knees on the hearth, concentrating.

"Orion!" she called, not taking her eyes off the fire. "Come quick! I need your help!"

He came running, banging the door open with a knife in his hand, scattering fish scales. "What is it?"

"Write down what I say!"

Orion glanced at the fire, and then scrabbled through drawers in the kitchen, until he found a pencil stub. He searched for something to write on, but Suli called, "Write on the tablecloth! Write this: *'PM using metal amulet to control soldiers—third kind of magic, ask Coalfeather. War on Portjean will be declared in a week. King and queen are imprisoned, charged with treason. Gather the wise women to help you. Can't leave. Tala.'*"

Suli's eyes were smarting from trying not to blink. She reread the lines—yes, she'd gotten them all. They began to fade until they were gone. "Did you get it?"

He straightened up. "Yes." He read the words back to her from the faded red cloth. "How does she know all this?"

It was only then that Suli noticed Benno, standing in the open doorway. How long had he been there? She held out a hand. "Benno, come sit by me."

He closed the door and walked slowly toward her, his face pale, his mouth in a grim line. "How do you know the king and queen are in prison?"

So he'd heard. "It was a message from my teacher, in Lofton. I think it's true, Benno."

"We have to get them out," he said. "I should have rescued them by now, and I haven't even started!" Tears slid down his face, and he turned away to hide them.

"No, Benno, don't cry." She put an arm around him, but he shook it off.

She threw Orion a pleading look, and he came over and touched Benno's shoulder. "You can't fight soldiers, and you can't overpower the guards of the prison. Neither can I. We need help and a plan before we can help your parents."

"Orion's right," Suli said gently, "we have to gather our forces, just as the prime minister has gathered his."

"Tell me what we have to do, to help my parents," Benno commanded. He folded his arms across his chest and stood there, waiting. For the first time, Suli saw a prince instead of a little boy.

"The first thing *I* need to do is talk to Coalfeather, but I haven't seen him. Perhaps the Animal Council could help. The wise women can't do this alone, not if our magic doesn't work around the amulets."

"What's an Animal Council?" Benno asked, distracted for a moment.

"Every animal nation that lives here sends an ambassador to represent them at the Council, then they decide things that affect everyone. They don't meet very often, only when something important happens, or there's a terrible threat."

"This is important," Benno said. "Will they help us?"

"Some will, I think. Especially when I tell them it's related to the magic that's killing their children."

Benno frowned. "The prime minister is killing their children?"

"I'm afraid so."

"Then we have to help them," he said.

Suli nodded. "Yes, that's the plan."

Benno looked up at Orion. "You'll help, too, won't you?"

"Of course, Benno. I already said I would." He rested his hand lightly on the boy's shoulder and asked Suli. "Do you want me to look for Coalfeather?"

She shook her head. "It's getting dark. Tomorrow."

Benno sat by the fire. "I've never seen messages in the fire like that. Can you do that?"

"No." Suli said. "Tala is too busy trying to stop the prime minister to finish my education."

"How can my parents be charged with treason? That *is* treason."

Orion sat in the chair across from Suli and spoke gently. "The prime minister wants to make everyone afraid. He thinks if they're frightened enough, they'll see enemies everywhere, and they'll believe his lies. They aren't thinking clearly." He glanced at Suli. "The prime minister probably said they're conspiring with Portjean. Makes no sense, of course, but if people are afraid of the enemy—"

"And then he'll kill them?" Benno asked. There was a shocked silence.

"It's possible," Suli said gently.

Arta came into the room, rubbing her eyes. "What's going on? I heard loud voices." She saw Benno's face and demanded, "Why is Benno upset?"

"Ask him," Suli said. "Orion, come outside for a moment."

As Suli went out the door, Arta and Benno had their heads together.

Suli followed Orion to the stump where he'd been descaling the fish. It stared mournfully up at him.

"Tala said to talk to Coalfeather about the amulets," she began, "but I already know about magical objects. So what did she mean? I wonder if it has something to do with Arta's magic."

"But he's not allowed to help us," Orion pointed out. "He'll get in trouble."

"He won't turn his back on me," Suli insisted, hoping she was right. "His flock is worried about the sickness. Even if they're angry at humans, they expect me to be there for them. And I'm worried about Tala. What if she sent that message now because she thinks she'll be caught? Magda said she's in danger."

Orion shrugged. "Well, so are we. There's nothing we can do to help her, is there? Except what she's asked. We should be trying to find any wise women still free."

"Agreed. I think they should come here, but then where can they stay? Tala's house isn't safe."

"It's not safe anywhere," Orion said. "But if we get rid of the amulets on the soldiers in Weatherstone, our village might be safer than anywhere else. And the prime minister will assume all the wise women have already been captured here."

"Maybe," Suli said doubtfully. "But how can we get the wise women here without anyone noticing—" She fell silent. The answer was obvious, once she thought of it. The question was, would he do it?

19

THE CROW TRAITOR

THE WIND WAS BITTERLY COLD, numbing Suli's face as she flew down the side of the mountain, a small glass jar of lake water bumping against her chest. Magda would need it. And she'd want to hear Tala's message.

Suli circled the house, searching for any sign the soldiers had returned. Smoke rose from the chimney and from the beehive-shaped oven behind the house. Everything looked normal enough.

She landed behind the barn and changed. The smell of baking bread drifted from the oven. Watching for any sign of movement, she crossed the yard and climbed the steps to the kitchen.

Sergeant Lito sat at the table, a steaming mug in his hand. He looked up and met her eyes.

She regarded him in silence for a moment. "Where's Magda?" she asked, standing in the doorway, ready to flee. Amulet or no amulet, this was the man who'd threatened to break her face.

"She's out tending the animals. Come in, girl, you don't need to fear me, although as a rule I don't hold with witches." He smiled ironically and drank a long draught from his mug. "But since you two freed me from a cursed spell, I suppose I'm grateful, witches or no."

His drank again, his dark eyes watching her over the rim of the mug. "The prime minister gave those amulets to every man in the army. The prince hasn't got a chance." When he lowered the mug, Suli saw he was grinning. "Unless he happens to find some loyal witches."

"And you aren't still searching for the boy?" Suli asked, unconvinced.

"Catch up, girl. I'm no traitor, nor would any of my men be if we hadn't been magicked. The prince has my loyalty. For all the good that will do either of us. Here," he pushed the teapot toward her, "have some tea. I just made it."

Suli pulled a chair out and sat down. "Magda's out feeding the animals you say?" She pulled the teapot toward her.

He laughed. "And she's baking bread. You might want to check the oven. She's been gone long enough."

She hadn't decided whether to believe him when the door banged open and Magda came through, carrying bunches of kale and a clump of turnips, their roots dripping mud.

"The sergeant's been telling me he doesn't hold with witches."

Magda gave a bark of laughter and dropped the vegetables in the sink. "So you're getting acquainted. You've naught to worry about with him. We have an understanding Sergeant Lito and I. He won't arrest us and I won't turn him into a goat."

"Very fair," the sergeant said, nodding. He pushed back his chair and walked to the stove. "Now I'm going to make you my famous lobscouse, guaranteed to grow hair on your chest."

Magda waved her hand toward the stove and the pots hanging on the wall, "Help yourself. I have to check the bread." She walked back out the door which banged behind her.

Suli watched the sergeant set a pot of water to boil on the stove and begin to wash the vegetables in the stone sink. "What

about the rest of your men? Won't they come looking for you?"
she asked.

"Aye, they will. And we've got to be ready for them," he said.
He turned to face her, a knife in his hand. "You witches will have
to spell them, like you did me, to get those amulets off."

"Aren't you afraid of the prime minister?" she asked in a low
voice.

"A pox on the prime minister and all his doings!" he said, his
face reddening. "I don't take kindly to any man or woman putting
a spell on me against my will. That includes you too, witch."

Suli kept her eyes warily on the sergeant's knife. "You were
going to smash my face." Suli said. "We had every right to protect
ourselves." She didn't really care what the man thought; if she had
her magic back, she'd use the Voice on him in a heartbeat. He was
a violent man who'd probably hurt women and children without
thinking twice about it. The amulet had only used him; it hadn't
made him that way.

He snorted and turned back to the stove. "I've given you fair
warning: Don't do it again."

The door opened and Magda came inside with a basket piled
high with crusty brown loaves, the steam rising from them. She
set the basket on the table and the smell of fresh bread filled the
room.

Suli's stomach growled. She inhaled deeply and closed her
eyes, trying to pretend things were the way they'd been a week
ago, before she'd left with the wild geese. All she wanted was for
things to go back the way they were. She wanted to live at Tala's
house peacefully baking bread, making remedies, and helping the
villagers with their problems. Instead, she was involved in a war,
not against Portjean but with the strongest witch the country had
ever seen.

Suli rose and asked Magda quietly, "How do you plan to get
those amulets off the other soldiers without magic?"

"That's the question, isn't it?" Magda said, not bothering to lower her voice. "Sergeant Lito has some ideas. But we'll need help."

"Can I speak with you—privately?" Suli tilted her head at the door. Even if Magda trusted the sergeant, she didn't.

Magda nodded and they went outside, their skirts flapping in the freezing wind.

"I brought you a gift," Suli said. She handed Magda the glass jar. "It's lake water. I haven't tried it, yet, but I thought you might need it."

Magda smiled. "How did you know? That's *exactly* what I wanted."

"I have a message for you, too," Suli said. "At least, I think it was meant for you. Tala sent a message in the fire: she says war will be declared in a week, and that the king and queen are in prison for treason. She knows about the amulets, and wants us to tell the wise women about them. I'm sending the flock to look for any wise women still free and ask them to come here."

The sergeant stuck his head out the door. "I don't like my new friends keeping secrets from me. What are you talking about?"

"Women's concerns, Sergeant; nothing for you to worry about," Magda said. She turned back to Suli. "You'd best do it now then."

Suli nodded and headed for the pond. They had to let the wise women know what they were up against. Some wouldn't come, she knew; they'd try to stop the soldiers in their own villages. And the ones who *could* come would have to travel in secret.

The geese gathered around her, the wind making the reeds by the pond rustle and ruffling their feathers. Seven geese volunteered to look for wise women in hiding to give them her message. Suli told them which villages she guessed might still have their wise women.

She had a special job for Flax; he was the strongest and could fly the farthest. "His name is Master Swift. Look for a long caravan of wagons traveling across the plains; I don't know exactly where they'll be. Once you find him, tell him we need his help to carry wise women secretly to Weatherstone. Tell him the two girls he helped in Winton are fighting back."

Flax nodded and said only, "If he's there to be found, I will find him." Then he leapt into the air.

Her message to the wise women explained the danger of the amulets, and asked them to join Master Swift's caravan if it came to their town, or to arrive however they could. Beyond that, they'd have to improvise. The mountain would be a safe place for them to gather; there were plenty of places to hide near the cottage and the lake. At all costs the wise women and Benno had to stay free.

She was returning to the house when a loud *Caw!* sounded above her.

Coalfeather and his father, Kaark, landed on the brown grass beside her.

"We must talk," said Coalfeather.

"Thank the Sisters! I need to talk to you, too. Hello Kaark, how are you?" She was afraid Kaark had come to tell her to stop involving Coalfeather in her plans.

"I am well, Mistress Suli," Kaark replied. "But what is this I hear about a powerful witch? My son says we must help you, in spite of our Law, but I will decide for myself. He thinks the Animal Council should be involved too. Everyone knows the Council should not get involved in human affairs, yet he wants me to call a meeting and tell them to break the Law. What have you done to him? Is it true a witch threatens the entire country?"

Coalfeather calmly answered for her. "Whether we help them or not, we are affected. Have you not noticed, Father, the bodies of winged people on the side of the road? Do you not remember the rotted and broken eggs in our cousins' flock? There is a pestilence on the land, affecting water, air, and earth. The crops will not grow and the young will not thrive. If we don't help the humans stop this magical plague, our flock will die too. The humans have turned their back on the proper balance. We are already dying because of the witch."

Kaark glowered at Suli. "Is this true? Is witchcraft the cause of the sickness?"

Suli took a deep breath. "I think so, and so does Tala. The prime minister is able to controls thousands of people using magical objects."

"You know as well as I do, Father, that we need the wise women to control the magic," Coalfeather spoke urgently in a soft croak. "They are the ones who can focus it. For that reason alone we must help them. I have seen the camps where they are kept. They are terrible places and these women have no magic now. We must help them."

Kaark was silent. He paced away, his head bowed low. When he returned, he said to Suli, "Tell me of this boy you're hiding. Is it true he can fly?"

"Yes," Suli said, wondering at the change of subject. "Both Benno and his mother, the queen, are part of Sigur's flock. We think the prime minister has accused the queen of witchcraft because of it."

"Hmm. And the soldiers invading our village are searching for him?"

"For the boy, for me, for anyone who knows magic. If they find a wise woman, or a girl learning magic, they take her to the camps."

"So you are in danger, too," Kaark mused to himself.

"Our Law was not made for times like these, Father. The threat of the soldier's amulets is greater than the threat of their violence. Then there is the girl. She knows secret animal magic, which the wise women don't know. If *I* don't teach her, she might become dangerous."

"What girl?" Kaark asked. "First you talk about a boy who can fly, and now there is a girl. What are you running, a human nursery?"

Suli remembered Kaark's message that crows were not human nursemaids and shifted uncomfortably. "I've acquired an apprentice," Suli said. "Arta can talk to animals silently. Coalfeather says it's a kind of animal magic. I've never seen anything like it."

Kaark rumbled his displeasure. He paced up and down on the dead grass, muttering to himself. "Teaching a human *our* magic?"

Suli remembered when Coalfeather had refused to teach *her* Crow magic, although he had shown her how to see through the Crow invisibility spell. It was Tala who had taught her how to use that spell because Tala had figured it out for herself. That was the only animal magic Suli knew. So how was this different? Why did Coalfeather want to teach Arta what he had refused to teach her? Because Arta could misuse it?

Kaark stopped pacing. "This is much worse than I thought. Revealing our magic to humans is absolutely forbidden, and for a very good reason. Used incorrectly, it could endanger everything!"

Coalfeather's feathers lay flat against his back. "Forbidden or not, the girl already knows it. Without training she may not be able to control it, and that makes her dangerous. The soldiers already suspect she bewitched their dogs. She must be taught to protect herself and the rest of us. Then she can help the wise women—and us. *She* may be able to stop the sickness."

Suli looked at him questioningly. Did he really believe that, or was he saying that to convince his father? Could Arta heal the animals?

Kaark paced away again, his head bowed. For the first time, Suli saw the resemblance between them. Before, in her dealings with Kaark, he had always made fun of her, determined never to let humans become too important in his world.

She remained silent. It was better for Kaark to be persuaded by his son, not a human, if he was going to break Crow Law. A request from Coalfeather, a revered teacher, was the one thing that might work. She heard him muttering, "becoming human nursemaids."

Kaark lifted his wings, hopped into the air, and floated back to face his son. "If you do this," he warned, "your enemies on the Crow Council will rejoice. You will lose any chance of being re-elected. It is even possible the flock could vote to expel you as a traitor."

Coalfeather opened his wings wide to emphasize his words, "I know. But the witch's magic is killing the animals around us. Our lives are already in danger. And he imprisons the wise women who have helped us in the past. If all wise women are imprisoned or killed, what do you think will happen to us?"

Kaark nodded. "It is your choice, then. I will help you as I can, but I will *not* be able to sway the Council." He turned to Suli. "Good luck, Wise Woman!" He leapt into the air, with a harsh cry of farewell.

Coalfeather and Suli stared at each other in silence a long moment.

"I wish he'd made a joke," Suli said. "When your father is serious, I know we're in trouble." When Suli first met him, Kaark kept calling her a witch, and laughed at her all the time. Now it seemed witches were no longer a joking matter.

Coalfeather hunched his shoulders. "Well, I am, anyway." He made a croaking sound. "But I have good news, for a change. I spoke with a wise woman in the camp nearby. She came to Tala's trial and speaks Crow. She knows a way to smuggle people into the camp. Once inside, we could remove the amulets and help the women and girls escape."

"Does she know about the amulets?"

"Everyone in the camp knows about them, Netil says. There are wild rumors about what they make the soldiers do, but she's certain it keeps them from questioning orders. She knows a man who wants to help; he offered to let us use his carts to bring people into the camps."

"Well, that's a start," Suli said. "I've thought of a way to remove the amulets without using magic."

She glanced at her friend, wondering if his flock really would expel him. "Thank you for your help, Coalfeather. I was afraid I'd have to do this alone." She smiled grimly. "I'll do whatever it takes to convince the Crow Council you're a hero—because you are. We *need* you."

"And there's something else I need to tell you," Suli said hesitantly. "I didn't want to say it in front of your father. Remember when I said Tala and Magda thought something was stealing magic? Well, we've found it. The amulets the soldiers wear steal any magic nearby. I can't Heal or use the Voice now, Coalfeather."

He squawked in dismay. "Netil did not tell me that."

"She may not know," Suli said.

Coalfeather began to pace. "This is bad, very bad."

"Well, of course—"

"If the amulets are stealing all the magic around us then *they* are the cause of the sickness. Once magic is ripped from the pattern where it belongs, it is difficult to restore."

I didn't know that, Suli thought. "What do you mean? How can it be restored?"

Coalfeather became very still. "Only a wise woman can restore the magical balance." He wouldn't meet her eyes, and abruptly flew away.

That was odd, Suli thought. *As though he didn't want to tell me the answer.*

20

MAGDA AND THE SERGEANT

WHEN SULI RETURNED to the house, Magda and Sergeant Lito were drinking tea and eating fresh bread slathered with honey from Tala's beehives. Suli poured herself tea and joined them, spreading honey on a generous slice of bread.

"Once we can get the amulets off your men," Magda was saying, "the prince will have a group of loyal soldiers to defend him."

"They'll be cut to pieces," Sergeant Lito predicted grimly. "As soon as reinforcements arrive. Unless you witches can help some other way."

"Your men are the immediate threat. Let's remove their amulets first, then worry about what happens next."

"It won't be easy," he said. "The idea of taking it off is frightening. I never took mine off, not even to wash." The sergeant's mouth twisted bitterly. "You'll have to trick them, using your magic. I don't see another way."

Magda sipped her tea. "If we're somewhere private, I can use the Voice on them. We could work on the highest-ranking officers first; then they can order the men to do what we need."

Suli kept her eyes on the table so the sergeant wouldn't see her surprise. Magda couldn't use the Voice anymore, but apparently she hadn't shared that information with the sergeant. Suli thoroughly approved of not telling him everything; let him think they had all their magic. She hoped Magda would test whether the lake water actually restored the Voice before she tried it on the soldiers, and that the small amount of lake water she'd brought was enough.

Sergeant Lito was picking his teeth with his knife. "Maybe. I'll ask the officers to attend a meeting at the inn, say I've got new information. Getting the amulets off will be your job."

Magda nodded.

Suli wasn't convinced they should trust the sergeant. She thought he was telling the truth when he said he wouldn't forgive being magicked by the prime minister, but that didn't mean he'd forgiven Magda for using the Voice on him. She sighed and kept her doubts to herself. They had to trust him for this to have any chance of success.

Sergeant Lito rode into Weatherstone alone. He would send word to the officers to meet at the Holly Branch Inn.

Before Magda left on foot, she and Suli stood in the yard, their skirts flapping in the wind. "Be careful," Suli said. "I don't trust him. Besides, too many things could go wrong."

Magda smiled faintly. "Don't worry. I understand the sergeant pretty well. He's got his own business with the prime minister. You be careful on the mountain. Send Orion if there's news."

Suli nodded and in a heartbeat she was winging her way to the mountain.

~

MAGDA PUT the jar of lake water in her pocket, wrapped her warm cloak around her, and set out on the short walk to the inn.

Inside, pale daylight fell through mullioned windows and

gleamed on the tables' dark wood. Pipe and wood smoke drifted upwards toward the oak beams overhead.

Magda ordered a mug of ale and sat down. She drank it slowly, watching the villagers. They huddled in groups, whispering with their heads bent close together.

One old man was beyond caution. He shook his head and said loudly, "In all my born days, Teveral has never gone to war, and for good reason. We have everything we need, and we're willing to trade for what we want. Why should we fight?" A younger man, probably his son, told him to hush, his eyes shifting to see who was listening.

A farmer in a battered hat, his skin weathered to the color of old leather, muttered softly, "We don't know for sure. The mayor's received nothing official."

"Aye, but messengers arrive every day for the soldiers, curse 'em," said another farmer, who grimaced as though about to spit.

The door opened with a blast of cold air. The heads of the old men huddled by the fireplace turned, but when they saw it was a group of officers, they looked away. The soldiers' boots clattered as they climbed the stairs.

"What do you think they're up to, then?" the old man asked loudly. His son told him to hush.

There was the sound of boots coming back down the stairs and everyone turned to look.

The sergeant stood on the bottom step, gesturing for Magda. She rose, her tread slow and heavy, to follow him up the stairs.

Sergeant Lito was supposed to explain her presence by saying she was spying on the witches for them. If he had warned them, they would arrest her as a witch. Still, if it *was* a trap, Suli and the others were safe. The sergeant didn't know where they were, and he certainly didn't know some of them could fly.

She could take the risk. Every amulet she removed would be another loyal soldier for Benno.

SULI FLEW to Magda's cottage on the mountain, wondering if she should have gone with Magda to the inn. If the soldiers arrested her, it would be hours before they'd know. But Suli had her own work to do.

In the cottage they were cleaning up after the midday meal.

"Any left?"

Orion handed her a bowl of roasted fish and turnips.

In between mouthfuls, Suli said, "There are only a few hours of light left, but I think we should start the lessons."

"Orion says you're finally going to teach me magic." Arta said, her eyes shining. "Benno and I want to learn how to stop the soldiers."

"Good." Suli smiled. "But I'd like to teach you Crow first. It will make your other lessons easier."

Arta looked interested. "Is it hard to learn?"

"Not hard, but you have to think differently. It includes sounds, but it relies on wings and beak, too."

"I don't have a wing or a beak," Arta pointed out. "And I can't change shape. So why do I need to know it?"

"So you can talk to Coalfeather directly. He's offered to teach you how to use your listening. He calls it animal magic. So you see, you already know some magic."

"Oh."

"Orion was the one who first taught me Crow. Perhaps he can teach you."

Orion was tilting his chair off the floor, his face noncommittal.

"No," Benno said firmly. "Orion will teach me how to fight."

"I thought you wanted me to teach him to defend himself while he's in winged form," Orion said.

"Fine," Suli said. "You teach Benno, and I'll teach Arta Crow."

"If I learn Crow, then can I learn the pidgin so I can talk to *all* of the animals?" Arta asked.

"That's a good idea," Suli said. "But learn Crow first, so you can start your lessons with Coalfeather."

"Why does Benno have to learn to fight?" Arta asked.

"Geese fight differently than humans. You may not realize it, but we're very strong. Using our long necks like a whip, a goose can break bones or kill a man."

"Oh," Arta said, subdued. "I didn't know that."

"Not to mention the fun of diving down on someone from the air." Orion said. "It scares people silly. And it really hurts when you're bitten." He grimaced as though he knew this from personal experience.

"I don't think a prince should have to fight," Arta said, a stubborn note creeping into her voice.

"Of course I should learn to fight," Benno corrected her. "How else will I save my parents?"

"He'll be a lot safer if he can defend himself," Orion said quietly to Arta.

"Let's go," Suli said, rising to her feet. She'd wolfed down the food and wanted to get started. Ever since Tala's message in the fire, it felt like time was running out.

Suli draped a heavy shawl over Arta's shoulders, and threw on her cloak.

Orion and Benno flew ahead, saying they'd meet them at the lake.

Suli trudged through the deep drifts of snow across the forest path, resenting having to walk. It wasn't Arta's fault she couldn't change, but Suli was too tired to be fair.

When she and Arta arrived at the banks of the lake, Benno was diving and soaring in the air, the younger wild geese calling encouragement.

Orion called for him to come back.

Arta watched Benno fly toward them with a wistful expression. "I wish I could do that."

"You can do something no one else can," Suli reminded her, "talking to animals the way you do. You should be proud of that. You don't even need the pidgin."

Arta frowned. "But I don't know how I do it, or if I'll be able to use it when I need to."

Suli nodded. "That's why Coalfeather wants to teach you. He doesn't make that offer lightly; he's breaking the Law of his people to do so. His flock could even expel him for helping you."

Arta frowned. "Then why—"

"Because the prime minister's magic is killing animals. Your magic could help them."

Arta's eyebrows rose in surprise. "I'd like that."

"Good. Now, here's how you say, 'Hello, I'm here!' in Crow." Suli made a croaking call. "Now you try."

From the corner of her eye, Suli saw Benno and Orion fall like rocks from the sky, diving at the ducks floating on the lake. The ducks dived beneath the surface and the two geese pulled up at the very last moment. Orion and Benno flew off laughing. The ducks protested, calling loudly, then swam away, deeply offended.

Suli taught Arta a few basic sentences in Crow, but she was distracted by Benno and Orion attacking each other. It was frightening to watch, even though she knew they weren't really trying to hurt each other.

The sun sank behind the high cliff above the waterfall and it grew much colder. Suli called that they should go back. They'd made a good start, she thought. Arta could say a few phrases to Coalfeather tomorrow.

Then she remembered Magda, alone with the soldiers, and felt her stomach knot. Magda had no way to send a message if something went wrong.

21

TIME FOR SCHOOL

THE NEXT MORNING Suli was awakened by the squeal of the rusty hinge on the stove door, followed by a loud *thump.*

She sat up from her pile of sacks by the hearth and rubbed her eyes. Orion was throwing logs into the stove, building up the fire. She rose stiffly to her feet and went outside to wash, sputtering in the icy water from the pump. Arta and Benno were sitting at the kitchen table when she returned.

"Morning," she said. "Ready for lessons?"

Benno nodded, bleary eyed. Arta seemed excited. "Will Coalfeather teach me magic today?"

"That's what he said. Orion will take you both to the lake."

"What about you?" Arta asked.

"I need to check on Magda first, to make sure she got home safely. I'll be right back, I promise. Orion can help you translate Crow if you get stuck. Can't you?"

Orion shrugged, and ladled barley porridge into their bowls.

Suli wasn't hungry. She grabbed her cloak and went out the door. "See you at the lake."

When she reached the pond below Tala's house, she circled it cautiously before landing. She wasn't going to be ambushed by soldiers again. A few members of the flock huddled beneath the trees, using each other's bodies to block the wind. She landed near them. "Any news?"

Tessa lifted her head. "Magda's back. She's up at the house with that sergeant fellow."

"Do you know how it went?"

"Well, she's not a prisoner," Tessa said. "You'd better ask her."

Tessa was one of the geese who hadn't forgiven Magda for kidnapping members of the flock years ago. She was the last person Magda would confide in, especially if she was worried.

"How's the boy and your apprentice?" Tessa asked, changing the subject.

"Orion's teaching him to fight like a goose," she said, "And Coalfeather's teaching Arta."

"Teaching her what?"

"I'm not sure." Several of the geese were missing. "The others haven't returned?"

"Flax hasn't returned from his search for Master Swift. The others are still looking for wise women. I'd guess it will be a day or two yet. The roads are swarming with soldiers."

Suli flew up the hill and circled the outbuildings, looking for signs of booted feet in the melting snow. She saw only one set, and they led to the kitchen door.

Making sure to keep out of sight of the windows, she changed into human form, wrapping her cloak more tightly against the cold.

Inside, the heat was stifling, waves of heat blasting from the stove and the fireplace at the opposite ends of the room.

"There you are," Magda said. "Finally came to see whether I'm a prisoner? Took you long enough."

Sergeant Lito was there, staring glumly at the wall. He snorted. "As if those lazy louts would ever have that much initiative." He met Suli's eyes. "Our plan worked well enough; we removed the amulets from four officers, but we can't do it that way for the enlisted men. For one thing, there's too many of 'em. For another, they're spread out across the country. I don't see how a few people could slip inside every camp or barracks and get close enough. Even if we could, it would take forever. Magda can't be everywhere at once, so I hope you have a better plan."

"I *do* have another idea—but I need more information. You didn't by any chance bring the amulets back with you, did you?"

Magda gave her a considering look and then rose from her chair. "I wrapped 'em in moss and layers of cloth. You should take them to the lake."

"Oh, I will," Suli said, picking up the bundle. "But I want to test something, first."

AT THE LAKE, she set the bundle down on a rock. Orion was demonstrating flying tactics to Benno, and Arta was alone, not looking particularly happy.

"Ready to start?" Suli asked. She made a harsh croaking sound, a phrase in Crow. "Can you imitate that?"

Arta made a strangled croaking sound.

"*Caw! Caw!*" Coalfeather landed and hopped toward them, his talons leaving V-shaped tracks in the snow. He listened for a moment, pacing back and forth, as Suli demonstrated another call and Arta imitated it. Finally he observed, "You are making progress, Arta."

Suli translated and Arta beamed at him.

"Unfortunately, Suli," Coalfeather continued, "your accent is terrible when you're human."

"Thank you. May I remind you I don't have beak, and that my throat is different than yours?"

"That is true," he conceded. "Perhaps Arta should listen to me, then."

She smiled sweetly. "Good idea. Please take over. I have something I need to do." She turned to Arta. "Coalfeather wants you to practice with him."

"Okay," Arta said. "And then you'll teach me animal pidgin, right? I want to be able to talk to all the animals, too."

Suli sighed. She heard giggling and turned to look. Benno and Orion were trying to hit each other with their necks, and laughing each time one of them lost their balance and fell. Benno fell and lay in the snow staring up at the sky, laughing as though he couldn't stop. It was good to see him act like a child for a change.

"I'll be right back," she said, picking up the bundle of amulets.

Coalfeather bobbed his head and turned to Arta. "Here's how to be polite in Crow..."

Suli trudged through the snow until she reached Orion and Benno. They fluttered their wings, snow flying from their feathers. "Orion, I need your help."

He waited, cocking his head in a question.

"I want to test whether the amulet will work on me while I'm in winged form. But in case it does, I need someone to watch me to see what happens—and to tell Magda if it goes wrong."

"If you're worried, why risk it?" Orion asked.

"Because I suspect the prime minister's magic only works on humans. If that's true, the animals could remove the amulets safely, without becoming bewitched."

She untied the bundle's corners and laid it on the ground, unfolding the cloth carefully. "I'm going to change. Once I have the amulet in my beak, ask me questions about the prime minister and the royal family. I'll nod yes or no."

Orion nodded. Benno looked worried.

Suli changed and bent over the pile of amulets. Selecting one, she picked it up with her beak. The metal had a harsh taste, as though it had been bathed in something bitter, but she didn't feel any different.

"I think we should help the prime minister take over the country, don't you?" Orion drawled.

No, that doesn't seem like a good idea. She shook her head, *No.*

"And we should get rid of the royal family. Who needs 'em telling us what to do, anyway?"

There was a gasp from Benno, but again, Suli shook her head, *No.* She dropped the amulet on the ground, and spat. The horrible taste lingered in her mouth. "It tastes foul! Wait a moment."

She walked to the bank and dipped her beak in the lake water, taking a long drink.

"I didn't feel different," she announced when she came back. "And it was easy for me to drop it."

"So what does that prove?" Orion asked.

"It proves that it's safe for the flock to touch it, at least, because the spell didn't work on me in winged form. But we need to test it on another animal to be sure." She glanced around her. "Who else can we ask?"

Orion tilted his head at Coalfeather. "What about the learned professor?"

She hesitated. Coalfeather had already risked his reputation and his place in the Crow Council to help them. She didn't want him harmed by witchcraft, or humiliated if the spell worked. But he noticed them looking his way and glided over to join them.

"What are you doing with those amulets, Suli? You should get rid of them."

"I will. But I have good news, Coalfeather. When I hold one in my beak, the magic doesn't affect me. I'd like to be certain the spell doesn't affect other animals. Would you be willing to touch one, so we can see if it affects you?"

Coalfeather made a low rumbling noise in the back of his throat. "Hmph. If that will get you to come translate for Arta—she doesn't understand enough Crow yet, Suli—of course I will help."

"Thank you," Suli said, smiling.

"Very well." Coalfeather selected an amulet from the pile, tilting his head back so he could get a grip on it. He walked back and forth before his audience. Suli saw Arta coming toward them, looking worried.

"How do you feel?" Orion asked.

Coalfeather shrugged, and indicated nothing was wrong by extending his wings.

Arta came running over to join them.

"Shall we turn Benno over to the soldiers?" Suli asked in Crow. This time Benno didn't react, but Arta looked horrified.

Aha, Suli thought, *she understands more Crow than she lets on.*

Coalfeather shook his head and spat out the amulet. "That is disgusting!" He snapped up some snow. "Ugh! You are correct—it only works on humans. What are you planning? I know that look."

"What are you talking about?" Arta demanded, unable to contain her curiosity any longer. "Why did you ask if we should turn Benno over to the soldiers?"

"It was a test," Coalfeather said, "to see if the amulet worked on me. It did not."

"Oh," Arta said. "What does that mean?"

But Suli had seen something out of the corner of her eye. She turned to look at the forest behind them.

A group of animals watched them silently from the protection of the trees. A herd of deer, their ears pricked forward, stood together, with turkeys and squirrels practically under their feet. A jay called above them. Suli looked up and found the branches full of vultures, raptors, and songbirds, all watching in silence.

Coalfeather landed on Suli's shoulder and tugged a strand of her hair, none too gently. "Are you going to help me or not?"

"Ow! Of course I'll help," she said, pulling her hair free.

He fluttered back to the ground. "Arta, Crow etiquette is

different depending on whether you are with your flock or not—"

Suli was certain Arta understood, but she translated anyway, her mind elsewhere.

Arta repeated what Coalfeather said, but her gaze drifted toward their animal audience too.

Their animal audience confirmed Suli's suspicion that word was spreading about humans living in Magda's cottage. Their animal neighbors would be curious to know what was going on, especially if they were worried about the sickness. That could be useful.

Maybe they'd be curious enough to listen to the plan taking shape in her mind.

22

THE MERRY BAND

BENNO AND ARTA practiced their new skills for the rest of the day, Benno grimly determined to rescue his parents single-handedly. Arta seemed willing to listen to Coalfeather no matter how long he went on, fascinated with crow life. Suli wanted to talk to Coalfeather alone to ask if he really thought Arta could heal the sickness affecting the animals, but she never got the chance.

By late afternoon, dark clouds had rolled in, and the light was fading. It was colder, and the air smelled of snow. Coalfeather said he had to get back, promising to continue Arta's lessons the next day. "But I may be delayed. The Crow Council meets tomorrow morning." Before Suli could ask what that meant, he'd flown off.

"Well, we've done a good day's work," Orion said. "I'm ready to go back and get warm." Suli didn't argue; her fingers and toes were numb.

Inside the cottage, Suli piled wood into the stove and stood before it, shivering, while Orion built up the fire on the hearth.

The fish and potato stew Orion had left to simmer all day on the back of the stove was ready to eat. They each took a cup of hot tea to warm their hands, and sat down at the table to eat. The stew was spicy and good; Arta had two bowls, and Benno three.

Arta's eyes closed and she nodded where she sat.

"Time for bed," Suli said. She handed Arta and Benno each a cloth dipped in hot water, and they washed their faces and hands. Suli wrapped each of them in a separate quilt with a hot stone at their feet, and put them in Magda's bed. "Good night. See you in the morning."

"Good night," Benno replied softly.

"I like Coalfeather," Arta murmured sleepily, her eyes already closed. "I hope he doesn't get into trouble."

"So do I," Suli said softly. She left the door open a crack and returned to the kitchen. Orion was doing the dishes, so she sat down in the rocking chair beside the hearth. She wondered where Tala was and what she was doing at that moment. If Orion was right and she was spying on the prime minister, she was in more danger than any of them.

"What was your experiment with the amulets supposed to prove?" Orion asked. He put away the last dish and came over to stretch out on the rug beside the fire.

Suli hesitated. Now that it was time to explain it to others, she wasn't sure her idea would work. "Sergeant Lito says soldiers alone can't remove all the amulets in the country, and I agree. But what about animals? The soldiers won't notice them. They can go anywhere, without arousing suspicion. Crows, mice, raccoons, and foxes—they live among us and no one thinks twice about seeing one. What if they helped us?"

Orion shook his head. "You know that isn't likely. The crows aren't the only ones who think dealing with humans is danger-ous. Besides, they blame us for the diseases and the strange storms."

She fell silent, wondering how she could persuade them. "I wish Tala would send another message, so I'd know for sure this is what she wants me to do. Magda is worried about her, and Magda's the one who knows what she's doing in Lofton."

They fell silent, watching the fire and listening to it crackle and hiss.

The silence was broken by the sound of scratching on the cottage door, tentative at first, then becoming more insistent.

As one, Suli and Orion turned to look at the door.

Soldiers wouldn't scratch on the door, Suli thought. Crows would call out, and besides they would be asleep by now. Mice?

She crossed the room, opened the door, then hastily stepped back. "Uh...hello. What can I do for you?" She spoke in animal pidgin.

A huge grey timber wolf was framed in the doorway. "How are you, Suli?"

There was only one wolf who would call her by name. "*Ralph?*"

The wolf smiled hugely. "You *do* remember. Thank goodness. I'd hate to have to remind you how we met. Unfortunate circumstances and all that." He craned his neck to look past her. "Who's here with you? Magda isn't here, is she?" he asked nervously.

Orion joined her at the door. "What's going on?"

Ralph tilted his head as though he didn't understand human speech, but Suli was certain he did. He'd once been human, after all. She was grateful that she could still use her Seeing; he seemed genuinely glad to see her. But without the rest of her magic, she had no protection if he wanted to harm them.

She replied in pidgin, "This is Ralph. We met when I was searching for the geese Magda imprisoned. Ralph was their guard, but he was Magda's prisoner, too."

"Until Suli released me," Ralph said, nodding. "Quite decent of you. I haven't forgotten, you know. And now I hear you're in trouble and I think *we* can help."

"We?" Orion asked, switching to pidgin. He peered out into the darkness.

Looking for more wolves, Suli thought.

"My Merry Band in the forest. Maybe you've heard of us? We're quite well known—they make stories about us. Stealing from the rich, giving to the poor, that sort of thing."

"A merry band of wolves? A wolf pack?" Suli asked. "I thought the wolves refused to accept you."

"Well, yes, that *was* true," Ralph acknowledged. "But I finally convinced them. They like my stories, you see. And my ideas for getting food. We play tricks on the humans and they become so confused they leave us alone."

"Are we inviting him in or going outside?" Orion asked without bothering to use the pidgin. "Only, you're letting in the cold air. We're almost out of wood, too."

Suli hesitated. It was one thing to talk to a huge wolf in the forest when you didn't have a choice, but quite another to invite him into your home.

Ignoring her hesitation, Ralph shouldered past both of them easily, muscles rippling. For a heart-stopping moment Suli was afraid he was attacking, but Ralph padded over to the fire.

"Now what?" Orion whispered to Suli.

"We hear his offer," she said under her breath. "If he wanted to eat us, he could've done that already."

Ralph curled up beside the fire, like an oversized dog. He panted, his long tongue lolling, the open mouth revealing large and pointed canine teeth. Suli tried not to stare. Snow matted on his thick pelt began to melt in the heat of the fire. The air was soon filled with the smell of wet wolf.

The large golden eyes seemed to follow Suli's every movement, making her uneasy. She tried to act as though a wolf on the hearth was a normal occurrence, but she took the chair furthest from the fire—and from Ralph. "You said I was in trouble. What have you heard?"

"Well, you'd know that better than I, but the animals in the forest are worried. They say soldiers are capturing *all* the wise women, and they're looking for you 'specially. They're also angry that their young are sick and dying because of witchcraft. They expect you to fix it."

"Did they say *how* they expect me to fix it?"

Ralph shook his head. It was a strange gesture for a wolf, but then Ralph had been a man until Magda had changed him into a wolf, saying he was becoming one anyway. "No, but that's your job, isn't it?"

Orion returned from the kitchen with two mugs of tea; he handed one to Suli. She sipped it cautiously. Chamomile. Well, she could *try* to relax.

Ralph watched Orion hopefully and looked disappointed when he wasn't offered anything.

Orion sighed and returned to the kitchen. He filled a bowl with water and placed it beside the wolf. Ralph lapped the water delicately.

"Tell us about your Merry Band," Orion said, lowering himself into the rocking chair.

Ralph licked the traces of water from his muzzle, his long tongue reaching all the way around. He grinned hugely, revealing all his teeth. "They're good-hearted rogues, the best friends a wolf could have," he said. "I know you'll like them, too, Suli. I've taught them to play jokes on the farmers in Grass Village. They enjoy it as much as I do now. The farmers think it's witchcraft and are terrified, so they leave us alone."

That sounded like the Ralph she remembered.

"What kind of jokes?" Orion asked.

Ralph's grin grew wider and Suli found herself leaning back.

"Oh, this and that. We hide things, around the farm. Or we put them in some strange place where no one would think to look. And when we liberate chickens—"

So you do *steal chickens,* Suli thought.

"We make sure to hide one at a neighbor's farm. Now the

farmers suspect each other, but they can't be sure what's going on. It's great fun."

Suli decided this wasn't the moment to comment on wolf ethics. "How could your Merry Band help us?"

Ralph nodded and became solemn. "The soldiers are capturing wise women, and that's just wrong. I've seen them using dogs. Well, dogs are afraid of us, and they'll do as we say. I've also heard these men carry bad magic with them. So I thought, why not play tricks on men who really deserve it? They're afraid of witchcraft, right? Well, by the time my band of tricksters are through with them, they'll be terrified."

"Let me see if I understand," Orion said. "You want to play tricks on angry and frightened men with weapons, so they'll be even more dangerous?"

"He has a point," Suli said. "Frighten them and they may become violent."

"Perhaps. Or perhaps they'll be so distracted by their fear they'll make mistakes—or flee. And they won't get near you, Suli. Not with my friends and I leading them astray and guarding you." He added as an afterthought, "And their dogs aren't going to follow a trail once we've threatened to eat them." He grinned.

"Isn't this too dangerous?" Suli said. "The soldiers have swords, and bows and arrows. They might shoot you."

"Not if they never see us," Ralph countered.

"I don't want the dogs to get hurt," Suli said. "Promise me."

"No one will be hurt," Ralph said patiently. "The dogs will smell us and run away. The soldiers aren't that smart, but wolf tracks, nervous horses, frightened dogs—they'll be afraid. Besides, we plan to do most of our work in the village."

Orion frowned. "People will notice wolves invading a village. They'll panic."

Ralph stared balefully at Orion until he flinched and looked away.

"Did I say everyone in my Merry Band was a wolf? Not at all.

My friends can get in and out of the village easily. No one will suspect a thing."

"You can't steal from people in my village," Suli said firmly, imagining wolves roaming freely throughout Weatherstone. "The soldiers have already taken their food without paying for it. It's going to be a hard winter for them."

"Wait," Orion said in disbelief, "you're going along with this madness?" He turned to Ralph. "How do we know you won't simply steal from everyone and then run away, laughing at us for being gullible? Aren't you still angry about being turned into a wolf? Maybe this is your revenge."

A growl began in the back of Ralph's throat, his hackles rose, and he stared fixedly at Orion. Then the growling ceased abruptly. "I suppose I can't really blame you. Normally, that would be the sort of thing we'd like to do. But I owe Suli, and the last thing we need on the mountain are bewitched soldiers roaming the forest. That's a threat to everyone. We in the Merry Band treasure our independence. No evil witch will control *us*. Besides," he said, grinning wolfishly, "it will be fun. Suli knows I like being a wolf. So you see," he concluded, "you can trust me."

He added, "The soldiers have food in their wagons. We *might* relieve them of their ill-gotten gains. I promise," he said, raising one huge paw in the air, "that we won't steal from your villagers."

The idea she'd been reluctant to tell anyone earlier had solidified in her mind while Ralph spoke. "There *is* something I need help with, and your talk of hiding and moving things made me think of it. But I doubt a wolf could do it. What other animals are in your Merry Band?"

Ralph cocked his head to one side. "Oh, we take all sorts. Anyone can join if he or she can prove they have what it takes. We have squirrels, raccoons, even mice. They've turned out to be very handy for stealing things."

"Aren't the wolves tempted to eat them?" Orion asked.

"Not once we've hunted together. The wolves think of them

as part of the pack," Ralph said piously. "Wolves are careful hunters. We don't hunt if we're not hungry. Only humans do that."

"Huh," Orion said. He didn't look convinced.

"I think you *can* help me," Suli said. "There's something we need to steal from the soldiers, an amulet they wear around their necks. That means getting close to them and it will be dangerous."

Ralph was silent. "We'll need a good plan, then, with loud distractions so my fellows can get close. More than one, probably." He stared into the fire.

Orion shifted uneasily in his chair. "There's something I don't understand, Ralph. How did you know Suli would be here? She flew here; there was no trail to follow, so you couldn't have followed her scent. How did you find out?"

Suli waited for the answer.

"Oh, everyone knows Suli's here. But it was Kaark who told me. He said we should help you."

"Kaark! But he was against helping us, I thought." Orion turned to Suli.

Ralph shook his entire body, spraying them with drops of melted snow. Suli wiped her face with her sleeve.

"Oh, that can't be right," Ralph said. "He's convinced the Crow Council to allow Coalfeather to help you and now he's called for the Animal Council to meet, saying everyone must decide whether to help the wise women." He gave Suli a shrewd look. "You look surprised. Didn't the crows help you last time? Isn't Coalfeather your teacher?"

Suli sighed. "The teacher doesn't always feel the need to explain things to the student. I *do* know that Coalfeather is breaking Crow Law to help us, but I didn't think Kaark—" She hesitated. "I hope it's not too dangerous for both of them. The last thing I want to do is to prove Kaark right, that humans are a danger to everyone else."

Ralph barked twice, short and sharp, then whined and rolled on his back, wriggling.

He's laughing. "What's so funny?"

Ralph rolled over and sat up. "I assure you, my Merry Band and I are far more dangerous to the soldiers than they are to us." In the firelight his eyes shone green.

"About the Animal Council," Suli said. "When is it to be, and where?"

"Tomorrow night," Ralph said. "Absolutely *everyone* who's anyone will be there. Kaark said to meet in the clearing in the forest by the tall cliff. You know, where the geese were held prisoner. Quite convenient for you." He yawned and looked as though he were about to fall asleep beside the fire.

Orion stood and stretched, yawning. "I'm ready for bed." He threw a meaningful glance at Ralph.

"Thank you, Ralph," Suli said. "I accept your offer. The special talents of the Merry Band are exactly what we need."

23

CROW MAGIC

THE NEXT MORNING SULI, Arta, Orion, and Benno stood beside the shores of the lake, waiting for Coalfeather to appear. Early morning light cast a rosy glow on the blanket of snow shrouding the banks, but Suli wasn't fooled. Those blue shadows in the hollows of the snowdrifts were a reminder that the cold and snow would return. She pulled her cloak around her more tightly, shivering. "Where in the name of the Sisters is that bossy crow?" Suli muttered stamping her feet to keep them warm.

Coalfeather had woken her *very* early, tapping on the window of the cottage. Suli had said crossly that they would meet him by the lake *after* they'd eaten. He had squawked impatiently, saying they had to start right away. Then he'd flown away without any explanation.

Orion and Benno spoke quietly in Goose. The day before they'd asked permission to listen to Arta's first lesson in animal magic, before they resumed fighting practice. Suli didn't ask permission. She had to know more.

She noticed their footprints, human and goose, were obvious in the snow; if soldiers came to the lake their footprints would lead them straight to Magda's cottage. They needed a lookout.

Of course, if soldiers did come, the three shape-shifters could hide among the geese on the lake, and Coalfeather could fly away, but how could she protect Arta? She was wondering if her invisibility spell still worked when Coalfeather fell from the sky and glided down to land beside them.

He greeted everyone with the *Hello* call, and then turned to Arta. "Hello, Arta. Our real lessons begin today."

"Hello," Arta replied in Crow.

"Let us talk about the kind of animal magic you already know —the kind that relies on listening," he said. "Humans and winged folk are noisy. But to hear what your friends or enemies are doing far away, you must be quiet and listen."

"How do you know that when you spend so much time in the air?" Suli asked. "You're winged folk too."

Coalfeather tilted his head to look down his beak. "Crows are observant. We watch what others do. We learn many things simply by paying attention. Have I never mentioned that before?"

Suli grimaced. *Only about a hundred times.*

Arta watched them uncertainly. "I hear things," she offered. Everyone looked at her.

"Good," Coalfeather said. "Tell me what you hear."

Arta blushed, suddenly self-conscious. "I hear the wood of the trees crackling in the cold. I hear the animals moving slowly in their burrows beneath the ground, gnawing on the roots in their dens. The fish in the lake are drowsy and sleeping, but I hear them breathing, very slowly."

"You can hear fish breathe?" Orion asked, incredulous.

Arta nodded. She looked so solemn, even Orion didn't dare make fun of her.

Coalfeather smiled. "You have a gift, Arta." He said to Suli, "Even without touching the earth, or using an amplification stone, she hears the animals around her. Tell me, Arta, can you hear what these animals are thinking?" He regarded her with one bright eye, his head cocked.

"I've only done it when I'm afraid they'll hurt me. Most of the time I don't try. It feels—strange."

"Well, try now. Pick one of the animals in a burrow. A hare, perhaps. Tell me what it is thinking."

Arta nodded and squeezed her eyes shut. Frowning, she said, "There are a lot of...oh! This one had babies recently, so she's awake. The babies are pulling on her with their mouths, looking for milk. She thinks it will be a long winter and she hopes there will be enough to eat. She thinks warm, slow, muzzy thoughts. But nothing else is very clear."

Suli exchanged a look with Orion. It had been easy for her. Did that mean she could hear the thoughts of anyone?

Coalfeather hopped across the snow, leaving his V-shaped prints. "Very good, Arta."

Arta looked worried. "Is it wrong to listen to their thoughts? They can't hear mine. It feels like I'm spying on them."

Coalfeather bobbed his head in approval. "Good question, young human. You should respect their privacy—and you must *never* try to control them or tell them what to do unless it's to help them. But right now you are simply learning and your listening does them no harm. This is practice."

Suli added, "Sometimes—you said it yourself, you're afraid of them, and you need to talk to them so they won't hurt you. That helps both of you, making sure no one gets hurt. You saved Benno by telling the dogs what to do. And you explained to the dogs, didn't you? They had a choice."

Arta didn't look convinced, so Suli said, "Your listening could help them. You should be proud of that."

Arta said to Coalfeather, "Tell me more about listening."

In the corner of her eye Suli saw two geese gliding down to land on the lake. Even from a distance she recognized Flax and Wilo. Suli realized she hadn't had to translate once. Coalfeather didn't need her.

Suli stepped away to change, then flew across the lake,

landing beside the two geese. A cold breeze wrinkled the surface of the water, biting into her skin in spite of her feathers.

"Messages are arriving at the house: the free wise women say they'll be here soon," Flax said to her when she arrived. "Magda wants me to remind you they can't stay at the house. That's the first place the soldiers will look."

"There's no room there, anyway. How is removing the amulets in Weatherstone going?"

"Slowly," Flax said. "Magda's exact words were: 'tell our child wise woman that she'd better come up with a faster plan. Otherwise the war will be long over before we've taken more than a handful.'"

Magda was right, unfortunately. It was time to put her plan into motion.

"Where *will* you put the wise women?" Wilo asked.

Suli hesitated. "I don't want to offend the flock, but I thought we could use the cave in the woods. We can fix the lock so it works from inside; it would be a safe place to sleep, and they can cook in the clearing."

"They'll be cold," Flax commented. "But don't worry about offending the flock. You aren't asking *them* to stay there. They'll understand. The animals of the forest all know where it is, and I doubt the soldiers do."

"What do you think, Wilo?"

Wilo nodded. "It's well hidden, and that's the main thing. What will the wise women do once they're here?"

Suli took a deep breath. If her idea didn't make sense to the flock, it might not to anyone else, either. "I need their help to remove the amulets when we're in the camps—but most of all to restore the flow of magic. That's the tricky part. That reminds me, I need to ask another favor from the flock: could someone keep watch on the path up the mountain? The soldiers may keep looking for the boy. Perhaps two-hour shifts on the main trails? I don't think we need them at night. Once our plans are underway, I'll ask other birds to keep watch too."

"Leave it to me," Wilo said, and then she and Flax lifted off, flying over the trees.

When Suli returned, the snow was melting, turning to slush in the warmth of the sun. Arta's eyes were closed. Coalfeather paced silently back and forth in front of her.

"What's going on?" Suli whispered to Orion.

"Coalfeather asked her to find animals further away, in Weatherstone. He wants to know if she can hear at a distance."

Arta held a shiny black rock cupped in her two hands, gingerly avoiding its sharp edges.

"What's that?" Suli whispered, nodding at the stone.

"Amplification stone," Orion muttered, not taking his eyes off Arta.

"Can you hear anything, Arta?" Coalfeather asked at last. "If not a soldier, are there animals in the village you can hear?"

Arta's serious expression broke into a smile. "I found a group of horses! They're bored and longing for new grass and clean water, but they're stuck on the village green."

Serves them right, thought Suli, remembering the arrogant mare she'd met.

"Can you ask them not to help the soldiers?" Orion asked aloud. "Or at least ask whether the soldiers are still searching for a boy?"

Coalfeather opened his beak to speak, but waited to hear Arta's response.

"Yes," she said, her eyes closed in concentration. "One horse doesn't like the man who rides him and thinks the soldiers are bad men. He says he'll throw the man the next time he tries to ride him. The others won't cooperate. They're loyal to their riders.

"Oh! The dogs are there too. They already know they shouldn't help the soldiers. They like being in town. The villagers wait until their trainer isn't looking to feed them scraps so they won't attack them. The dogs would run away if they could."

Coalfeather nodded. "Very good, Arta."

"Wait!" she exclaimed and her eyes flew open. "This is wrong!" She closed her eyes again and concentrated. "I have to help her."

Suli waited, afraid to interrupt.

"No, no," she was murmuring, "it's going to be all right. Leave the village. Go back the way you came, to the forest. Please, I know it's hard." Tears ran down Arta's face. "She's a wildcat whose babies died, all at once," she explained without opening her eyes. "She carried one in her mouth and brought it to the village, then laid it beside the fountain. She doesn't understand the danger she's in, or that she doesn't belong there. She's confused—I'm trying to get her to leave, without her baby."

Arta was silent a moment. "I'm telling her she's one of the cougar people and she must go home to the forest, and stay away from humans. I promised we'd make everything better soon and then no more babies will die. She's still unhappy, but she's leaving." Arta sighed deeply then opened her eyes. "The villagers saw her and ran away, but she left before they hurt her."

Coalfeather appeared stunned. "That...that is very good, Arta. I am glad you were able to help her." He ruffled his wing feathers, then flattened them along his back, collecting himself.

"I was going to wait before asking this—but you have just proven you are capable of doing more." He bobbed his head and stared fixedly at her. "Would you be willing to see if you can heal other animals? The ones who have forgotten who they are? Their minds are unbalanced by witchcraft, so it is their minds we must reach. It must be your choice; I cannot compel you to do this. It could be dangerous."

"Why?" Suli demanded. "I mean, how could it be dangerous?"

He preened a feather beneath his wing. Apparently it was hard to reach, because it took a long time.

He doesn't want to answer, Suli thought. It *must* be dangerous.

Coalfeather's head emerged and he said, "Arta has a strong personality. I don't think she will become confused helping just one animal. But if she tries to help a family, or a herd or a flock, she might be overwhelmed. There are techniques she can learn, to focus on just one mind, and block out the others. But until she has more experience, there is a danger she could forget herself."

"I won't," Arta declared stoutly. "I've been doing this for a while. I know how to come back to myself."

Arta was probably right, Suli thought. She *had* figured out how to user her magic on her own. She was a fighter, and stubborn. She wouldn't lose herself, Suli thought, no matter how many confused voices were in her head.

"We shall practice, then," Coalfeather said.

"I'm ready," Arta replied, gripping the obsidian amplification stone tightly.

24

THE ANIMAL COUNCIL

After lessons were over, Coalfeather said the Animal Council would gather at sunset, in the clearing by the tall cliff.

Suli couldn't decide whether the location was a bad idea or not. Many at the meeting would remember that during Magda's long campaign against her sister, Magda had used the cave in the cliff as a dungeon. As a witch, Magda had been a danger to every animal in the forest. No one would ask tonight why she wasn't invited to the meeting. They all knew.

But the former prison was also a reminder of how Suli and the animals on the mountain had worked together to stop her. Suli had help from the shape-shifters, from Coalfeather and his flock, and from Andragora, queen of the mice. Without them, Suli couldn't have saved Tala from hanging, or helped Magda to stop being a witch. She had needed her animal allies then, but she needed them even more now.

Suli arrived at the clearing by the cliff just as the sun slipped below the horizon and shadows spread from under the trees.

Many were already there, seated around the fire Orion had built in the center. They watched as she landed and changed, and took her place beside Orion. Benno was on Orion's other side in goose form, and Arta sat beside him, entranced by the different kinds of animals gathered peacefully together.

The branches of the surrounding fir trees were filled with small birds chattering and chirping. Herons and cranes stood behind the circle, elegant but wary.

Representatives from animal nations that normally avoided the wise women were there, too, looking uncomfortable, the raccoons among them. They smiled mockingly at Orion and Suli when their glances met. To them, humans were useful but absurd, a source of easy food.

Suli badly wanted the raccoons on her side. Those clever fingers could remove amulets or open doors or windows.

Coalfeather and Kaark floated down from the star-filled sky together. Kaark perched on a rock outside the circle, watching the others with an unreadable expression.

Coalfeather strutted and hopped around the fire, opening his wings to jump aside when a floating ember drifted his way. He, too, seemed to be reading the mood of the Council members who spoke quietly amongst themselves.

When full night had fallen and everyone was there, Kaark called loudly in pidgin, "Hear me!"

Everyone fell silent.

"Members of the Animal Council, thank you for coming," Kaark began. "I have called this meeting to address a grave matter. Our land is under attack. A powerful witch is using the third kind of magic to control humans. This witchcraft also steals magic from where it belongs, destroying the normal balance. Because their magic has been stolen, the wise women cannot protect us. It is our turn to help them."

At a nod from his father, Coalfeather spoke. "Many of you know me and my family. We have always followed our Law:

never to depend on humans, and never to become like them. Humans do not understand balance; they do not understand that they create danger when they try to control everything. In normal times, we would never interfere with their foolishness. But these are not normal times. Humans threaten not only themselves, but all of us."

He paused and Suli heard the rustling of wings and feet and soft squeals of surprise.

Kaark spoke again. "This land is about to go to war. War is a human insanity that we on the Council of Animal Nations neither share nor understand. Our Law says this alone separates us from them. It is a horrifying example of their ignorance of the pattern. Yet war is the least of our worries now. It is only a symptom of the underlying disease."

There were murmurs of agreement. Heads large and small turned toward Kaark, waiting for him to say, as he always did, that they should stay out of human affairs. "You have undoubtedly heard that my son, Coalfeather, is prepared to help the humans. I will let him speak for himself."

Coalfeather bobbed his head. "Do not misunderstand. I do not advocate fighting a war. But *survival* is our right within the Law. Outwitting a predator is our right. Humans are the most dangerous predators we know. Just as any crow will attack a hawk or eagle if their nest is threatened, we are allowed to defend ourselves."

Kaark waited a beat and said, "I know you are all waiting for me to say I disagree with my son."

There were chuckles at this.

"But I do not. Coalfeather is right: we are allowed to outwit predators by playing tricks on them. We can steal their food, set prey free, attack them if they come near our nests. That is our right."

"But our survival is not at stake," the weasel ambassador pointed out.

"I believe it is," Kaark said. "Animals all over the country are forgetting who they are, and what they need to do to live. They no longer remember that they belong to the animal nations. Many flocks have discovered their eggs will not hatch. Young foxes, moles, and mice are born dead. Fledglings sicken and die for no reason we understand. The magic that once kept us healthy is being drained away, stolen by the witch who threatens every living thing. With no wise women to protect us, we will die of disease or hunger. The humans' crops are being destroyed by disease, insects, or storms. And all of these disasters have the same cause.

"When the crops die, it is not only people who starve. The small animals who depend on the fields starve too, and the animals that eat them go hungry." His glanced at the raptors in the trees. "Our web of life has become a web of destruction. Your young may be the next to die. We are linked together, whether we wish to be or not. We are embedded in a web of life that the witch is taking apart, strand by strand."

"That is the threat we are here to consider tonight," Coalfeather said, nodding at his father. "I say the Law allows us to help the wise women, to save ourselves."

Wings and paws shifted uneasily, but he had their full attention.

"Soldiers have invaded our homes, the fields and forests and mountain passes once made safe by the wise women. You see these young humans?" Coalfeather stood before Arta and Benno, and all heads turned toward them. "The soldiers are searching for them. This male fledgling—if he survives—will be the ruler of the humans of this land. This girl has magic greater than anything the wise women possess: she can heal the animals who have the forgetting sickness. We must protect these children at all costs. And we must help the wise women to bring the magic back."

"No," the raccoon ambassador said in a silken voice, "I

disagree. These are human affairs and not our concern. Let them kill each other. We do not care."

"Truly?" Coalfeather asked quietly. "Our stories tell us that when the balance is disrupted by evil magic, it affects everything: the weather, whether plants live or die, whether our young will live. Do none of these concern you? And what about the garbage humans provide, the gleanings in the fields, the chickens they raise—don't these feed you?"

"We can live without them," the ambassador said smoothly. "We do not need humans."

"Perhaps not," said Coalfeather. "But the soldiers infesting our land will obey *any* order from this witch. Their minds are not their own. An object of power has taken away their free will."

A loud murmur of fear greeted this news. Everyone knew magical objects were dangerous; that's why they were forbidden.

"But what do you expect us to do about it?" the raccoon ambassador asked. "My people don't need or use magic, and everything you've said proves we're right to avoid it. This is a *human* problem. Let the wise women deal with it."

Suli watched the faces of the fox and weasel ambassadors who sat either side of the raccoon. They nodded in agreement. They would follow the raccoon's lead, voting as he did.

"I have just explained," Coalfeather said, "the wise women have lost most their magic. They cannot do this alone."

"But humans are not one of us! They do not belong to our Nations, and do not follow our Laws. By using witchcraft, they have broken the treaty with our Nations. They are Outlaws. Let them die. Perhaps things will be even better for us then." The weasel ambassador spoke with passion.

Coalfeather shook his head sadly. "You are ignoring the web, the pattern we are part of. This fledgling here," he nodded at Benno who was in winged form, "does he not look like one of us?" He paused a moment, raising his eyes to the starry sky above the clearing. *Pausing for dramatic effect,* Suli thought.

"Both the Queen of Teveral and her son are one of us," he said. A hushed silence fell.

"They are winged folk, part of Sigur's geese, part human it is true, but also part winged folk. The boy flew here to escape his jailers. For that reason alone we should help him."

"The prince is one of us!" a hawk exclaimed.

"We *should* help them," a sparrow chirped.

The raccoon ambassador interrupted. "I'm sure this is all very gratifying for the winged folk, but my people keep their feet on the ground, where the food is. Kings and queens are nothing to us—they simply create better garbage." At these words some of the weasels and raccoons sitting beside him chuckled as though he'd said something clever.

"Then perhaps we should leave you to your garbage," Coalfeather said calmly, "if that is all that interests you. But know this: the prime minister's witchcraft is disrupting all magic. It is destroying the pattern that sustain us. The storms and diseases caused by the witch's spells may kill both you and your children, one way or another. The pattern is broken."

Suli heard horrified gasps, then everyone spoke at once, a wave of loud chitterings, squeals, chirruping and yips that went on for some time.

The weasel and fox ambassador shifted away from the raccoon ambassador, with sidelong frowns. Everyone had heard about the broken eggs and dying young, but this was new.

Coalfeather called loudly and the fox ambassador gave her eerie, penetrating call to quiet everyone. The vixen kept her eyes on Coalfeather, waiting for him to continue.

"Let me sum up," Coalfeather said, pacing again. "The entire animal community is threatened by witchcraft, the like of which we've never seen before. The prime minister controls an army of soldiers who will do whatever he commands. He does not fear the consequences of the third kind of magic, believing himself invincible. All he cares about is power; the power to control everyone, whether human or animal. He might say, 'murder all the foxes,' and the bewitched humans will do it."

"But why don't the wise women stop him?" the rabbit ambassador asked. "I still don't understand why they can't use their magic."

Suli spoke up. "Many wise women have been imprisoned by soldiers wearing an amulet. This amulet steals their magic. That's why the wise women need your help.

"Mothers are refusing to teach their daughters the most basic magic, to keep the soldiers from taking them away," Suli said. "It's possible that wise women's magic will be destroyed forever, I don't know. I *do* know the prime minister thinks anyone who knows magic is his enemy. He has imprisoned all the wise woman and girls he can find, to keep them from fighting his magic. But I am going to fight him, and I'm going to free the wise women from the camps any way I can."

"Well, I for one will help the wise women!" declared Queen Andragora, "and so will my people!" Loud squeals of approval came from the mice sitting behind her.

"I thank you," Coalfeather said, acknowledging Andragora with a dip of his head. She nodded regally in return, and Suli smiled at her old ally. "Will anyone else help us free the wise women?"

"Not I, and not my people," the raccoon ambassador said. "We don't need them."

"Well, *I* think our wise woman and Coalfeather are right," the weasel ambassador said unexpectedly. "We *should* help the wise women; they've always helped us when we needed them. The sooner we come together to stop this witchcraft, the better our chances. If we wait too long, the witch will be too powerful to stop."

"Ambassador Weasel speaks the truth," Coalfeather said, "The sooner we remove the threat of the soldiers and free the wise women, the safer we will be."

"I have heard enough—"an owl began, but voices had risen excitedly and her words were drowned out by grunts, squawks, and squeals of excitement.

"Quiet! Quiet!" called one of the geese. "Continue, Ambassador Owl."

"I have heard enough," the owl repeated, "to decide how I will vote. Surely what the Council must decide is how our people can help? If the wise women's magic can't protect them, how are *we* to fight witchcraft?"

Everyone turned to look at Suli.

She took a deep breath. "Once the amulet is removed, the soldiers listen to reason and no magic is needed. We need your help to remove the amulets. The wise women will do the rest."

"But that means getting close to their hands and feet!" a mouse wailed. "That's dangerous!"

"Yes," Suli agreed. "Yes, it is. But we have plans to make them safe. The amulets don't affect animals; I think the prime minister never thought to include them in his plans. Once freed from the amulet's power, the soldiers are horrified to find they were bewitched to become traitors. Some have already agreed to help us."

"Have you actually done this?" a haughty falcon asked.

"Yes. Magda has removed the amulet from several officers, and they're helping us to remove more."

"What did you do with them—the amulets?" Ralph asked. "Is it safe for my Merry Band to touch it or carry it in their mouths?"

At last, a practical question. "Both Coalfeather and I have carried it in our beaks without harm. I assume it will be safe for others, too. If you are worried, wrap it in moss, or leaves. But I believe the prime minister's spells are meant only for humans. It hasn't occurred to him that the animal nations might oppose him. He doesn't know about *your* power. That's our advantage."

Ralph nodded, satisfied. Suli saw many heads nodding—

squirrels, rabbits, weasels and geese, their eyes flashing in the firelight.

"I hear wisdom in these words," growled a brown bear, "but my people will not go among humans. They will kill or trap us and treat us cruelly."

"I wouldn't ask that of you, nor of the other forest predators such as the wolves or bobcats," Suli said. "Villagers would be afraid if they saw you and we don't want to cause a panic. Only the animals the villagers won't notice will be sent there, or into the witch camps."

"There are other ways to help," Coalfeather said. "Some can remove the amulets—but only those who volunteer and whose skills fit them for the task. Soldiers won't notice crows and mice in their camps, or expect us to sabotage them. We can spy on them easily, sabotaging their work when the opportunity arises. Ralph, the leader of the Merry Band, will advise us on this. I understand he's our expert on fooling humans."

Appreciative smiles appeared on the faces around the circle, and heads nodded.

So it's true, Suli thought, *stories of the Merry Band are going around.*

"For myself," Coalfeather continued, "I have promised Suli I will help the wise women in any way I can." He called loudly, "Who is with me?"

A cacophony of voices rang out, agreeing to help. The raccoon ambassador rose stiffly and slunk away, the rabble of raccoons following him, glancing furtively behind them.

Coalfeather stood before Suli. "I've done what I could to persuade them, Wise Woman. Now it's up to you. Take my advice and listen to their ideas." He cocked his head, his eyes glinting in the firelight. "We have been fooling humans for centuries. Every animal here knows tricks of escape and camouflage."

Always the teacher, she thought. Aloud she said, "Yes, Coalfeather."

She rose to her feet. "Everyone? We need to plan. I have some ideas, but I want to hear yours, too. Everyone who wants to help, gather 'round." The animals moved closer.

"Here are my ideas…"

Ralph yipped sharply. "This is going to be so much fun!"

25

THE TWILIGHT CARAVAN

THE NEXT EVENING, a long caravan of brightly painted cottages snaked up the road to Weatherstone in the blue twilight. No soldier stopped it on the road, and no villager hailed it. Those still abroad in the streets swiftly ducked inside, locking their doors and dousing their lamps, afraid to be seen talking to strangers. Weatherstone was an occupied village under martial law.

The caravan stopped at the bottom of the hill that led to the house of the wise woman of Weatherstone. An older woman opened the gate and stepped into the lane. She spoke briefly with someone on the steps of a blue cottage with red wheels. That wagon, pulled by a team of horses, left the others behind and headed across a field for the steep mountain trail, bouncing and jolting as it went.

Suli heard the creaking harness and the rumble of the iron-shod wheels long before the caravan cottage came into view. By then the lake was turning red, mirroring the fiery band of sky above the western horizon.

Arta, Suli, and Coalfeather waited as the cottage rolled up beside them. The two horses snorted, breathing heavily, their flanks lathered from the long climb. Master Swift sat on the driving bench. He waved. "Hallo, Suli and Arta! We've come for a visit."

Coalfeather turned to Suli. "You know this person? He looks like a crazy peddler."

"It's Master Swift!" Arta exclaimed. She scooped up Tekka the wooden horse from a tree stump.

"He's the one who brought us home safely," Suli explained quietly. "His sister, Molly, gave Arta the carved horse."

"Then it seems the lesson is over for today," Coalfeather said. "I must go home. Father wants to hear about what Arta can do."

"Tell him Arta says you're her favorite teacher," Suli said with a grin. She knew that would please Coalfeather and irritate his father. *A win all around.*

Coalfeather made the chuffing sound that meant he was pleased and flew away.

Suli picked her way across the snow, glancing toward the far shore where Orion and Benno had been only minutes before. They'd disappeared—to change, she hoped.

When she reached the cottage, Molly came down the steps to embrace her. "Arta has been telling me everything that's happened since we last saw you. You've been busy."

Suli felt a stab of panic. What had Arta told her? They shouldn't involve the Swifts more than they already were, and they definitely didn't need to know about the shape-shifters. "And how have things been with you? Any trouble on the road?"

"Well enough," Master Swift replied. "We got your message, and a few wise women who'd been in hiding managed to find us. We just delivered them to the house below. Your cousin Magda told us we'd find you here. She said she'll send the women up here tomorrow."

"I'm sorry you had to come all this way—you could've sent word for us to come down to the house," Suli said, perplexed as to why they would risk their axles and wagon wheels on the mountain road.

"Oh, but we brought you a gift and we wanted to deliver it personally," Master Swift said, stepping inside. Mistress Swift took her by the hand and led her into the cottage.

Everything inside was the same as she remembered it, the high bed with the trundle bed beneath it, the table and the rug—except the puppets on the walls were gone, delivered to their new owners.

Arta sat on the high bed, swinging her legs.

With a flourish, Master Swift bent over and twitched away the rug. He pressed down on a section of floor with his foot. A metal ring popped up from its hidden compartment. He pulled on it, and a trapdoor rose up from the floor.

A head emerged from the opening, grinning. Then a very tall youth, who looked like Suli except for his golden-brown hair, climbed out. "Well, Sister, aren't you glad to see me?"

For a moment Suli stood grinning like a fool. Then her brother, Eb, pulled her into a long crushing hug. When he stepped back, he had a smug look on his face. "Surprised you, didn't I? Grandmother bet me I couldn't pull it off."

"But what are you doing here?" Suli asked.

"The countryside is rising against the prime minister. Seems he's the one making folk afraid of witches, so I'm here to help. And to see that you're all right."

Suli shook her head, smiling, and hugged him again. "I don't believe it! But you left Grandmother alone. Who'll take care of her?"

"She can take care of herself, as you well know. So can I, Suli. I'm a second-year 'prentice and a man now," he said with great seriousness. "I'll fight when my country needs me. From what I've heard, you're going to need my help."

"But—"

"Besides, you've been having all the fun while I've been stuck making tables and cabinets."

She couldn't stay worried with him grinning at her like that. She heard a sound behind her and turned.

Orion and Benno, both human, were watching from the doorway. Orion stepped forward. "Good to see you again, Eb." They shook hands. "We need someone with a level head on our side."

Eb glanced at Benno.

Orion said, "This is Benno. He's staying with us for a while."

Eb smiled. "Hello."

Benno nodded, his eyes wary.

Then Eb picked up Arta off the bed and swung her around, much to her amazement. "You haven't introduced me to the pretty lass."

Arta giggled with pleasure and smiled at Eb with shining eyes.

"That's Arta. My apprentice." Suli could say it with a straight face now. "I'm really glad you're here." *And I really am glad*, she realized, even though she shouldn't be. Now Eb was in danger, too. But Arta needed someone to make her laugh. She and Coalfeather put so much pressure on the young girl, it only made her more serious. Suli had to admit she wouldn't mind having someone cheerful around herself.

Behind Eb's back, Orion motioned for Benno to join him outside, and the two of them disappeared, whispering.

Eb performed a magic trick for Arta, making a coin disappear in his hand.

"Are you a witch now, Eb?" Suli teased.

"I'm sorry to interrupt," Master Swift said, reminding them he was there, "but is there somewhere I can stable the horses out of the cold? They need a good rub down."

"Of course, I'm sorry. I'll lead you to the clearing by the cottage. There's a shed behind the cottage with some stalls. We've oats, but no hay I'm afraid," Suli said. "And of course you must join us for dinner." She walked to the door. "Orion and Benno!" she called. "Didn't you go fishing for supper?"

"Yes, Mistress Suli," Orion called, exchanging a look with Benno. "We'll get them." He and Benno ran toward the lake, sharing some joke. She was pleased to see they remembered not to change in front of the Swifts. No sense in giving away *all* of their secrets, although Eb of course knew she and Orion could change.

"I'll lead the horses—" Suli began, but Arta interrupted.

"No, I will," Arta said firmly.

"All right, but remember the horses are cold, so let's go quickly."

When Suli stepped outside, Arta was nuzzling up to a dark horse that towered over her, a blissful expression on her face. She led the horses, and everyone else followed the wagon until they reached Magda's cottage. Suli showed the Swifts the weather-beaten shed with two horse stalls, and a trough full of rainwater behind the house. "I'm afraid it's the best we can do. But we do have oats, and some apples."

"That's fine. We have hay," Master Swift said, pulling an armful from the nets attached to the side of the wagon to fill both mangers. While he rubbed down the horses with flour sacks, Suli and Arta led the others to the pump.

While the travelers washed, Suli placed pots on the stove and Arta set out mismatched dishes on the faded tablecloth. There was the bread baked the day before, and a pot of vegetables that had simmered all day. When Benno and Orion returned, Orion added the cleaned fish, fresh rosemary, and juniper berries to the pot, then set it back over the heat to finish cooking.

Arta made nettle tea, and once Master Swift returned from tending the horses, they sat beside the hearth, mugs in hand, waiting for dinner to be ready.

"Tell me what you saw on your way back," Suli said to the Swifts.

Master Swift's face darkened. "Nothing good, I'm afraid. Everywhere we went, soldiers were rounding up wise women and taking them to camps. We've heard conditions are terrible. No real buildings or heat, only temporary barracks or tents, and in this terrible cold, too. I'm sure there will be deaths simply from cold and hunger."

"They aren't feeding them?" Arta asked, frowning.

"Well, to speak truth, yes they are, but it's poor fare. Not what you need when it starts to snow, I'm thinking, only handfuls of porridge and thin goat's milk now and then. No meat. No vegetables besides turnips. We have to get them out of there."

"The question is how," Eb said. "When they came for Hedith, Grandmother and I talked about what to do, and we hid her in our house. They were looking for you, too, Suli; they came and questioned us. I expect one of those spiteful girls in the village told them you were a witch. Some things never change." He stared into the fire, frowning.

Hedith was the wise woman in Suli's home village, and she was quite old. She would never have survived the cold with little food. Master Swift was right, the older women and young girls could die simply from cold and hunger. "Eb, how will Grandmother be safe if soldiers continue to arrest women? What if she says something, or does something—" Grandmother wasn't one to let soldiers bully her.

"She said you'd worry. I wouldn't have left if I thought she was in danger. She promised if they began rounding up the dangerous old ladies, she'd find a market cart heading for the mountains and come here. We're both more worried about you. After all, you're a known associate of two former witches." His eyes crinkled with mischief.

"What's this?" Master Swift's eyebrows rose.

Suli sighed. "He meant it as a joke, only it's not funny. My teacher, Tala, was falsely accused of witchcraft two years ago. She was acquitted and the man who accused her was put in prison.

He had falsely accused—and killed—several innocent women. Since I was her apprentice—"

"And the second witch?" Mistress Swift asked, frowning.

Suli sighed more deeply. "You just met her. Magda actually *was* a witch when she accused her sister of being one, and the judge forced me to live with her. She pretended I was her apprentice. So I suppose if anyone wants to overlook the truth of the matter, they can say I lived with a known witch."

"But Suli fooled Magda," Eb explained. "She kept Magda from doing more harm. And in the end, Magda risked her own life to save her sister." He stared challengingly at the Swifts. "You should remember that. Suli has a good head on her shoulders and she's had more experience than most in fighting witchcraft. In case you had any doubts."

Master Swift lifted his hands in mock surrender. "I don't need to be convinced, Master Eb. I'd never heard about Magda, but I can see it might be useful to have a former witch on your side—if you're fighting one."

"I agree," Suli said.

"Magda used to be a witch?" Arta asked. She glanced from Suli to Orion.

"Hush, don't worry," Suli said. "She's not one now. And she's risked her life several times over to help Tala and stop the prime minister, so we know she's on our side."

"She *is* scary though," Arta said in a small voice.

Everyone laughed.

"Time to eat," Suli announced.

They rose and found places at the table; Orion and Eb brought chairs from the hearth so there'd be enough.

Suli passed bowls and baskets around and everyone was quiet as they served themselves.

They bowed their heads and Suli said, "Thank you for this bounty, Sisters. Bless us and protect us from harm."

Everyone began to eat, and it was quiet while they paid serious attention to their food.

When he was finally full (after several helpings of the fish stew) Eb pushed his chair back with a sigh of contentment and said, "I think we should make plans—"

"No," Master Swift said, interrupting him. "Please don't say anything. We can't know what your plans are. Safer for us, and safer for you. If we're stopped by soldiers, there's nothing we can reveal. We gave a lift to a young man who wanted to visit his sister. Where's the harm in that?"

Suli nodded. The Swifts had risked imprisonment several times already. "You're right, of course." She began carrying the bowls to the sink. "What are *your* plans? You're welcome to stay as long as you like."

The Swifts exchanged a glance. "Thank you, but we're traveling to Lofton in the morning," Molly said. "I haven't seen my husband in months, and Samuel has a delivery schedule to keep. I'm glad we could help, but it would look suspicious if we don't keep the schedule. I'm sorry we can't do more."

"I will always be in your debt," Suli said.

"Me, too," Eb said. "Thank you for bringing me here."

"Our pleasure, young man. Good luck with your plans." Master Swift stood and said formally, "Thank you for the meal, Mistress Suli. We'll turn in now, if you don't mind. Our bunks are waiting in the caravan."

"Goodbye Arta," Molly said, bending down to hug her. "Take good care of Suli."

"I will," Arta said. "And she takes good care of me."

Molly turned to Suli. "I'll say goodbye now. We'll be gone by sunup. You be careful." She leaned in and gave Suli a hug.

"I will." She had a sinking feeling as she watched those two good people step outside into the night. They'd done more for her than she'd any right to expect, so why did she feel abandoned? Eb was here now, after all.

She glanced at him, sitting by the fire, talking softly with Orion. His presence made her feel more vulnerable, she realized. Everyone she loved was at risk now. Even Grandmother might be in danger.

She straightened her shoulders and walked to the sink, telling herself not to be a fool.

But as she scrubbed the first plate, she knew why she felt alone, in spite of Eb, in spite of the arrival of more wise women and the offer of help from the Animal Council.

Tala had laid the burden of deciding what to do on *her*. How would she know she was doing the right thing?

26

WITCH CAMP

IN THE MAIN supply tent for Internment Camp #12, an hour's ride from Weatherstone, the quartermaster was checking his inventory of stores for the morning report. The canvas walls of the tent billowed and collapsed as the wind plucked at them. He checked the shelves again, but it was true: the boots were gone. Every morning something new was missing, broken, or discovered in a bizarre place. A nameless dread had settled over the camp. Everyone said it was witchcraft, that the witches were fighting back.

He heard men cursing outside, and the raucous sound of birds calling loudly. He stepped through the tent flap, a sinking sensation in the pit of his stomach, looking for the source of the disturbance.

That strange flock of birds was back. The men who'd been working on a broken wagon axle had stopped to watch them, their faces uneasy. He heard mutters about witchcraft.

That was foolish talk, the quartermaster thought. Yes, witches were a threat, but birds? He refused to be afraid of birds. So what if there were different kinds of birds in the flock? Yes, that was unusual, but who knew why birds did anything? They were just birds. The men needed something to keep them occupied, that was the problem. Guard duty was boring.

The missing boots and other supplies, they were the real worry. Not to mention the holes in the sacks of beans and grain that were their main food allotment for the month. As far as he could tell, they'd lost half the shipment to leakage. And if he didn't figure out what was causing the problem, he was for it. He'd brought in several cats from the neighboring village, hoping it was simply a rat problem, but the cats seemed content to sleep all day *and* all night. It was as though someone had told them not to bother.

One of his men came out of the tent behind him. "Sarge, you should come look at this."

The quartermaster followed him back inside. The man pointed toward the corner where the hogshead barrels were stacked, the ones containing perishable food. The lid was off one. He went over to look inside.

Instead of oysters in brine, brought from the coast, there were boots floating in the salty water.

"How in the name of—you're not to tell anyone else about this, see? Let me report it to the captain."

"Yes, sir." The man saluted nervously. "But how do we explain—"

"We don't. It's not our job to explain. Let me handle it. Clearly there's a saboteur in the camp. Maybe someone working for Portjean, who knows?"

"But why sabotage boots, sir?"

The quartermaster glared at his subordinate, his face reddening. "I dunno, do I? I'm not a saboteur. Now look sharp and check the other barrels. I have a feeling those cursed breeches will turn up, too."

"Yes, sir."

Men were shouting outside. The quartermaster heard the sound of running feet and hurried out the tent flap.

Outside, he had to stifle a laugh; a score of horses pounded past at a gallop, trailing their picket ropes, with four frightened and angry men chasing them.

"The horses are loose *again*?" someone called. "That's the third time this week. Maybe we need a guard on the guards!"

Yes, there was a saboteur in the camp. But how were they able to get away with so much without being seen?

⌇

WHEN IT WAS ALMOST MIDNIGHT, Andragora gave the signal.

The mice crept under doorways and through the gaps between floorboards, climbing up from beneath the hastily constructed barracks. Andragora had brought twenty of her best scouts and soldiers to the witch camp.

Once the mice had removed as many amulets as they could, they would meet up with the others. Ralph's Merry Band was busy hiding swords and arrows and would join them later. The wise women would handle the more difficult cases. They wouldn't have much time.

⌇

EB CREPT FORWARD on his elbows, wriggling through the damp grass. All he could see through the blackberry brambles was a lone sentry on the barrack's steps, outlined by orange lamplight from the window. Orion should be in position by now, but the signal hadn't come.

Where was he? Eb wished he'd been the one to get the lieutenant's uniform. It would make bluffing the soldiers much easier. But Orion was right, he was older and looked more like a soldier. The only reason Eb could get away with wearing a uniform at all was because he was so tall.

Eb waited a few more minutes, debating whether to move

without the signal. Dawn would come soon and their hope of surprise would be gone. Then he heard it: the soft *huh-hoo* of an owl. He grinned to himself. For someone who could fly, Orion was lousy at birdcalls.

Eb rose slowly and cautiously to his feet, stiff from lying motionless on the cold ground. He kept his eyes on the sentry on the porch, alert for any sign he'd been seen.

He rubbed his hands together to warm them, then removed a slingshot from his coat pocket, then a stone. The stone was smooth and round, smaller than a hen's egg. He inhaled deeply to calm himself, and took aim. Then, holding his breath, he let the catapult fly.

With a soft grunt, the sentry toppled over and lay motionless.

Eb waited to see if anyone had heard him, but no one came to investigate. He crossed the yard of trampled dirt and climbed the steps, treading as softly as he could.

Breathing through his mouth, he turned the handle and opened the door.

Inside, three soldiers lay sprawled on the floor by a fireplace, empty bottles strewn around them. There were more soldiers down the hall, Eb knew. The fire had burnt to ashes, but the dying embers cast enough light for him to see.

Something moved in the corner of his eye. His heart leapt in his chest.

Orion, in the hall doorway, nodded once and pointed at himself, then to the soldier nearest him.

Eb exhaled. He crept toward the man close to him, bending low. Orion was already kneeling beside his soldier.

Eb didn't move; he was looking for the amulet's cord. He didn't see it, and time was running out.

He slipped one hand gently below the man's collar; with the other, he pulled his knife from its sheath. He found the cord and grabbed it, yanked it free and sliced it with his knife. But the amulet had slipped inside the shirt. Cursing silently, Eb ripped open the shirt, searching frantically for the metal disc—there. He pulled it free and looked at it, the dull metal gleaming evilly in the dim light. His head swam. *I should call out, raise the alarm. Shouldn't I?*

Then Orion was there, knocking the amulet from his hand.

Eb remembered what he was doing and was horrified by how quickly and easily his thoughts had been controlled.

The man opened his eyes. "Hey! Whaddya think you're doing!"

Orion had removed the amulet from the man closest to him, and he slept on. But the soldier in the middle sat up, reaching for his sword. "Attack! We're under attack!" he cried hoarsely.

Then Orion's soldier woke, too, looking dazed.

Eb cursed himself silently. They'd forgotten to remove the swords before they began. The soldier who still had his amulet was the real threat, but the other two might attack simply because they were strangers.

"Quiet!" Orion roared at the top of his lungs. "No one gave you permission to speak!"

The freed soldiers were too confused to move for a moment, but the bewitched man rose and lunged at Orion with his sword. Orion quickly stepped aside.

Eb moved behind the man.

The amulet-free soldiers rose to their feet in confusion. "Who are you, sir?" one asked. "What's going on?"

Orion ignored them. The bewitched soldier thrust his sword now left, now right. "Help me," Orion grunted, dodging. "Disarm this maniac."

The two soldiers grabbed their comrade's arms and held him fast.

He struggled, cursing them. "Traitors! Witch-ridden maggots! Let me go!" He squirmed and kicked but could not get free. Eb quickly pulled the cord from his shirt and sliced it, pulling the amulet free and dropping it in his pouch.

The freed soldiers frowned at Eb. They looked as though they were trying to remember something. The third man hung limply in their hands, staring glassily at the floor. "What's going on?" he mumbled, raising his head to stare at Orion. "Who are you?"

"I'm your superior officer," Orion replied, breathing hard. He wiped the sleeve of his greatcoat across his face. "And *you've* been insubordinate, soldier," he continued in a threatening tone. "What's your name and rank?"

Abashed, the soldier muttered, "Diggs, sir. Private."

"Well, Diggs, I've a job for you and your mates here, if you'll stop trying to kill me long enough to listen."

Diggs shook himself free of the others and stood at attention, saluting smartly. "Yes, sir." He glanced at the other two, moving only his eyes. "We're ready for your orders, sir."

The other soldiers snapped to attention.

An officer appeared in the doorway from the hall. He, too, wore the insignia of a lieutenant.

Eb nearly groaned aloud.

"What's all the racket?" the real lieutenant asked, frowning. "I heard someone yell we were under attack."

"That was me," Orion said. "Pvt. Diggs here attacked me. I expect you to put him on report, Lieutenant." He glanced at Eb. "We've been waiting for you to wake up. Now that you're here we can discuss the new orders from headquarters."

The real lieutenant stepped into the room. "Who are you? I've never seen you before. Why weren't these orders sent to me directly?" he asked, his face reddening.

Eb stood clear of the three freed soldiers, so he could move toward the real lieutenant quickly. If the soldiers now free of the spell helped them, they could take him.

"Why do you think?" Orion said sarcastically. "The usual mix-up, of course. Right hand doesn't have a clue what the left is doing, at least not at HQ. It's left for us to sort out, as usual."

A sergeant appeared in the doorway, rubbing his eyes. "Are we having a party? Where are the dancing girls?"

Eb fervently hoped that Orion had already removed his amulet.

"Is everyone here now? Good," Orion said crisply. "Here are our orders, gentlemen. There's a big push to consolidate the camps. Too many men are being tied up on guard duty, when they're needed to fight Portjean. We've been ordered to commandeer transport and escort our charges to a main camp at the foot of the mountains. All the females will be rehoused within two weeks. That doesn't give us much time, so let's hop to it. Once resettlement is complete, I'm happy to say, we'll be assigned to real duty!"

The sleepy men looked pleased. The real lieutenant commented grudgingly, "About time."

Eb exhaled softly in relief. The lieutenant wasn't going to question the order, or their presence.

"Aye," one of the men said, "kicking our heels babysitting old women and girls is no work for soldiers. I was trained to fight men."

"And what's the point of it, anyway?" another man asked.

Eb glanced quickly at the lieutenant to see if he noticed the traitorous talk, but the lieutenant only nodded. "The sooner we start moving the prisoners, the sooner we can put this behind us." He looked faintly disgusted, as though remembering a distasteful task he'd been forced to do.

Clearly Orion had removed the amulets from these men. Eb relaxed a little. The danger wasn't over; there were plenty of other bewitched soldiers nearby. They'd resist if ordered to release the prisoners, unless Andragora's mice or Ralph's Merry Band had gotten to them by now.

～

THE SOLDIERS WORKED QUICKLY, hitching horses to wagons, eager to be on their way. Once the lieutenant had relayed Orion's orders, sleepy soldiers began to herd women and girls from their tents into the wagons beneath the cold starlight, their breath forming clouds in the air. A few of the soldiers were pushing and shoving the women roughly, and Eb took note of their faces. They probably still wore the amulet.

"I need volunteers for special duty!" he called. "If you want to make sure these witches can't escape, step forward!" Most of the men rolled their eyes, but a few, including the men Eb had already noted, took a step toward him.

He smiled. "Good men! Follow me. I have information for you." He caught Orion's eye and tilted his head toward the wise women. It was time for them to help.

He led the men to the deserted quartermaster's tent. Three wise women followed them, each drinking a vial of lake water. In the darkness, Eb heard the sound of a scuffle and what sounded like a dog barking and mice squealing. Then silence.

EB HAD WONDERED if the wise women, who hadn't been involved in planning the mission, would try to take charge. But when he returned from the quartermaster's tent, he heard Orion order crisply, "Two girls to each wise woman. Mistresses, you're responsible for keeping them quiet. We want to be long gone before anyone notices. And I'll need your help when we reach Weatherstone. Explaining the new postings to the soldiers will be tricky."

The girls counted off by twos, then fell silent. Some looked hopeful and excited, but a few looked about to cry.

Queen Andragora appeared, leading a troop of mice. They were almost invisible, their grey fur blending into the darkness. Eb touched Orion's arm and pointed to them.

Orion and Andragora spoke briefly in pidgin, then she and her band melted back into the darkness beneath the wagons. Eb guessed they'd climb up to ride beneath the wagon bed on the return to Weatherstone. Orion turned to Eb. "Looks like everything's gone according to plan. Ralph's band has hidden some arms in the wagons if we need them, and Andragora's team has removed the last of the amulets. We can leave now."

"What will you tell the soldiers once we reach Weatherstone?" Eb asked. They'd debated this at the cottage with Andragora and Ralph, but since he didn't understand pidgin, he never heard the final decision.

"They're to report to Sergeant Lito at the Inn in Weatherstone for orders," Orion whispered, grinning. "I understand he has a way with new recruits."

~

EARLY THE NEXT MORNING, Ralph and his Merry Band arrived in the village of Weatherstone. The villagers and the soldiers were asleep. Many of the soldiers bivouacked there still wore the amulet. Ralph and Andragora had made their own plans to change that.

"All I need for you to do is get us past the sentries," Andragora had said to Ralph. "My soldiers can do the rest. We'll slice the thongs that hold the amulets and remove them. Then your lot can help us carry them to some safe place where they can be collected and taken to the lake. The wise women should help."

Ralph nodded sagely. "Honestly? That's a little boring for us. But we'll keep the sentries quiet." He grinned at the queen of the mice and she grinned back.

"Good," she said.

Andragora's mice flitted past the wolf, waving at the mice in the Merry Band. A fox came up and asked Ralph, "When do we begin?"

"Now, I think," Ralph said with a low growl. He leapt into the air, and the sentry they'd been watching was suddenly on the ground, with a wolf on his chest. Wordlessly, he stared at the open jaws, and the long, pointed teeth.

"You probably shouldn't move," a voice said somewhere nearby. "That wolf is a friend of mine and he gets *very* annoyed when soldiers don't do as he says." The voice was high-pitched and strangely childlike. Slowly the sentry slid his eyes sideways. He saw a small figure a few paces away. It was a boy of about eight, smiling pleasantly. It was the prince! He opened his mouth to call out when something hit him on the head.

"Thanks," Benno said to Arta, who dropped the rock. "Did you have any trouble with yours?"

"Naw, ours is tied up in his guardhouse already. I just came to see if you needed help. Where's Andragora?"

Before Benno could answer, Arta let out a surprised squeal. Ralph had climbed off the sentry to lick her face.

"I think he likes you," Benno said with a smirk. "Andragora and her troops will bring the amulets. Then I'm going to fly with them to the lake."

"I wish I could fly," Arta said wistfully, as Ralph wandered off.

"So do I," Benno said. "These things are heavy. I'll have to make two trips."

27

TALA'S LAST CHANCE

AT BREAKFAST, Arta and Benno reported that no soldier in Weatherstone wore an amulet, and that Weatherstone had become the safest place for wise women in all of Teveral.

"How did you convince the soldiers to let the women and girls go?"

Orion laughed. "Sergeant Lito pretended he was in charge of a secret assignment, and ordered the soldiers from Camp #12 and all the soldiers in Weatherstone to ride to Lofton to set up a camp outside the town. One of the soldiers asked who was escorting the women and girls, and the sergeant said loudly it was a secret assignment, and he should thank the Sisters it hadn't been given to him. The other soldiers were so happy to be leaving, they didn't ask questions."

Suli was about to ask who had told Benno and Arta they could go on a midnight raid into Weatherstone while she was at the witch camp, but Orion and Eb were grinning at her, too obviously waiting for her to ask, so she sighed and shrugged. "Where are the women now? At the cave?"

Eb replied, "A few of them said they had to go home, and they left with the girls from their village, but most are going on to help liberate more camps with Ralph and Andragora. We brought the ones who were sick to the cave for now, but I think they need a warmer place to stay. Can they stay here?"

"Then we could go back to your house!" Arta said happily. "I want to take care of the animals."

"Do you really think Weatherstone is safe now?" Suli asked Orion and Eb. "Arta, it might not be—"

Arta frowned at her. "You're the one who told me your goats are sick. Don't you want me to help them?"

Suli thought of Silky who didn't know she was a goat, or that she had to eat. "Of course I do. But I have to keep you and Benno safe." *Which won't be easy if Orion and Eb keep taking you on raids.*

Eb interrupted, "It would be easier to stay in touch if we were near your flock. Sergeant Lito wants us to free one more camp before we head for Lofton. That would make space for the sick wise women to sleep here."

Suli sighed. She *would* like to sleep in her own bed again. And Magda's cottage *was* far away from everything. She needed to be closer to the flock. "All right. Let me talk with the wise women in the cave. Some may want to come with us now that it's safe to go into Weatherstone for supplies."

So it was decided; they'd move back to Tala's house. Eb and Orion carried food from the cave to Magda's cottage for the wise women to use, then they promised to bring the wagon, and more wise women, down to the house. Suli and Arta simply left, carrying what they'd brought with them down the mountain. Magda was busy in the kitchen when they reached the house and Suli sat down at the table to talk to her.

Arta left her things in Suli's room, and headed for the barn.

It wasn't feeding time yet, but Arta wanted to visit the goats. She would practice her listening on them. She was getting better at it, and she knew all about goats. Her mother said there was always something wrong with goats, some infection, some parasite, some mange irritating their skin. If the goats were sick, she could try to Heal them, even though Suli said she couldn't teach her that yet. When Arta had asked her why not, Suli looked as if she was about to cry.

Arta stepped inside, inhaling the comforting smell of hay and manure. It was a familiar smell, anyway. The pen needed mucking out. She'd need help with that. Maybe Benno would help her. She giggled at the idea of a prince shoveling manure. But he and Orion always seemed busy with the soldiers, and aside from letting her go on the raid in Weatherstone, they weren't letting her help. And that wasn't fair. She *could* help, she knew she could. Her magic was useful. Both Coalfeather and Suli had said so.

Arta decided no one would mind if the goats ate early, and it was a good way to make friends. She scooped grain from the bin into three buckets, then poured piles in the trough that sat against the side of the pen the way she'd been shown. Strangely, the goats didn't move. They simply stared into space, as though she wasn't even there.

She bowed and said, "Please enjoy your dinner."

The goats would rush to the piles to eat after she bowed, Magda said. But they didn't. They continued to stand there. Staring.

"That's not good," Arta said aloud. *Only a sick animal refuses to eat.*

She moved closer and reached through the bars to touch a yearling's head, closing her eyes to concentrate. Then she stepped back, shocked by what she'd found.

The poor goat didn't *know* she needed to eat. For that matter, she didn't know she was a goat. Her mind was a blank, a frightening blank. If she didn't remember who and what she was soon, she would starve to death. Arta opened her eyes and saw ribs sticking out beneath the shaggy coat, and the sunken eyes on every goat in the pen.

Arta closed her eyes and tried to send Healing energy to fight whatever had affected the goat's mind, although she didn't know how. But nothing happened.

She shook her head at her foolishness. She had her *own* magic. She could talk to them in their thoughts.

She made her way into the yearling's mind, careful not to frighten her. "You're a young goat," Arta told her. "You love to eat. You're hungry and want to eat the grain I've put out for you. When spring comes again, you'll eat new grass, and leaves, and shoots. You want to stay healthy now so you can feel the warm sun and eat the fresh grass. So you have to eat now. Eat."

The yearling stared at her, but where before there had been a blankness, Arta thought she saw a *person* behind the yearling's eyes. The goat remembered who she was. She lowered her head and began to eat.

Arta nodded, satisfied. She closed her eyes and focused on *all* the goats in the pen. She smiled, her face lit with excitement. *It was working*; she could heal them. She could stop the sickness the prime minister's witchcraft had created. She was more powerful than he was. *He* couldn't stop her from healing as many animals as she could find. This was *her* magic, the kind no one else knew.

MAGDA WAS WASHING turnips in the sink while Suli chopped vegetables at the table. Magda cleared her throat, and without turning around said, "We should talk about how to get the magic back."

Suli put her knife down and wiped her hands on her apron. "I'm listening."

Magda sat down across from her. She was silent a moment, staring at her clasped hands on the table. "I think I know why

Tala is still in Lofton. She mentioned once that it was possible the prime minister has a magical reservoir of his own—just like the lake. Tala is searching for it."

"How would she do that?" Suli asked, with a sense of foreboding. If what she and Orion had guessed was true, Tala was spying somehow on the prime minister.

Magda hesitated, looking guilty. "Have I mentioned Tala is the prime minister's housekeeper? She lives in his house. I'd expect her to search it from top to bottom."

"*What*? How could you let her take such a risk? She's right under his nose! She'll be caught!"

"I don't *let* Tala do anything; Tala does whatever she wants, as you well know. If the stolen magic is hidden away, she won't return until she's found it—or destroyed it. What if the amulets don't simply steal magic, what if they send it to be stored in the prime minister's magical reservoir? That's why the loss of magic doesn't affect him. He's causing it, deliberately. He's *stealing* the magic so he can use it himself. That's why the spell on those amulets is so powerful."

Suli's hands had gone cold and when she reached for the knife, they were shaking. If Magda was right, the wise women would only grow weaker, while the prime minister grew stronger. Even if they removed *all* the amulets, the prime minister had magic stored away, while they had none, except what they could draw from the lake. The magic *couldn't* return.

Tala might release the stolen magic, if she could find it. But she was in terrible danger. Suli just wanted her to come home.

HIDDEN BY LACE CURTAINS, Tala stood to one side of the window and watched the prime minister step into his carriage. She'd been preparing for this moment for weeks.

Coming out of the spy-hole passage the day before, she'd

almost been caught by a footman who always seemed to be nearby. Assigned to spy on her, probably.

It was now or never. She'd seen the suspicion growing in the prime minister's eyes and knew it was only a matter of days before she was arrested. Maybe hours.

The desk contained the master amulet that controlled the ones the soldiers wore, but then what controlled those idiotic flag pins? She was certain the pins, like the one Merrill wore controlled their wearers. Hallard was the key. He was the only one not wearing one—and the only one not cowed by the prime minister. But how were the pins controlled?

Perhaps the desk itself controlled the pins. She remembered the prime minister tracing the inlaid patterns with his finger. What if that had been more than an idle gesture? What if that renewed the spell?

She'd only get one chance. Once she breached the protective spells around the desk, the prime minister would know for certain she was a spy and she'd have only have minutes before she had to flee. Once she neutralized the spells, she'd change and fly away. She hoped the prime minister had never discovered she could change shape. Surely, he would have arrested her by now if he had.

She waited ten minutes after the carriage had left, then entered the study, softly closing the door behind her. She closed her eyes and *felt* the webs of power emanating from the desk, like prickles of irritation against her skin, then opened her eyes.

The webs encircling the desk glowed green, an intricate weave of crisscrossing threads. But where—

She smiled. *There.* Inside the green, a pattern of red, trying to hide behind the green lines. She'd been right: the desk itself was an object of power. It controlled the pins handed out to patriotic citizens, telling them what to think. No wonder it needed protection.

She waited, unmoving. Something else was hiding there.

Beneath the green webs of protection, just on the edge of sight, strands of violet and indigo flickered, their colors so intense they made the eyes ache.

With a sense of shock she realized what they were. The stolen magic had been there all along and she'd missed it.

If that were true, what would happen if she destroyed the desk? The magic itself couldn't be destroyed, but once it was released, where would it go? Would it become wild, rogue magic that no one could control? Or would it return to where it belonged? She shook her head, debating. She didn't know the answer, but she couldn't delay. She would have to risk it.

The wood and expensive inlays would burn nicely. She watched the flickering webs a moment longer, mesmerized by the pulsing of the blue and purple strands. Then she shook herself free, raised her hands and stepped inside the web of power. Her hands moved quickly, creating a new pattern in the air, now glowing white, now gold.

An oil lamp sat on a corner of the desk. Tala raised it over her head and smashed it down. The glass reservoir shattered, the spilled oil spreading across the desk's surface, filling the air with the sharp smell of kerosene. With only her hands, she struck a spark, setting the oil alight. The blue flames went *whoosh* as they spread across the surface of the desk. Murmuring softly, Tala coaxed the flames to spread until the entire desk was a burning pyre, and the smoke threatened to choke her.

The smoke was changing color, now blue, now violet, now green. *The magic is escaping*, she thought, returning to the world where it belonged. The flag pins would cease to work, freeing the people of Lofton. *If they even want to be free*, she thought acidly.

The sound of rattling carriage wheels stopping beneath the window startled her. She ran to the window, and looked down through the iron bars of the grille.

The prime minister had returned. Breaking the protective webs must have alerted him. She couldn't wait to make certain the controlling amulet was destroyed. She just hoped the fire would finish the job.

It was time to run for her life.

She opened the door, checking the hallway. No one was in sight. She fled down the servants' staircase, breathing fast. She hurried through the kitchen and out the scullery door. No one gave her a second glance.

She was out the door, and in the kitchen garden, where the leafless trees offered no cove. She slipped behind a tall juniper bush to change.

And was grabbed from behind. Strong hands whirled her around to face three angry soldiers. Before she could say a word, a gag was thrust into her mouth and her hands were tied with leather bindings.

The prime minister came out the kitchen door, his face red with fury. "I thought so," he spat. "I suspected all along what you were, witch."

He stepped closer, his hands twitching convulsively as though he longed to put them around her throat. "You've wrecked months of work and planning—and you'll pay for that." He nodded to himself. "Yes, you will. But most of the amulets will work, and that's all I need to become king. I have plenty of magic left—even though you destroyed the desk. You revealed yourself for nothing, Witch. And now you'll die for it."

Tala felt her skin crawl. Was he telling the truth—that destroying the desk hadn't affected his power—or was he bluffing? With a sinking sensation, she realized her Seeing no longer worked; she couldn't tell if he was lying.

"Of course," he continued, controlling himself, "I must admit I'm grateful. A traitorous spy, caught right in my own home, is better than I could've hoped for. It will make everything simpler. And you never came close to stopping me, did you?" He smiled. The flat coldness of his eyes was more frightening than his anger.

Was he right? Her legs felt shaky. Breaking the webs around the desk had drained all *her* magic. If he decided to kill her then and there, she had no protection.

She thought of Suli and Magda. She'd failed them, unless he was lying about the desk. She could only hope that by releasing the magic, she'd given them a fighting chance.

28

ROGUE MAGIC

SULI CURLED DEEPER beneath the quilts, reluctant to leave the warmth of her bed. She'd stuck her nose out and her room was freezing cold. There were benefits, she thought wryly, to being awakened by someone starting a fire. She glanced at the empty pillow where Arta should have been and sat up. Reluctantly she lowered her feet to the freezing floor.

Another camp had been liberated, and no one hurt, except one foolish soldier Ralph had bitten in self-defense. The freed wise women would be liberating more camps, or returning to their villages with the girls. A few had chosen to stay and help, camping in a field near the house.

With all this help, could they stop the prime minister? Suli wanted to believe it, but every time she remembered she had no magic she felt hopeless. It was a constant shadow at the edge of her thoughts. *What if the magic never returns?*

The wise women camping in the field argued about ways to ask the magic to return. Suli didn't join them. What was the point? She didn't think any of their plans would work. If the prime minister had hidden the magic where they couldn't find it, they might never get it back. Not unless his magical reservoir was destroyed.

Why hasn't Tala come back yet? That was her greatest worry, since Magda had told her that Tala was living in the prime minister's house. Suli needed to see her, to know that she was safe. It was someone else's turn now to risk trying to stop the prime minister's deadly magic. If she knew how, she'd send a fire message to ask Tala to come home.

There was a thunderous rapping on the roof, as though thousands of rocks were falling on it. The same sound clattered against her window and Suli leapt out of bed. The sharp sound was everywhere, as though the house was under attack. She ran to the window and opened the shutter.

Hailstones as big as her fist were falling. The ground was covered with them. The sky was cloudless and sunny, yet the hailstones hammered down, ricocheting off the ground. The yard soon was buried beneath a layer of white ice. *The winter vegetables will be torn to shreds,* Suli thought, and any human or animal caught outside might be hurt, maybe even killed.

She pulled on her clothes and boots and ran into the kitchen. Magda stood in the doorway, watching the falling hailstones. The sound of the storm faltered, and finally stopped, the sun shining brightly.

"Was that natural?" she asked Magda. "Or magical?"

Magda shrugged.

Suli stepped outside, shivering at the icy coldness in the air, her boots slipping on the hailstones.

Just as she feared, the dead bodies of sparrows and chickadees lay beneath the trees surrounding the garden. There would be more deaths because of this storm. More deaths because of one man's selfishness.

She splashed her face and hands at the pump, watching the sky for signs the hail would return. The storm *could've* been normal weather. But Suli felt a gloomy sense of certainty that it wasn't.

A terrifying screech shattered the silence.

Someone calling the Crow alarm call was flying up the hill. A moment later Coalfeather and Kaark appeared.

"What's the matter?" Suli called, running toward them. "Is your flock all right?"`

"No, Wise Woman, they are not!" Kaark screeched angrily. "Three members of my flock were just killed by human stupidity!"

Suli had never seen him so angry.

"I should not have to explain this to you, but that was no ordinary storm. The magic is *back*, but it is out of control! *You* must fix this, before anyone else dies!" Kaark spat.

Coalfeather said, "Wait, Father. I will tell her the rest." He turned to Suli. "We were on our way to tell you, when we were caught in the storm. It was just announced in the village. War has been declared."

"No! We aren't ready—"

She broke off when saw Magda coming down the steps. At the same moment, Benno and Arta appeared, coming around the house from the garden, their cupped hands full of hailstones. They were laughing, but when they saw Suli's face their smiles disappeared.

"Coalfeather says the war's begun," Suli said to Magda. "We're at war with Portjean."

Benno's face went pale. "My parents! We should've rescued them by now."

"We will, Benno. This makes no difference," Magda said calmly. "Now that we have enough loyal soldiers, we can leave for Lofton. Remember, the prime minister has the support of most of the town as well as the soldiers. They won't be persuaded by anything we say. We'll need soldiers to fight."

"But we're out of time!" Benno shouted, angry tears in his

eyes. "This time *I* give the orders! We leave *now* to rescue my parents. I'll go alone if I have to."

"That's exactly what the prime minister wants you to do," Magda said quietly, placing a hand on his shoulder. "You'd be playing right into his hands."

"But now he can kill them," Benno cried in an anguished voice. "It might already be too late."

"We don't know what he'll do," Suli said gently. "The prime minister has to have support for the war. He'll probably wait, Benno."

He shook his head. "You're only saying that to keep me quiet."

"No, I'm not. Think: If he kills your parents while you're free, *you* become king—a rallying point for the resistance. Folk who might not have wanted to be involved before will be angry that he killed the royal family. They'll support you. Loyal soldiers will flock to your banner and the entire countryside will join them. The last thing the prime minister wants is an open, organized resistance behind a new king. But that's what will happen if he can't prove your parents are alive. Until he has *you* under his hand, the risk is too great. He won't kill them—not yet. We still have time."

"She's right," Magda said. "He'll use your parents as bait to lure you to Lofton. Until he has you under lock and key, your parents are useful to him. He won't lose them as bargaining chips. As long as you're free, he'll keep them alive. Right now I'd say *you*, more than the war, are what keeps him awake at night. Or rather, you and the mystery of how the wise women are escaping from the camps. That should worry him." She smiled with grim satisfaction. She'd been on two raids so far.

"*Aaah!*" Benno cried, stomping away from them. "I need to do something! I can't sit around waiting much longer." He turned and walked around the corner of the house. Arta went after him.

Suli started to follow him, afraid he'd change and fly back to Lofton.

"Let me go," Magda said. "He's angry and afraid, and who can blame him? And he's right; it's not too early to plan what we'll do in Lofton. Sooner or later we have to confront the prime minister." She followed Benno into the garden behind the house.

Kaark croaked harshly. "Suli, listen to me. You must stop the wild magic. That is something only you can do."

"Maybe there is another way," Coalfeather said. "You're asking her to risk her life."

"But it *is* her responsibility," Kaark said. "The animal nations need her protection. Many have died from the disease and more have died today in this storm. Many more deaths will follow. The rogue magic cannot be stopped unless she asks for help on our behalf. She asked for our help; now we ask for hers."

"She is too young," Coalfeather protested. "She could die. There is no air where the guardians live. How can she go where there is no air?"

Suli felt an icy chill down her back. *I could die?*

"Others have done it before," Kaark answered impatiently, "so it must be possible. Remember, she is a shape-shifter, not just a wise woman, and she *is* young, young enough to survive the cold and the thin air. There is no one else to ask. She must do this. And *you* must help her, whatever your fears."

"Who is this 'she' you keep talking about?" Suli demanded angrily, trying to hide her fear. *Coalfeather thinks I could die.* "If you mean *me*, then you should talk *to* me. Stop talking over my head."

"I did not wish to say anything to you unless it was necessary," Kaark explained. "But the magical storms have begun because no one can control the released magic. You are our wise woman, and I am asking for your help."

She remembered asking Coalfeather how they could restore the magic. He'd avoided her eyes and flown off without answering. This must be why. He didn't want to tell her she had to risk her life to bring it back.

But wouldn't you do anything *to have your magic back?* "Wait, are you certain the hailstorm was caused by magic?"

Coalfeather paced impatiently. "Yes, of course. Someone released the stolen magic, but once the magic is stolen the pattern is broken. It can't return to where it belongs. Now it cannot be controlled. It is far more dangerous than anything the prime minister can do."

Magda joined them. "What are they saying?"

Suli turned to Magda, her stomach knotted in fear. "He says he's certain; the storm was caused by magic. Someone freed the stolen magic; now it's out of control."

Magda turned pale. "It must've been Tala. So why isn't she here? If she were free, she would have flown back. The prime minister must've caught her. She might already be—"

"We don't know anything for certain. If she was caught, he probably just locked her up. Listen, I can be in Lofton by tonight, and find out what happened."

"No, Suli," Kaark protested, screeching. "You will not. The magic will kill more of us, bringing more sickness and more storms, unless we ask for help. You must do something *now* Suli. You must fly to ask for help."

"Fine, I'll do whatever you want, *after* I find Tala. I have to go to Lofton." Suli said angrily. "Tala's in danger! I can't just wait here while the prime minister kills her." Her voice cracked. "You can't ask me to leave her there."

"*Everyone* is in danger now," Coalfeather said quietly. "The storms are everywhere and many will die. We've received messages that earthquakes are happening out in the plains for the first time. A wildfire is burning on the other side of the mountain, and nothing can stop it. No one is safe. My father is right. There is no one else who can go. It must be you."

Then Coalfeather explained what she had to do. Suli stared blankly at him, too shocked to argue.

Why didn't he understand? She had to save Tala.

29

SULI'S CHOICE

"I CAN'T. Don't ask me," Suli whispered, tears running down her face. "Don't you understand? The prime minister may have Tala —I need to know she's safe. Then I'll do anything you want."

"No!" Coalfeather said. "You must do this *now*. There can be no more delays. You must prepare for the ceremony. Let the others go to Lofton."

Kaark croaked his agreement.

Suli said to Magda, "I'm the one who can fly; I can be in Lofton tonight. You and the others will take at least two days on the road. Once I find Tala and free her, we can *both* come back for this ceremony."

Magda shook her head. "So you can fly, so what; so can the rest of the flock. You can't go, Coalfeather is right. Tala would expect you to do this. You have to perform the ceremony."

Suli narrowed her eyes. "I thought you didn't understand Crow. How do *you* know about the ceremony?"

"Coalfeather explained it to the wise women, and we've discussed it. We agree it has to be you."

Suli stopped breathing for a moment. "What?" *They talked about it without her?*

"Suli, the rest of us will find Tala. But you're the only one who can do this."

"Lofton is not your concern now," Coalfeather said. "The ceremony must happen now, and as our wise woman, you must go."

Suli scowled at Coalfeather, tears running down her face. *Of all the times for Coalfeather and Magda to agree.* "Fine, let the others go to Lofton. I only hope Tala is still alive when they get there." She walked away, trying to escape him.

"Suli, we are asking you to save us, to save our families," Coalfeather croaked, gliding after her. "Tala would say the ceremony is more important than rescuing her. You know that. The wise women are preparing the circle. When they are ready, I will come and get you."

Suli grunted, keeping her back turned so he couldn't see her face. He'd said she could die. What if she refused?

"I will tell the wise women she is coming," Kaark said. He flew off.

Suli whirled around and yelled at Coalfeather, "I thought you were my friend! But you and Kaark are plotting behind my back, with Magda no less. You want me to risk my life. You seem to think I have no choice, but I could say no!"

Coalfeather made a sad rumbling sound. "You do have a choice, Suli. But you are our wise woman and you said you would always protect us. If you say no, many more will die, not just here but all across the country. What do you think Tala would say if she heard you were using her as an excuse not to help us?"

"It's not fair," she said under her breath. She gave a shuddering sigh. "But I will do it."

Coalfeather was silent for a long time. "Thank you, Wise Woman." He flew away.

Suli wiped her nose and eyes and took a deep breath. Now

that she'd agreed, she felt calmer. She'd have to trust the others to find Tala.

She climbed the kitchen steps. Inside, Eb and Benno sat on the floor packing supplies. Eb greeted her cheerfully, but Suli could tell he was worried and trying to hide it. He was packing Orion's things as well as his own.

"Going somewhere?" Suli asked.

Eb flushed and muttered something about bivouacking with the soldiers.

"You're going to Lofton, aren't you? Without me. Who else is going?" Suli demanded.

"It's not decided yet. We're just—getting ready."

Something scratched against the kitchen door. Suli marched over and threw it open. "What?"

Coalfeather was on the top step. "We are ready for you. The ground is prepared for the ceremony. You will fly to the guardians to ask for help. As we walk to the circle, I will explain what you must do."

Suli wrapped herself in her cloak and stepped outside.

ARTA AND BENNO sat beside the fire, watching Eb and Orion prepare for their journey to Lofton. They were feeling left out. Something important was happening, but no one would explain. Everyone looked grimly serious.

"Do you think Suli is afraid of Coalfeather?" Arta asked Benno in a low voice, glancing at Eb who was putting food into sacks.

He shook his head. "No. She's afraid of what Coalfeather wants her to do."

Arta chewed her lip. "They should tell us what's going on. We could help."

Orion burst through the door, looking frightened. "Arta,

Benno—get your things! We're leaving. A wildfire is headed this way."

Eb looked startled. "What? There's snow on the ground!"

"We have to leave fast," Orion said. "The fire is coming this way and moving fast—pretty sure it's not a normal fire. I'll drive the wagon for the heavier stuff. It's a good thing most of the wise women came down from the mountain for the ceremony. I've already asked Flax to fly to the mountain and warn the others." He looked around. "Where's Suli?"

"She and Coalfeather went off to argue about something," Arta said. "She looked mad. And scared."

Eb exchanged a look with Orion, cursed quietly, and ran out the door.

"Come on, we're leaving," Orion said.

Benno asked, "Should we warn the animals too?"

Arta's face brightened. "I can do that! I just have to find who's on the mountain."

Eb found Suli easily. She and Coalfeather had barely started down the path to Tala's fields. As he approached, Eb heard his sister yell, "How can I do this without magic?"

"As a shape-shifter, you have all the *animal* magic you need," Coalfeather said. "You are a messenger for both the animals and the wise women. This is the only way to get your magic back."

"All right, but I don't understand why the magic can't return," Suli said.

"You have only known magic when it flows in the normal patterns. The wise women can use it then, focusing it, like a lens focuses light," Coalfeather said patiently. "Once it is ripped from the fabric of magic, the web is broken. You cannot put it back together again. Wise women cannot fix this. Someone outside the world must intervene. Otherwise cause and effect will harm us all, even the innocent who have nothing to do with human witchcraft."

She flinched.

Eb interrupted. "Suli, you can't stay here. There's a wildfire on the mountain. It's rolling through the forest like a storm, and there's nothing to stop it. Weatherstone's in danger, too. You have to leave, *now.*"

Coalfeather said, "You see? This is exactly what I mean. Another magical storm. The magic out of control."

"Whatever you two are arguing about has to wait, until you're somewhere safer," Eb said, grabbing Suli's arm and glaring at Coalfeather.

"There is nowhere safer," Coalfeather told Suli. "The fire is caused by magic, and the magic cannot be controlled. There is nowhere to run."

Suli nodded. "I can't leave, Eb. Go get the others."

30

THE NORTH STAR

Netil, the wise woman, tapped the drum in a slow rhythm, like a beating heart. Seated on the ground near the fire, Suli's heart slowed to match.

A woman Suli didn't know sprinkled lake water from an evergreen bough, on the circle of wise women. She gave Suli an extra shake, spattering her face so she had to close her eyes.

Suli didn't believe this would work, even with lake water.

She closed her eyes, inhaling the curling smoke of burning sage, while the wise women shuffled in a strange, slow dance around her. They chanted:

Bring our prayers to the ones who watch over us.

Fly to the North Star.

Find the Frost Goose. Find the animal guardians.

Do not be afraid.

Find them and tell them what has happened.

Explain our magic was stolen and ask for their help.

Tell them the animals are helping us and we are helping them, as it should be.

Tell them the magic is wild, and we cannot protect ourselves or anyone else.

Suli let the chant wash over her, remembering Coalfeather's words.

"A young goose must fly to the North Star and ask the spirit guardians for help, but they may not be able to help us. You may have to risk speaking with the World Guardian."

"But I don't know about the guardians! Why didn't you tell me about them if they're important?" Suli demanded. "Why can't someone who knows about these things talk to them?"

"There is no one else. I would not ask this if I thought you would not return. It must be a young person, one willing to sacrifice herself for the earth, or the guardians won't listen." He sounded certain, but Suli noticed he shifted uncertainly from talon to talon. "It *is* dangerous. If you don't fly fast enough, the air might run out before you reach them."

"Did you say *sacrifice?*" she asked. He meant willing to die.

If Tala were here, would she ask her to do something so crazy? Of course she would. Asking her to do something dangerous without an explanation was Tala's favorite way of teaching. But Coalfeather had helped her when she was friendless and alone. She considered him her friend, as well as her teacher.

And that means something, she told herself. He was asking her to do this, to protect the animal nations from the rogue magic. He was asking her because she was *their* wise woman. It was her job to protect them.

She remembered Hedith insisting every year that they gather around the fire to hear the winter stories. But it had never occurred to her that the guardians in the stories were *real*, or that someone could ask them for help, as she was about to do.

"What do I say when I get there?" she asked. "You expect me to fly to this mythical place, where I could die, then convince mythical people—"

"They're not mythical people, they are *our* guardian spirits. First, find the guardian for Sigur's people: her name is the Frost

Goose. She is the guardian of all the geese on earth, but especially the shape-shifters. You will humbly ask for her help, and if she asks you to do something—*anything*—you will do it. If she refuses to help you, ask to see the World Guardian. Tell them everything is out of balance now and that the magic is wild and all beings are suffering. Only someone from Sigur's flock can reach the North Star. No one else can fly so far or so high. It must be one of you. That is your honor."

Suli had fallen silent, and that's when Eb had interrupted to warn them about the wildfire. There was so much she didn't understand. Why had neither of her teachers mentioned the guardians before?

The women who'd been dancing and chanting in a circle paused, and then began a new chant.

We fly north, we follow the trail of stars.
We fly north, we follow the trail of stars.
We fly north, we follow the trail of stars.

They chanted over and over again.

Suli grew drowsy, and her eyes closed. The smoke, the drum, and the chanting made her sleepy. How could she fly to the guardians if she was asleep? She struggled to open her eyes but couldn't. Surely someone would notice and wake her up.

Then all of sudden she was lifted up. She was in the air. She *was* flying. Her wings were beating in time to the drum, and cold air slapped her face. She opened her eyes and the stars greeted her like old friends. *There she is*—they called—*the one who seeks the guardians. Follow us to our sister, the Brightest One! She will guide you. Safe journey!*

Suli called her thanks and kept flying, pointing up and up, aiming her body at the brightest star, her wings beating powerfully, her heart strong, her mind focused. She would carry Coalfeather's words to the guardians. She would explain that neither the animals, nor the wise women, nor even the people of Teveral, were to blame for ripping the fabric of magic.

The rhythm of the drum shifted and the chanting stopped.

Below her, a blue haze curved around the earth; the air every living thing needed to live. Beyond it lay the blackness of night, filled with stars she'd never seen before.

Her breath faltered and her wings missed a beat. Was she already too high, too far beyond the air she needed to breathe? Would she die here?

She flew on, feeling her breath coming in gasps, struggling to keep her wing beats steady. Panic threatened to overwhelm her. If she didn't find the guardians soon, her flight would be in vain. And many others would die.

Then, floating on a cloud, she saw a mountain ahead, gleaming white and glowing with a greenish light.

She flew toward it, her fears forgotten in her fascination with the glittering city as she drew near. At its center an enormous tree sprang so high she could see the branches even at a distance. Every branch was filled with birds of all kinds: songbirds, raptors, scavengers, sparrows, parrots—every bird she knew was there, as well as many she'd never seen before.

She headed for the wide circle of grass below the tree. Animals of every kind lay beneath it or strolled together. Bears, foxes, beavers, lynx, cougars, moles, even tiny shrews seemed content in each other's company.

A loud call came from the tree, a goose crying, "Come here, little one, come here."

Suli obeyed the summons, landing awkwardly on a branch beside a snow-white goose whose wing tips shimmered the blue-green of thick ice.

"I've been waiting for you," the goose said. "I'm the Frost Goose, the guardian of Sigur's people."

Suli curled her neck in a respectful bow. "I'm honored, Frost Goose. It is you I've come to see." Raising her head, she gazed around her in wonder. In the distance she saw palaces of ice where the streets glittered like diamonds, and colorful gardens of strange plants. Suli wanted to see everything at once. It was hard to tear her eyes away, but she had to remember why she was there.

"I'm a messenger," Suli said. "I was sent to tell you that the magic was stolen from our land by a witch. Now it's been set free, but it's wild and uncontrollable and the wise women can't remake the pattern. Humans and animals are suffering. We humbly ask your help to return it where it belongs."

"But it was humans who misused the magic, wasn't it?"

So this wasn't going to be so easy. "Yes," she admitted. "That's true, but one man, alone, is responsible, using witchcraft to steal magic. We need your help to get it back."

"I see," the Frost Goose said gravely. "All of us—all the guardians—have been wondering what to do. The animal guardians are angry with *all* humans, you know, even the wise women. They say they must learn their lesson by suffering the consequences of this folly. The floods, diseases, and storms— you've brought them on yourselves."

"But innocent animals, as well as people, are dying! Why should they be punished? A wildfire is burning the mountain near my village as we speak, and all animals are in danger. It's not the villagers' fault—truly it's not. Without your help, more animals and humans will die. Won't you help us?"

"And why exactly do you deserve our help?" The voice behind her sounded bitter.

Suli turned. A small yellow songbird glared at her from a nearby branch.

"Your magic killed many of my people," the songbird chirped angrily. "And now you think we should help you? Arrogant humans, they never grow up! Do you think we're here to save you from yourselves? You don't even show the proper respect, yet you assume we'll help you!"

"Forgive me," Suli said, "I mean no disrespect. I don't know the proper way to address you, or to ask for help. Please advise me: What can we do to set things right? *All* beings below are suffering, including your children."

"We know perfectly well our children are suffering." The songbird sniffed, and turned to the Frost Goose. "*You* explain it to her. Explain why there is nothing we can do." And with a disdainful glance at Suli, the songbird darted into the sky.

"Explain what?" Suli asked.

"That it is too late for us to intervene," the Frost Goose said. "Once the humans break the pattern, the consequences follow. We cannot change cause and effect. I am sorry, Wise Woman."

Suli felt numb. She'd assumed the Frost Goose would help her, or at least tell her what she had to do. She was glad Coalfeather warned her this might happen. "The animals and the wise women are working together to stop the witch. They've removed the cursed amulets from many men, which stopped the flow of magic to the witch. Then someone—probably my teacher—set the magic free. But now it's out of control and we need help to stop it. Could you help me ask the World Guardian?"

The Frost Goose pondered a long moment before she said, "Tell me more about the witchcraft."

Suli explained how the prime minister used amulets to control others, while stealing the magic the wise women needed. She spoke quickly, afraid Weatherstone was already burning.

"We can try," the Frost Goose said. "You're correct: only the World Guardian can help you now. Follow me."

The Frost Goose opened her wings and soared into the air, with Suli following close behind. They flew above the tree, until they were ascending the side of the dazzling mountain. The Frost Goose swooped low, heading toward a green valley. There was a sweet fragrance in the air, and the sound of waterfalls. They descended to a meadow, surrounded by tall trees, where deer, elk, and wild turkeys grazed in the high grass.

"I shall speak with the World Guardian first," the Frost Goose said. "Wait here until she sends for you. If I don't call you, it will be because she's too angry. Then you must leave quickly and return home."

Suli swallowed nervously. There was no reason why the World Guardian *shouldn't* be angry, she thought.

A quarter of an hour passed before she heard a voice calling from the trees. "Suli the wise woman, approach me."

Beneath her feathers, Suli's skin was covered in goose bumps. She entered the trees cautiously and found the Frost Goose talking in a low voice with a strange figure. The World Guardian saw her, and beckoned her forward.

The World Guardian shimmered, changing form constantly, now transparent, now solid. Suli looked into her eyes and they, too, changed color from moment to moment.

"Why are you killing my children and destroying the gifts I gave you?" the World Guardian asked gravely, her luminous eyes shifting from deepest black to gold to the blue of the deep ocean, then becoming the colors of the stones at the bottom of a creek.

"One man alone is responsible. He wants everything for himself. He doesn't respect the magical balance or the pact between humans and animals. He thinks he should command everyone, human or animal," Suli replied in a small voice. "We're trying to stop him, but he's stolen so much magic the wise women are powerless. They sent me to ask for your help."

"Will this man repent of his evil actions?"

Suli swallowed hard, trying to control her dismay. If that was what was required, there was no hope. The prime minister would never confess he'd been wrong.

"If this man is too selfish and heedless, I cannot stop the curse on the land." The World Guardian spoke kindly but her words were like stones raining down on Suli's heart.

A goat emerged from the trees. "World Guardian, you should know that one of the humans is healing the animals cursed by the evil magic. She reminds them who they are and what to do. They are no longer dying."

He must mean Arta. Suli's hopes rose.

"Ah. That speaks in your favor," the World Guardian said. "I wish I could help you."

"But there must be something you can do! More will die from the storms!"

"What storms, child?"

"The storms caused by uncontrolled magic. The magic was released from the witch's control, but it won't return to the pattern. Couldn't *you* return it to where it belongs?" Suli asked.

"Hmm. I shouldn't interfere with cause and effect, but... perhaps I *could* fix that," the World Guardian said thoughtfully. "Restore the proper pattern. But as for the witch, humans must deal with him. They allowed this to happen. Tell the wise women to deal with him."

Suli bowed her head. "I understand. Thank you, World Guardian."

She turned and walked back the way she'd come,. Her legs had begun to tremble and she felt strangely weak.

The Frost Goose said, "You must leave now, Suli. Even Sigur's geese can't stay here long." She quickly explained the ceremonies the wise women would have to perform to be able to use magic again.

Suli repeated the instructions and the Frost Goose nodded. "Go now, or you won't be able to leave."

Suli thanked her again, and then leapt into the starry blackness, plummeting toward the blue globe of her home.

If she reached the blue haze surrounding her home before the air ran out she'd survive. But she already felt dizzy. Black spots appeared before her eyes.

I'm going to crash into the earth and die, she thought.

For a moment, she felt terribly sad.

Then she lost consciousness.

31

FIRE ON THE MOUNTAIN

Rows of wagons headed west toward the plains in orderly lines. In Weatherstone, there were no tears except for a few crying children. The grim-faced adults left their homes to whatever fate awaited them.

In the central square, Eb was urging three stragglers to climb aboard a wagon. The fire's roaring sound grew closer, and drifting smoke obscured anything beyond a few feet away.

"I wish I knew Suli was all right," Eb said hoarsely, raising his voice to be heard over the fire.

Orion shoved an old lady into a wagon against her will. She walloped him over the head with her walking stick, and a grinning soldier shook the reins and urged the mules to move, heading for the only road out of town. Benno and Arta sat in the last wagon, watching the smoke and glancing at Eb and Orion nervously.

"Suli's probably safer than we are," Orion said, rubbing his head. "Coalfeather won't let anything happen to her."

Eb didn't believe that for a second. In his opinion, magic always seemed to involve dragging his sister into dangerous situations and expecting her to escape without help. He wished he could see what was happening at this ceremony the wise women expected Suli to be in, but they'd told him to go help the villagers.

"Look, if you're really worried, I can finish here," Orion offered. "I'll take Arta and Benno outside of town. We'll wait for you while you go back to the house. But don't stick around if the fire's already there. Suli can fly away. You can't."

Eb didn't need to be told twice. Walking quickly, he headed up the village street toward the hill where Tala's house sat outside the village.

The smoke grew thicker. A shard of blazing bark fell onto the path in front of him and he looked up. The trees beside the road were smoking, with more smoke seeping through the branches of the trees behind them, until the sky was capped by a dome of smoke. It seemed to Eb that the entire village would be in flames soon.

He heard cows lowing in fear nearby, but couldn't see them. *I should probably turn around.*

Pounding hooves were coming toward him down the path. Without thinking, he leapt aside. A herd of deer thundered past, the whites of their eyes showing.

The fire sounded close now, a threatening roar that made every hair on his body stand up. *What am I doing? If I go any further, I'll die.*

But he thought of Suli, doing Sisters-knew-what because a crow had told her she had to. *I have to get her out of here,* he decided, pushing away his fear. He stepped into the smoke, tying his shirt over his nose, his eyes streaming.

What he could see of the sky, past the thick spirals of smoke, shocked him. Flames shot up higher than the trees, and seemed to engulf the sky. The clouds reflected the firelight, staining the mountain a bloody red. It looked like the sky was burning.

Cinders and bright orange embers floated down; one landed on his bare arm. He yelped in pain, brushing it off. It was hard to breathe, and his heart beat too fast. He broke into a run. *The pond,* he thought, *I can stay below the surface of the pond*. He knew he'd never make it to the field where he'd left Suli. Maybe she was already dead.

The trees thrashed in the gusting wind of the firestorm. The hot air seared his throat and lungs. He stumbled against the gate, pushed through, and sprinted toward the pond. With a final leap, he fell through the tall reeds to plunge into the water.

When his head broke the surface to gulp a lungful of scorching air, he saw he wasn't alone. Animals of every kind were watching him calmly. A wild horse, a family of wildcats, even a wolf—all politely ignored each other. He wished he spoke pidgin.

～

THE WISE WOMEN held wet kerchiefs or shirts over their faces. Instead of watching the towering flames speeding toward them down the mountainside, they kept their eyes on the sky. Above the pillars of smoke, the clouds were gathering thickly in serried ranks of grey, blotting all light from the sky.

Lightning stabbed down without warning, and thunder echoed in every valley, rolling down the mountainside to crash over the fields and house. Then the rain came, pouring in solid sheets like white curtains moving across the fields, obscuring all in its path and dousing the flames. It rained steadily, a hard, pounding rain that churned the dirt to mud and soaked the charred trees and grass into sodden, inky ruins.

～

WHEN SULI AWOKE the first time, she was lying on a sodden clump of grass. She tried to move and found she was stiff and cold. She sat up and looked around, but didn't recognize anything. The ground around her was frost covered and tussocky. A white mist lingered in the hollows.

Where am I?

She rose stiffly to her feet and stretched her wings. Nothing was broken, thank the Sisters. The numbness in her feet gave way to tingling pins and needles. She smelled wood smoke and the bitter tang of burnt grass.

In the distance, a large flock of unfamiliar geese was watching her. One of them called, "You did well, young one." For a moment she wondered if it was Grisa's flock, until she realized they were all white.

Dawn was coming. The stars disappeared as the sky turned pale grey and the unseen sun waited below the horizon. A charred smell lingered in the air, but the wind shifted, and now she could see where she was: Tala's field near the foot of the mountain. She began to walk back toward the house, wondering where the wise women had gone and feeling dizzy and unsteady on her feet. Between one step and another, she fell asleep.

When she awoke the second time, she was lying beside the sodden ashes of a fire, shivering and drenched to the skin. "How did I get here?" she croaked, pushing herself up on her elbow.

Someone tucked a shawl around her soaked clothes. Magda pulled her to her feet and rubbed her arms. "Let's go back to the house," Magda said. Wise women patted Suli on the shoulder, smiling. A few were laughing, apparently delighted to be soaked to the skin on a cold November day.

"What happened?" Suli asked.

Coalfeather appeared from where he'd been hidden by the women's long skirts. He flapped his wings and croaked, "You did it, Suli. You saved us."

Magda bared her teeth in a fierce smile. "You convinced them. The wildfire has stopped and you're home. Welcome back."

Magda put an arm around Suli's shoulder and led her to the house. She sat Suli beside the hearth, tucked a blanket around her, and threw logs on the fire. When a wise woman handed her a cup of tea, Suli was shivering too much to hold it, and Magda held it for her to sip from as though she were a baby. Coalfeather remained perched on the windowsill outside, as if he wasn't convinced she was back. For that matter, Suli wasn't sure either.

Wise women brought what vegetables were left from the garden, and began to prepare food.

The wildfire had reached the edge of the fields, Magda said, but most of the village was untouched. Tala's house escaped with only burnt hayricks and a few charred patches on the roof. "We were extremely lucky."

The door opened. Everyone turned to look.

Eb stepped inside, soaking wet, with red-rimmed eyes and soot-streaked face. "Is Suli here? Is she all right? I tried to find her but I got caught—"

"Eb!" Suli threw off her blanket and ran to him. They hugged tightly.

"You're all right, then?"

"What about you?" she asked. "You look terrible. What happened?"

"I'm slightly roasted. Or maybe braised in my own juices. The fire almost got me, but I made it to the pond. I can now boast I've sat through a wildfire along with a horse, a wolf, and various small animals who decided I was a good place to perch above the water while they waited."

For some reason Suli thought this was unbearably funny. She began to laugh until the tears ran from her eyes and she started hiccupping. She and Eb laughed together, holding on to each other. The wise women smiled.

Suli pulled Eb to the fire, wrapped her blanket around him, and sat down beside him, one arm around his shoulder. One of the wise women brought Eb a mug of tea.

He gulped it down. "Oh, that's good."

～

AT MIDDAY, in the field where the ceremony had been held, Magda and Suli called everyone together to make plans. Orion had returned with Arta and Benno and the rest of the wise women. Arta had gone to the barn to comfort the animals who were still nervous.

"Most of you, I know, want to return to your villages to perform the ceremonies the Frost Goose gave us, to help the magic return," Magda said. "We wish you good luck. The rest will go to Lofton. Thank you to everyone who volunteered." She nodded to a small group who smiled back. "It's time to take the fight to the prime minister. We leave at sunrise."

"And we'll rescue my parents!" Benno said loudly.

"And free Tala," Suli added. *If it isn't already too late.*

"Benno will rescue his parents, and we will free Tala," Magda agreed.

"How do we get to Lofton?" Eb asked. "I know some of you can fly, but what about the rest of us?"

Orion spoke up. "Farmer Soko said we can keep his wagon if we'll save his animals and crops. Ralph's Merry Band and Andragora's mice are coming, too. Eb and I will be in charge of two squads of soldiers on horseback."

When the meeting was over, Suli went to find Arta. She was in the barn stroking Silky between her ears. The goat nibbled at her sleeve affectionately.

"Arta, we're leaving tomorrow for Lofton. Let's start packing."

To Suli's surprise, Arta shook her head. "I can't go, I have to stay here."

"What? Why?"

"Because I need to concentrate without being interrupted, if I'm going to take care of all the animals." She spoke with certainty.

"Some of the flock are staying here, they can feed the animals—"

"Not only the ones here. I am going to heal all the animals in

Teveral. I'm the only one who can. Wouldn't you do it if you could?"

Suli took a deep breath and let it out. "You're right. You have to do this. And *I* have to thank you. You're the reason I was able to stop the wildfire."

Arta looked skeptical. "What do you mean?"

"It was only after the goat guardian reported that you were healing the animals from the forgetting sickness that the World Guardian decided to help us. Without your magic, everyone in the country would still be in danger. But are you sure you want to be here alone?"

Arta considered that. "I'm old enough to be by myself," she said. "I've done it lots of times before. And I can save animals across the country. If I can hear them, I can heal them. I think Coalfeather was planning for me to do this all along."

When she thought about it, Suli had to admit Arta was right. Coalfeather had said something exactly like that at the Animal Council. Once again she was surprised by Arta's cleverness. She grinned. "Who am I to argue with Coalfeather? Very well, you can stay. I'll ask Wilo to keep an eye on you. And Arta?"

"Yes?"

"I'm proud of you. I think you'll be a great Healer someday. And I *will* teach you magic, once we stop the prime minister."

Arta smiled. "Good."

SULI COULDN'T WAIT ANY LONGER to test her magic. She went into the garden where a few rows of hardy winter vegetables had survived the fire. She squatted next to a row of cabbages, and touched one. Closing her eyes, she tried to See it. The black spots of disease were still there. Whatever the World Guardian had done hadn't changed that. Hesitantly, she tried to move healing energy toward the spot.

It shifted, but sluggishly, and she couldn't control it. The magic to Heal wouldn't flow, she realized, because *she* hadn't held the ceremony to ask permission to use the magic. She bit her lip, considering. There wasn't time; they were leaving for Lofton tomorrow. It would have to wait until after they brought Tala home.

A FEW HOURS LATER, while they were eating dinner, sitting on the floor, or perched on every chair in the house, there was a knock on the door. Suli answered it.

A human Lamisa gestured for Suli to come outside.

"What is it?" Suli asked.

Lamisa glanced at the window. "I didn't want everyone to hear, but you and Magda should know. The king and queen are to be executed for treason."

Suli's heart pounded slowly in her chest. "When?"

"In three days. I didn't want the prince to hear. If you're going to save his parents, you can't wait."

We can't tell Benno. Not yet, Suli thought.

32

THE ROYAL EXECUTION

Two days later, at a roadside inn outside Lofton, two wagons pulled up in the rear courtyard. Three weary travelers climbed down, carrying their belongings while the ostlers unharnessed the horses and led them away to be fed and watered.

Magda led the way; Suli, Benno, and Orion, in his lieutenant's uniform, trailed after her. Eb would camp with the soldiers by the side of the road that night.

"Welcome! Welcome!" A smiling, red-faced landlord rubbed his hands together. "What can I get for you folks?"

When they were seated at a table and Magda had ordered, she asked him for a room for the night. "Sorry, Mistress, but we're completely full. Lots of out-of-towners have come for the execution. You folks here for that, too? I've never seen the place fill up so fast. Maybe it's the witch-hanging that has people so excited—everyone's hoping to see some magic if she tries to escape."

Suli's shock must've shown on her face because Magda glared at her. She felt as though she'd been dropped into an icy stream. *A public hanging.*

"We hadn't heard about that," Magda said carefully. "Where did they find a witch?"

"Living in the prime minister's own house, if you can believe it," the landlord said, shaking his head in wonder. "No wonder he decided to make an example of her."

"When is the hanging to be?"

"Tomorrow, with the other traitors." He sighed. "It's so sad our royal family are traitors. I could hardly believe it."

"Landlord, we'd like something hot to drink now," Magda said curtly. "Cider if you have it."

"Right away, Ma'am." He scurried off.

"It's Tala," Suli whispered.

"That's fairly obvious," Magda snapped. She sounded angry, but her face was ashen.

"We have to find her and free her tonight," Suli said, rising from the bench.

Magda shook her head. "No, we don't. As long as she'll be executed with the king and queen, our plans don't change. We'd better make sure, though. Orion, wander over to the bar and ask those soldiers when the witch is scheduled to die."

Orion looked sick, but he nodded and slid off the bench, heading for the bar.

There were claws trying to tear their way out of Suli's stomach. Anything could happen to Tala between tonight and tomorrow. The prime minister might decide not to wait, or to torture her to find out what she knew, and Tala had no magic to protect herself.

~

IN THE CENTER of Lofton's town square, three scaffolds stood atop a high wooden platform. Three nooses hung from the scaffolds, their shadows falling across the faces of the King Sito and Queen Mora, who stood waiting to die.

The crowd surged against Suli, pushing her forward. She stumbled and shoved back to keep her place beside the steps to the platform. An honor guard of soldiers, in scarlet dress uniforms and plumed hats, stood directly across from her, waiting to escort the prime minister.

The crowd murmured and shifted, turning their heads to watch a squad of soldiers lead Tala to the steps. A soldier grabbed her roughly and pushed her up the steps. He winked at Suli as he passed, and her eyes widened. It was Orion.

Tala never looked at him, staring straight ahead, as Orion guided her to the third noose. He left her there with her hands bound before her, just like the king and queen.

Suli craned her head, peering around the town folk to find the others.

Magda would wait until Eb and Benno were in place before giving the signal.

There they were. Eb was on horseback at the edge of the crowd. She hoped no one else noticed the small bump under his cloak, where Benno rode behind him. Eb caught her eye and a smile flickered on his face. Then he faced forward, expressionless, the disciplined soldier leading his troops.

Suli scanned the edge of the square until she found Magda, dressed in her village clothes, on the driving bench of a wagon. Suli had argued that Magda should stay out of sight to avoid being recognized by the magistrate or one of his visitors. Magda dismissed the risk with a flick of her fingers. "You'll need me," she said. Unfortunately, that was true.

The town folk heaved against the platform, eager for the spectacle. Suli's face was smashed against the back of a large man who smelled strongly of fish. Next to him a fat woman wearing a dress stained with food gobbled sausages with gusto, her eyes avid with anticipation. Suli watched the crowd with a growing sense of disgust. They chattered and laughed and exchanged rumors; they hoped either Tala or the witch-queen would use magic to try to escape. The possibility added a delicious shiver of fear to their holiday entertainment.

F<small>ROM THE PLATFORM</small>, Tala saw Hallard standing at a window overlooking the square, wearing a look of disgust. He'd helped her without knowing it; because of him she'd figured out the pins controlled their wearers, or they had until she'd burnt the desk. Few people wore them now.

She'd hoped her magic would return after the destruction of the desk, but it hadn't. What had gone wrong? Had she been mistaken, and the desk wasn't where the magic was stored after all? But the prime minister had admitted it was, and in that, at least, she thought he told the truth.

She glanced behind her and started. She forced herself to look calm. *The soldier guarding me is Orion.* If he was here, were there others, too?

She scanned the crowd, inhaling sharply when she recognized the tall youth, far too young to be a soldier; Tala felt her hope rising. *If Suli's brother is here, then Suli must be too.*

S<small>ULI WAS FRANTIC WITH IMPATIENCE</small>. What was Magda waiting for? She glanced at the far side of the square, wondering if any crows would come. Suli had thanked the animal nations for their help in liberating the camps, but she told them only Andragora's mice and Ralph's Merry Band should come with them to Lofton, because they were used to hiding from humans. This would be more dangerous than slipping into the camps.

But Kaark had surprised her again. He'd argued that since the prime minister had broken the Law first, the crows could volunteer if they chose.

A hush fell over the crowd. The prime minister strode across the platform, wearing a sweeping surcoat of gold brocade that brushed the ground. *He thinks he's the King already,* Suli thought.

The honor guard arranged themselves behind him, their scarlet uniforms with gold braid dazzling in the sun. Orion's men, standing behind them in their everyday blue uniforms, seemed drab and out of place.

The prime minister addressed the crowd. "Some of you still deny that witchcraft is a threat to our country." He glanced up at the window where Hallard stood. "Today I bring you proof of that threat. Witchcraft eats away at our country, from the lowest village hut to the palace itself. This woman," he pointed to the queen, who stood calmly in the shadow of the noose, "has used witchcraft for years. She can change shape, and used that skill to spy for Portjean. But that isn't the worst of her crimes: she's taught witchcraft to her son! He's a witch, too!"

Suli heard angry muttering in the crowd, but were they angry with the queen or with the prime minister? Some of the faces around her seemed afraid, but many more continued to chatter and eat, enjoying themselves like groundlings at the theater.

The prime minister pointed at the king, who appeared bored. The skin hung off the bones of his pale face, as though it no longer fit.

"This man concealed her evil deeds; he knew there was witch-craft in his family and said nothing."

Magda still didn't move. *What is she waiting for?* Suli craned her neck behind her again. Where were the wise women?

There. She glanced away quickly, so as not to draw attention to them. They sat in carts full of cabbages or turnips, positioned around the edge of the crowd. The wagons would block more soldiers from coming into the square or from reaching the platform.

Magda, do it now, Suli thought. If she waited too long, the prime minister might release the trapdoors before they could stop him.

The crowd hissed and booed, but some were scowling at the prime minister. "Stop the war!" someone shouted. A soldier pointed toward him, and his men tried to push their way toward him.

Maybe others would help once the fighting began. Suli was certain there would be fighting now. Since the prime minister had denounced Benno as a witch, his life was in danger if anyone recognized him.

Magda waved a red kerchief over her head twice, then tied it around her head.

Finally!

Eb forced his horse through the crowd toward the platform, his soldiers behind him.

The prime minister's attention was fixed on Tala. He announced, "This witch is more dangerous than the queen. A spy hidden in my house, she used her magic to sabotage the war. I was lucky to escape from her spells alive." He leaned closer and said, "Any last words for us, witch?" He spoke softly and only those near the platform heard him.

He must think she's cowed because she has no magic, Suli thought.

"Yes, I *do* have something to say. People of Teveral!" Tala's voice carried to the furthest edge of the square. "You have been betrayed by a traitor who imprisoned your king and queen on false and ridiculous charges. The only reason he's kept them alive until now was to lure their son here. The prime minister is the real witch, a traitor and a coward, a man who will do anything to take the throne, including murder an eight-year-old boy."

The prime minister strode toward her.

Tala continued loudly. "This execution is not about justice— it's a trap for the boy. Once he has the prince, the prime minister can murder your entire royal family, and steal the throne."

The prime minister grabbed her arm, but Tala shook him off, moving to the edge of the platform.

"Stop her!" he shouted. "Don't listen to the witch!" He turned and gestured for Orion's soldiers to help him.

Orion and his men rushed forward. The bewildered honor

guard, unsure what was happening, waited for orders. Orion saluted and moved briskly toward Tala. The prime minister said, "Yes! Help me! Kill her!"

Ignoring Tala, Orion raised his sword and tried to hit the prime minister over the head. But the prime minister raised his hands and said something under his breath. There was a streak of violet light.

Orion was hurled across the platform. The prime minister crossed the platform toward him, intent on finishing him off, but by then the honor guard had drawn their swords and were attacking Orion's men, preventing the prime minister from reaching him.

Orion rose unsteadily to his feet, looking around him.

Then Benno was there, leading more soldiers, with Eb at his back. The loyal soldiers surrounded the honor guard circling in toward the prime minister. He blasted three of them with his magic, hurling them several feet.

With a protective shield of soldiers around him, Benno ran to his parents. He sawed at the ropes on the queen's hands with his knife, while Eb cut the king's bindings with his sword.

Suli was up the stairs and running to Tala. In the confusion no one noticed.

"Are you all right?" she asked, fumbling at the ropes, until she cut them with her knife.

"Once we're away from here I'll be fine," Tala said. "But first I have to deal with the prime minister."

Suli was about to ask what she'd do, but she never got the chance. The sky grew dark and she looked up. Storm clouds were hovering above the square but nowhere else. She closed her eyes and opened them. It was still there. More of the prime minister's witchcraft?

Then a bolt of black feathers plummeted toward her. Before she could move, Coalfeather pulled out of the dive to land on her shoulder, his talons gipping tightly. She winced.

"Our scouts will drive the soldiers from the square," he said. "They'll stop anyone else from entering," he squawked jubilantly. "Look!"

Now she could see the darkness was a huge flock of crows, swooping and curling like a moving cloud. Coalfeather cried out, calling encouragement, then took off to join them.

The flock of crows descended on the soldiers, beating hands and faces with their wings, and pecking at the soldiers' eyes before darting away, untouched.

Suli gasped. Now the cloud was shaped like an arrowhead, and *Kaark* was at the point of the arrow.

The crows plummeted straight down at the prime minister.

He raised his hands and spoke a word, but his magic had no effect. Kaark's sharp bill tore a gash in the prime minister's forehead, and blood ran down his face.

Then rest of the flock came on, swooping and attacking him, screaming, "Murderer! Betrayer! Witch!"

They pecked and tore whatever they could reach. First the prime minister covered his eyes, then he put his arms over his head, until finally he dropped to his knees, and curled up on the ground, trying to protect himself from the black swarm that engulfed him, rending and tearing.

Benno watched for a moment, then calmly approached the prime minister and hit him over the head with the hilt of his knife. The prime minister went limp.

The crows continued to bite and tear at his unconscious body, screeching "Murderer!"

Kaark strutted up and down beside the body of his enemy while Coalfeather and the others flew off to attack the bewitched soldiers.

Benno's parents kneeled beside him, wrapping their arms around him.

"We should go," Benno said. He pointed toward the stairs on the other side of the platform where Magda waited with her cart.

Too much was happening for Suli to follow it all. Officers shouted for the soldiers arranged outside the square to come to the platform, but the wise women's wagons blocked their way. The wise women began hurling cabbages and turnips at the soldiers, who raised their hands to protect themselves. The women yelled insults, saying their mothers were ashamed of them, helping a witch take over their country. The soldiers glanced at each other uncertainly.

People struggled to escape the square, afraid they'd be crushed or killed by the fighting. The market women, who'd watched it all from their booths, decided to join in. They threw rotting vegetables, sticks, cobblestones—whatever they could find—at the prime minister's soldiers.

Eb and Orion's men had disarmed the honor guard, and had forced them to sit on one side of the platform.

Holding tightly to Tala's arm, Suli led her across the platform to the opposite steps, where Magda waited in the wagon. Benno and his parents were already in the wagon bed. Suli and Tala climbed in, and Magda shook the reins. Orion appeared at the top of the stairs. "Meet you at the palace!"

To Suli's astonishment, the crowd cleared the way for them, clapping and cheering as the royal family drove past.

A group of wise women, carrying buckets of water, were removing amulets from the officers on the platform and throwing them in the buckets.

The unconscious body of the prime minister was thrown across the back of a horse, arms and legs dangling on either side. The crows went with him, still pecking at his hands and feet.

No one stopped them.

33

A SISTERLY INTERLUDE

IN THE DEPTHS of the forest beside a stream, two women chanted softly, asking the magic that belonged there to return. They asked the animals, the trees, and the spirits of the sky and water to forgive them, and to allow the land to heal. Then they lit a fire, and placed offerings beside it: a feather, a shell, and a tiny bag embroidered with beads woven into a pattern that looked like a swirl of cloud. They poured a cup of water over the fire and asked the spirit guardians for forgiveness. They put out the fire completely, covering the ashes with dirt.

At the crossroads between Beeshome and Falling Water, a circle of villagers had gathered, carrying boughs of greenery. Suli's grandmother was there, and so was Hedith the wise woman. Hedith chanted a prayer while one of the men built a bonfire in the center of the road. They used evergreen branches to sprinkle water, walking clockwise, asking the spirits for forgiveness, and for them to return and make the land whole. Then they all held hands and circled the fire, singing an ancient song of renewal.

TALA INSISTED on driving the wagon during the long trip back to Weatherstone. Suli sat beside her, watching the oxen swat flies with their tails, and the countryside slowly move past. She was impatient; she wanted to fly home and perform the ceremony so she could know for certain that the magic would come back, but it would be unfair to leave Magda behind. She was stretched out in the back, guarding a bucket of amulets, lost in her own thoughts.

Orion and Eb said they would follow, after they'd made sure the prime minister, bloody and wounded though he was, was locked up safely. Suli wondered if someone who could use magic should have been in charge of that, but Benno insisted it be them. She wished they were riding in the wagon, too, so she wouldn't be alone with the Wing sisters. Wise woman or not, she was never completely comfortable being around both sisters together.

Then she grinned, imagining Tala's reaction to learning that Suli now had acquired her own apprentice. She'd let Arta explain that; Arta just might be a match for her stern teacher.

Neither she nor Tala had thanked Magda for her help. Without Magda they could never have removed all the amulets, or neutralized them. She was the one who had kept the wise women from squabbling, and organized them for their plans. Magda had been uncommonly brave, too, dealing with the soldiers by herself. But so far, Tala hadn't thanked or acknowledged her sister. Not even for saving her life.

"You did very well, Suli," Tala observed, her eyes on the road. "Persuading the animal nations to help free the wise women from the camps was quite an accomplishment."

Her first reaction was, *Tala actually praised me!* Her second was, *Oh no, I have a teacher again. That will take some getting used to,* Suli thought.

"We would never have succeeded without Magda," Suli said. "She removed amulets from the soldiers by herself, and knew how to neutralize the magic. Without her, we couldn't have organized the wise women, or rescued *you*," she said with emphasis. "Magda, I never thanked you for helping me. We couldn't have done it without you." She turned sideways and gave Tala a pointed look.

"Hmph," Tala snorted. "What I don't understand is what caused that sudden burst of magical storms you mentioned, or why they stopped just as suddenly. Removing the amulets can't be the reason. And the animals are recovering too. Do you know why?"

Suli glanced at Magda. What should they explain first? "Coalfeather had an idea—" she began, but stopped. Magda had raised a finger, a smile spreading across her face.

"*Please,* Suli, let me tell her. I hardly ever get to explain things to her. Dearest sister, what did you think would happen once you destroyed the prime minister's desk?"

"I didn't know; I had to risk it. Why, what did happen?"

"Did you have a chance to speak with Coalfeather before we left?" Magda asked.

Tala frowned, her eyes on the road. "No, why would I?"

"Ah." Magda exhaled with satisfaction. "Then let *me* be the first to tell you: the magic the prime minister stole, that *you* released into the world, caused the magical storms, threatening to kill everyone in the country. A bit short-sighted of you, if I may say so."

Tala frowned, chewing her lip. "Hmph."

"To stop the storms and to restore the magic, Suli flew to the North Star to ask the World Guardian for help. Suli risked her life to fix *your* mistake. Thank the Sisters she succeeded. That's why the storms have stopped."

Tala turned to stare at Magda, the blood draining from her face.

"What?" she whispered, clearly shocked. Then more forcefully, "The minute my back is turned you put Suli in danger?"

"*I* didn't send her," Magda said, rolling her eyes. "Coalfeather and the wise women agreed there was nothing else to do."

Tala turned to Suli and said quietly. "I never thought that...I never meant for you to take that kind of risk. If it was my fault I'm sorry. Will you forgive me?"

Suli smiled faintly and cocked her head. "For that? Yes. For leaving me alone for two years? Ask me once we're home."

34

RESTORING THE BALANCE

ARTA WAS WORRIED. Two days had passed since everyone had left for Lofton without her.

There was no one to talk to at Tala's house except the goats and the chickens; Wilo and the two older shape-shifters who'd remained behind never became human, and she couldn't speak pidgin. The storms had stopped, thanks to Suli, but the prime minister might still kill Benno's parents. And maybe Suli's teacher. So many things could go wrong.

She missed her lessons with Coalfeather. He and his father, the really bossy crow, went to Lofton with the others. With no one to share her fears with, they grew. She imagined horrible things—the prime minister capturing all her friends and putting them to death. But she couldn't keep thinking about it. She had work to do.

Eb said Suli had stopped the wildfire, but Suli said she couldn't have done it without Arta. The guardians, whoever they were, helped Suli because Arta had healed the goats. That proved what she was doing was important, and she worked hard. By the end of the day she was so tired, she simply fell into bed.

All day long, when she wasn't cooking, eating, or feeding the animals, she sat at the kitchen table with the amplification stone, her eyes closed, concentrating. Tekka, the wooden horse kept her company on the table. Everywhere she listened, desperately sick animals were starving and wandering in confusion, unable to remember who or what they were.

With great gentleness, she reassured every confused soul she found, telling them who they were, what they should eat, and how to resume their normal lives. Sometimes she had to guess. What did voles eat? But she did her best, reassuring them that the world was being set right, that normal life would return. She promised them that no more babies would die.

Yes, her work was important, but when she remembered that the others could be dead or in prison, she had to stop for a moment. If something had happened to them, she'd never know! If everyone was all right, shouldn't they have sent word somehow? The hours dragged on. She tried not to lose hope.

She'd never admitted that she could listen to humans as well as animals, although Coalfeather suspected it, she thought. He was a clever bird.

It was wrong to spy on someone without their permission, she knew that, but she *had* to know. She searched all of Lofton until she found Benno and slipped into his thoughts.

Benno was happy! She saw his parents through his eyes; saw how ill they looked, but also recognized the joy in their eyes as they couldn't stop smiling at their son. He was leading them by the hand to the palace kitchens. He made them sit at the large pine table where the kitchen staff ate, while the staff watched with shocked faces.

He put on an apron and announced he was making them roasted fish. The king and queen exchanged startled glances, but murmured that they couldn't wait to taste it.

Arta laughed. Benno was showing off his new talents. If the king and queen were free, then everything must be all right.

Relieved, she glanced out the window. The sun was sinking. Time to feed the goats and chickens again.

She crossed the yard to the barn, calling to the goats. It had grown warmer and the snow had melted, so she had let them outside into the pen. She carried a bucket of grain and poured a pile for each one. They lined up, waiting their turn, their golden eyes watching her expectantly. She bowed and said, "Please enjoy." They bleated softly and happily before they began to eat. Their ribs had disappeared and their coats were shiny and their eyes bright. They knew who they were, and they ate with gusto.

TWO DAYS LATER, when Suli arrived home with Magda and Tala, the first thing she did was go to bed and sleep for twelve hours, worn out by all that had happened. When Arta climbed in beside her, she slept on.

The second thing she did, when she woke late the next day, was to gather feathers, water, and a bundle of sage, and take them to the field where the bonfire had been. She walked around the ashes in a circle, chanting and sprinkling water—from the pond this time—leaving offerings, as the Frost Goose had advised. She asked for forgiveness and for the magic to come back.

Then she went to the garden.

It was probably too soon, but she couldn't wait.

This time when she tried to heal the dark spots on the cabbage leaf, she could. The energy moved the way it used to. She sat back on her heels, grinning, with tears running down her face. She could Heal again—which meant she was a wise woman again. Now that she had her magic back, there was something she'd promised to do.

Suli led Arta back to the garden, and despite the cold, they sat on the ground. She called loudly in pidgin that the wise woman was back, if anyone needed Healing.

She told Arta, "It's time you learned about Seeing and Healing."

"But I already have my own magic," Arta said. "Maybe I don't need to. My mother said it's all nonsense anyway. Your magic didn't stop the soldiers; you had to ask the animals for help."

Suli was distracted; her patients were lining up cautiously, behind the row of leeks that had survived the hailstorm. A rabbit and a fox pointedly ignored each other, while a field mouse waited behind them.

"That's true," Suli said, beckoning the rabbit forward. "But do you know why the animals helped us? Because we've always helped them. Learning about Seeing and Healing will help you become a Healer of animals," Suli said. "That's what you want, isn't it?"

Arta looked stubborn. "I can already help them, when I look into their minds."

"Yes, that's very useful," Suli agreed. "And you saved many from dying. You have a great gift. But what if they have a different sickness? What if one of them is hurt by a fall, or was bitten, or has a fever? How will you help them then?"

Arta pursed hers lip, thinking. "You're right, I can't." She smiled wryly. "I guess I will be your apprentice after all. You'll have to teach me magic, just like I said."

Suli laughed. "I'm trying to." Then she spoke to the rabbit in pidgin. The rabbit replied, explaining what was wrong. Suli turned to Arta. "Now: look at this rabbit. What do you See?"

~

"Tell us again, Ralph!" a squirrel pleaded. "We want to hear it again." The owl, bear, and the other animals nodded their heads.

Ralph's gaze traveled around the circle where his Merry Band waited for him to tell them the story of the battle of Lofton. They'd heard it once already, and some had been there. But many of the forest animals had stayed behind. Ralph was the only wolf who'd gone.

"Suli, the wise woman, advised us not to enter the town. She was worried about us, you see. But I knew you fellows could do anything, and we had our own plan with the shape-shifters. So we crept along, silent as shadows, until we reached the soldiers' barracks beside the palace."

"And then what? And then what?" a snub-nosed mole asked excitedly.

"The shape-shifters opened the doors and we crept inside, quiet and careful. We hid as many of their weapons as we could and Andragora's mice removed many of the amulets. Unfortunately, there wasn't time to remove *all* of them because Mangus dropped a sword and one of them woke up. That soldier called out, and then *everyone* woke up."

The animals looked reproachfully at Mangus, a grey fox who hung his head.

"But what Mangus did was the best thing that could've happened," Ralph continued. "We started howling and yipping and barking and nipping at their heels. Then the geese attacked them, screaming the way they do. The soldiers were so frightened they fled without their boots or pants and didn't come back.

"So when the orders came for the soldiers to help the prime minister, no one was there." He smiled proudly at his band, and they smiled back. Even Mangus.

⁓

SULI SAT on the withered grass by the pond, watching the geese and the ducks swim on the sparkling water. Coalfeather strolled nearby. *You'd never know we rescued a king and queen and stopped a war.* Or that she'd spoken to the animal guardians. She could hardly believe it herself. She remembered the shifting eyes of the World Guardian and shivered, although the memory was beginning to fade. Maybe humans weren't supposed to remember such things.

"Coalfeather, I'd like your advice."

"Hmm?" He was pacing idly, pecking at the grass in case an interesting-looking speck turned out to be a tasty insect. Kaark and the flock had returned to Weatherstone the day after Suli had returned with Tala and Magda, but Coalfeather wouldn't tell her what they'd been doing.

"Now that Tala's back, and things are returning to normal, I'm not sure...I mean, I *am* glad she's back, but how will I know— what she should do, what I should do? After all, I'm not an apprentice anymore, but she's going to give me orders again, isn't she? And lessons."

"All wise women must keep learning, Suli," Coalfeather intoned piously.

She sighed and shook her head. Why had she bothered to ask?

"I *will* tell you what I think," he said, hopping closer, a mischievous look in his eye. "Arta has much more to learn from me about her magic. But she is only a fledgling. Perhaps you should learn with her, to keep an eye on her."

Suli sighed deeply. "Or she could live with Magda on the mountain and be *her* apprentice," Suli said. Magda had returned to her cottage on the mountain without a word of thanks for the good cleaning Suli and Orion had given it.

Coalfeather made a chuffing sound. "Why are you so hard on Arta? She's done nothing to deserve *that*. She's done her part, and saved many lives. My father has heard from many flocks that she saved their children. He said it *almost* makes him feel grateful to a human."

"Maybe that's what's so irritating. I never wanted an apprentice, and now I've got one who can do things I can't! I've started to teach her to See and Heal, but it's difficult. All she does is ask questions with no easy answers, and she's impatient no matter what I say. Not to mention she's insufferably smug about what she can do."

Coalfeather hopped away, his shoulders shaking.

He's laughing at me.

He hopped back. "And wasn't that lucky?" Coalfeather asked gently. "That she can do things you can't? Didn't her magic help us?"

"Well, yes," she admitted reluctantly.

"And did it ever occur to you that Tala and I might have found *you* irritating, once or twice, especially when you asked questions with no easy answers?"

Suli laughed and threw a handful of grass at him. "It has now, Teacher."

A FEW DAYS LATER, horses rode into the yard. Tala hurried down the kitchen steps with Arta on her heels, the door banging behind them.

Eb and Orion dismounted, still in uniform. Their faces were grey with weariness, but they smiled at the welcome.

"Well, we're back," Orion announced. "I can now say with painful sincerity that flying is better than riding." He rubbed his sore backside gingerly.

Eb threw him an unreadable look. "*You* tell her while I take care of the horses." He took Orion's reins and led the horses to the barn.

"Coward," Orion said under his breath.

Suli and Coalfeather had heard the horses and came to investigate. Suli appeared at the top of the path, out of breath from running. Coalfeather glided ahead of her to land beside Tala.

"Tell me what?" Tala asked.

Orion waited until Suli came up with them. "The prime

minister escaped. We think soldiers who still had their amulets helped him. As far as we can tell, he's left the country by ship."

Suli waited to see Tala's reaction.

Tala said lightly, "I'm not that surprised. He's a very powerful witch. Maybe we'll be lucky and he won't come back. How's Benno?"

Orion grinned. "Having a tremendous time. He and his mother are allowed to fly in public now. There was some proclamation about it, saying Sigur's geese have saved the country and we all have to be grateful, blah, blah. It will be good for the flock. Maybe hunters will think twice about shooting us."

"It's freezing out here," Arta said. "Can we go back inside?"

"Excellent idea," Orion said, and Suli heard the exhaustion in his voice. They trooped into the kitchen and Arta put the kettle on the stove. Orion fell into a chair in front of the fire.

Eb came in a few minutes later, smelling of horses, his boots loud on the wooden floor. He sat down in the rocking chair and pulled off each mud-caked riding boot with a grunt, and then stretched his toes toward the fire with a contented sigh.

"I could fall asleep right here," he said.

"Welcome back," Suli said, kissing him on the forehead and handing him a cup of tea.

THE NEXT MORNING Eb said his goodbyes to everyone, and Suli walked with him down the path to set him on his way. He was leading the horse he'd ridden from Lofton.

"Who does that horse belong to, anyway?" Suli asked, as she opened the gate that led to the lane.

"The prime minister," he said. "Believe it or not, Arta asked him whether he'd rather live on a farm with me, or go back to the city. He told her he'd like to live on a farm."

"A suspiciously convenient story!"

Eb grinned, then said seriously, "Grandmother will be worried about both of us, so I'd better get home and let her know we're all right. You *are* all right, aren't you? There hasn't exactly been time to catch up." He searched his sister's face.

"Why wouldn't I be? Everyone I care about is safe. But Eb, I don't think I've ever said thank you."

"For what?"

"For coming. For helping me. I'm so proud of you. Make sure you tell Grandmother what a hero you are. And come visit soon."

Eb made a scoffing sound. "'Course I will. I have a horse now."

They laughed, and with a final embrace, Eb rode off into Weatherstone.

Suli turned back up the path, trying not to feel sad. She paused beside the pond, thinking how peaceful it looked, the ducks and geese swimming or dozing in the sun.

Coalfeather landed beside her. "I like your brother," he said. "He understands the way things should be. He would make a fine crow."

Suli tried to imagine her brother with dark glossy wings and failed. "Thank you for the compliment. I like him too."

"We should continue your studies soon, so Arta doesn't get ahead of you."

Is he joking? "What are you talking about? With Tala here to be the wise woman again, I'm going to lie around the house all day being lazy."

He bobbed his head and wagged his tail up and down. "Do you really think you've learned all the magic you need to know?"

She was tempted to say yes, but whatever she said he would correct her. "It's possible isn't it? I am *extremely* wise already."

Then she changed and leapt into the sky, rising swiftly to get away from him.

Coalfeather took off after her. They swooped and dived playfully over the pond, while the ducks and geese pretended to ignore them.

ABOUT THE AUTHOR

Elizabeth Forest writes speculative and historical fiction for all ages. Find her on the web and join her newsletter at:
https://www.elizabethsforest.com

If you liked this book, please leave a review at your favorite bookseller!

ALSO BY ELIZABETH FOREST

Suli's adventures began in *The Third Kind of Magic, Crow Magic Book One.*
https://www.elizabethsforest.com/books-third-kind-of-magic/

Forced to become an apprentice wise woman for misusing magic,
twelve-year-old Suli must stop a witch's deadly plans.

Made in United States
North Haven, CT
13 August 2024

55974933R10167